THE COWBOY AND THE ACTRESS

He lunged for her at the same time she went for him, and they only narrowly avoided cracking heads before he started kissing her, and that was that. She straddled his lap and let him have it, her hands roaming over him, relearning every taut muscle in his body and luxuriating in the feel of him.

"Silver." He finally came up for air. "We shouldn't—"

"Shut up."

She bit his lip and kissed him, her fingernails scratching his scalp as he groaned and let her have her way with him. She inched one hand under his T-shirt and he shuddered.

"Silver." This time he held on to her hands. "We really do need to talk about this."

She undulated against him. "Then talk."

Ben struggled to draw a breath that didn't smell like Silver, and the heat of her, and the *need* . . .

Books by Kate Pearce

The House of Pleasure Series

SIMPLY SEXUAL
SIMPLY SINFUL
SIMPLY SHAMELESS
SIMPLY WICKED
SIMPLY INSATIABLE
SIMPLY FORBIDDEN
SIMPLY CARNAL
SIMPLY VORACIOUS
SIMPLY SCANDALOUS
SIMPLY PLEASURE (e-novella)
SIMPLY IRRESISTIBLE (e-novella)

The Sinners Club Series

THE SINNERS CLUB
TEMPTING A SINNER
MASTERING A SINNER
THE FIRST SINNERS (e-novella)

Single Titles

RAW DESIRE

The Morgan Brothers Ranch

THE RELUCTANT COWBOY
THE MAVERICK COWBOY
THE LAST GOOD COWBOY
THE BAD BOY COWBOY
THE BILLIONAIRE BULL RIDER
THE RANCHER

The Millers of Morgantown

THE SECOND CHANCE RANCHER
THE RANCHER'S REDEMPTION
THE REBELLIOUS RANCHER

Anthologies

SOME LIKE IT ROUGH
LORDS OF PASSION
HAPPY IS THE BRIDE
A SEASON TO CELEBRATE
MARRYING MY COWBOY

Published by Kensington Publishing Corporation

THE REBELLIOUS RANCHER

KATE PEARCE

ZEBRA BOOKS
KENSINGTON PUBLISHING CORP.
www.kensingtonbooks.com

ZEBRA BOOKS are published by

Kensington Publishing Corp.
119 West 40th Street
New York, NY 10018

All Kensington titles, imprints, and distributed lines are available at special quantity discounts for bulk purchases for sales promotion, premiums, fund-raising, educational, or institutional use.

Special book excerpts or customized printings can also be created to fit specific needs. For details, write or phone the office of the Kensington Sales Manager: Attn.: Sales Department. Kensington Publishing Corp., 119 West 40th Street, New York, NY 10018. Phone: 1-800-221-2647.

First Printing: August 2020
ISBN-13: 978-1-4201-4825-1
ISBN-10: 1-4201-4825-7

ISBN-13: 978-1-4201-4828-2 (eBook)
ISBN-10: 1-4201-4828-1 (eBook)

10 9 8 7 6 5 4 3 2 1

Printed in the United States of America

Acknowledgments

Huge thanks to Sian Kaley and Jerri Drennen for reading this book early for me and for having widely different opinions. I'd also like to thank professional bareback rider Kenny Haworth for answering my questions about trail rides and what to pack in the wilderness.

Chapter One

Miller Ranch
Morgan Valley, California

Ben Miller didn't know what was worse, sitting on the back of a horse in the middle of a field of bawling calves, or not giving a damn about sitting in that field because he didn't want to be there anymore. Now that his big brother, Adam, owned the whole ranch, what did that make him? A hired hand? A man without a purpose?

"Ben! What the hell are you doing?" Adam yelled. "You're supposed to be moving these calves toward the gate!"

He blinked the squalling rain from his eyes, angled his Stetson against the wind, and looked over to where his brother sat waiting by the fence. Adam never looked particularly happy, not having the face for it, but now he was positively grim.

"Come on!"

Ben gathered his reins, clicked to his horse, and went around the back of the bunch of complaining calves. With the help of his two dogs, he pushed the youngsters toward the gate. Luckily, the calves stayed tightly together and, as their mothers started to call out for them, they were more than willing to be funneled into the next field to find food and shelter.

Adam rode off to make sure they all got settled in, and Ben leaned down to secure the gate. It was hard to tell what time it was, as everything was gray, but he had a sense that it was getting late. Most of the delays had been his fault because he hadn't been concentrating, and the calves kept getting away from him.

Jenna Morgan looked up as he approached the covered area where she was completing the paperwork for the inoculations they had just given the calves. She wore a heavy jacket with a hood, fingerless gloves, and long boots over her jeans to keep out the chill and the mud.

"I think I've got everything. Thanks for your help."

Adam, who had dismounted and brought his horse into the shelter, grunted. "Not that you *were* much help, Ben."

Ben dismounted, patted Calder, brought him out of the rain, and studiously avoided his brother's gaze.

Jenna glanced uncertainly from him to Adam and stashed her paperwork in her bag. "I'll get back to you tomorrow if I have any issues. Keep an eye on the calves for the next couple of days to see if there are any adverse reactions."

"Will do. Thanks, Jenna," Adam said.

"Have a great evening." She slogged off through the mud toward her SUV, which was parked on the other side of the fence.

Adam waited until she drove away and then cleared his throat.

"You got something to say to me, bro?"

"Why would you think that?" Ben fussed around with the straps of his saddlebags.

"Because you're acting like an ass."

"Takes one to know one," Ben muttered, as he found a

cloth and went around to clean off Calder's nose strap, which was so splattered with mud that his nostrils were practically closed up.

"You've been salty ever since Dad announced he was leaving me the ranch and stepping back."

"Really? I wonder why?"

"Ben . . . will you just *talk* to me?" Adam asked. "If you hate the idea so much, I'll talk some sense into Dad and make it right."

Ben finally met his brother's gaze. They were almost the same height although Adam was slightly taller and leaner. "If Dad wants you to have the ranch, then it's yours. It makes a lot of sense, and you'll definitely run it better than he does."

"Just because something makes sense doesn't mean it's the right thing to do."

"Why are you arguing against yourself, bro?" Ben patted Calder's nose and put the cloth away. "I totally get why he did what he did. This is on me." He poked himself in the chest. "*I've* got to work out how I feel about it—not you."

Adam held his gaze. "I'll tell him no."

"It's too late for that. The paperwork was all done and dusted last week." Ben took off his Stetson and banged it against his thigh to shake some of the water off.

"I don't care. We can do it again. I'll even *pay* for it if you'll just stop walking around looking like someone kicked your favorite puppy."

Guilt coalesced in Ben's gut. "That bad, eh?"

"Yeah."

Ben could never say that his older brother wasn't a straight shooter. If he said he was willing to go back and renegotiate the deal, then he'd do it. But what would that give Ben? Maybe he should've stood up and voiced his concerns straight off rather than stewing on them for weeks and making everyone else feel bad.

"It's on me," Ben repeated slowly. "I didn't speak out, and it's not up to you to fix my mistakes."

Adam opened his mouth to argue, seemed to think better of it, and just nodded. "Okay."

"Thanks, Adam." Ben found a smile somewhere. He was the one who normally made everyone else in the family get along, but he wasn't doing it right now. "We'd better get back. Dad will be wondering what's for dinner."

After a hot shower and three cups of strong coffee, Ben was almost feeling like himself again. Adam had been right to point out that his attitude sucked; he just wished he knew how to change it. Ever since his mother had reappeared in their lives and everything he'd once thought true had been upended, he'd felt adrift. The last time he'd felt like that he'd done some really stupid shit, and he had no desire to repeat himself.

Adam taking control of the ranch and keeping it together for the next generation made perfect sense. Having six kids potentially dividing up a profitable ranch, and maybe fighting over it when their father died, would have destroyed their heritage. Ben didn't want that to happen, so what did he want?

He wiped the condensation off the mirror and stared at his bearded reflection. What was he going to do? Remain at the ranch as Adam's second-in-command, a job he was damn good at, or what? Leave? Ranching was in his blood and he couldn't imagine doing anything else.

Someone banged on the bathroom door.

"Hey, you finished in there, Ben?" Kaiden shouted. "I just got back and I need a shower."

"Yup." Ben opened the door, allowing a cloud of steam to escape. "Sorry."

"No problem." Kaiden went past him, smelling like a pine forest. "That renovation in town is taking way longer than I anticipated, but it's going to make a whole group of people a great home."

Ben was the only brother apart from Adam who worked full-time on the ranch. Everyone else, including their sister, Daisy, had other jobs. Kaiden was a master carpenter and always busy.

Ben got dressed and wandered into the kitchen where Adam had already started cooking dinner. "Need a hand?"

"You can set the table."

Ben completed the task and then took a moment to check his cell phone. Not that he ever got many messages, but he liked to keep on top of things.

Can you come over tonight?

Ben squinted at the text, wondering who the hell was talking to him, and scrolled back up to see he'd missed a few vital bits of information.

"I've got to go out," Ben replied to the last message, and shoved his cell in the pocket of his Wranglers.

"I'm cooking dinner here," Adam complained. "Can't you just eat fast, and go after?"

"Nope, sorry, I've got to go right now. I'll eat when I come back."

Ben ignored Adam's next shouted question and went into the mudroom to grab his heavy coat, boots, and his second-best Stetson that had been drying out on the heater from yesterday's rain. It was still pouring so he took the keys to his Jeep, and ran to where he'd parked it.

It didn't take long to drive back onto the county road and then along to the much bigger Morgan Ranch where BB, Blue Boy Morgan, lived with his wife, Jenna, and his daughter, Maria, in a newly constructed house on the family land.

Ben pulled up in the driveway behind Jenna's truck, and got out to a cacophony of barking. Between Jenna's veterinary business and Maria's love of taking care of creatures, their place was like a zoo.

By the time he reached the door, it was already open, and Blue "BB" Morgan, retired Marine and all around badass, was waiting for him. He wasn't the kind of guy who would let anyone creep up on him unawares.

"Hey, thanks for coming over." BB patted Ben's shoulder. "Have you eaten? Jenna made some vegetarian patties if you like that kind of thing. Me and Maria are going with the beef."

"I'm good, thanks." Ben ignored the low growl of his stomach. Working outside meant that he had quite an appetite and burned through a ton of calories without putting on weight.

"Well, sit down and keep me company, anyway," BB said as they came into the open-plan kitchen and dining area. "Jenna's got a thing about us all eating dinner together."

"Hey again, Jenna," Ben called out as he spotted the veterinarian. "Sorry to barge in on your dinner."

"It's all good." Jenna patted the seat next to hers. "Come and sit by me. How are the calves?"

"All doing okay the last I saw of them." Ben took the

seat and nodded at Maria who was sitting opposite him. "Hi."

"Hi." She blushed and hid behind her long dark hair.

"How's school?" Ben asked.

"Good."

"Any idea what you plan to do when you graduate?"

"Not yet."

Jenna winked at him. "She's thinking about ranch management."

"Awesome." Ben's stomach growled again.

"Here." BB pushed the plate over. "Help yourself."

"If you're sure . . ." Ben looked longingly at the big, juicy burger. He should've listened to Adam and eaten at home before he came out.

"Plenty more where that came from," BB joked. "Benefit of living on a cattle ranch."

"Dad, that's *so* lame." Maria rolled her eyes.

"Apparently, nothing I say is funny anymore," BB commented as he reached for the ketchup. "Teens, eh?"

Maria looked over at Jenna. "Can I leave the table, please? I've got a math test tomorrow, and I need to study."

"Sure." Jenna waved her away.

"Bye, Maria," Ben called out to her retreating figure. "Nice to see you again."

She stomped up the stairs and slammed her door so hard that everyone at the table winced.

"Was it something I said?" Ben asked cautiously. "She used to get along great with me."

BB grinned at his wife. "Well, Jenna's got a theory about that. She thinks Maria's got a bit of a crush on you."

Ben almost choked on his burger.

"It's okay," Jenna hastened to reassure him. "And it's

all good. I can't think of a better man for her to have a crush on than you. You're a great role model."

Ben wasn't so sure about that, so he concentrated on his burger. Jenna excused herself to go and finish some paperwork, leaving him and BB with the coffeepot between them and time to talk.

"I got this kind of weird request for a trail ride experience," BB said. "At first I ignored it because I thought it was some kind of windup, but the guy kept calling and eventually I sat down and listened to what he had to say. I told him I had just the right man for the job, but that I'd have to square it with you first."

"What kind of job?" Ben sipped his coffee.

"He wants someone to take his daughter out on an all-singing, all-dancing, trail riding experience as close to nature as we can manage."

"Like on foot?"

BB grinned. "Not quite that bad. Just horses and no motorized support. Apparently, she needs to experience what it would be like for a film role."

"You're kidding, right?" Ben stared at his friend.

"Nope." BB shrugged. "It's not unheard of for actors to want to immerse themselves completely in a role, and that's apparently what she wants to do."

"Okay, for how long?"

"At least a week, maybe ten days."

"With just the two of us and a couple of horses?"

"That's about it."

While Ben considered the idea, BB sat back to drink his coffee and didn't rush him.

"Why can't you or Jackson do it?" Ben finally asked.

"Because the guy wants to get it done as soon as possible, and I can't be away for that long at this time of year. Neither can Jackson."

Yeah, that was all Ben needed—a reminder that he wasn't as vital to the operation of his family ranch as everyone else. . . .

"What about your military buddies?"

For the first time, BB hesitated. "It has to be someone I trust one hundred percent. The father wants the whole thing kept under the radar so she doesn't have to worry about the press or any of that crap."

"He thinks they'd follow her here to Morgan Valley?" It was Ben's turn to smile. "Who is it? Meryl Streep?"

"There's more to it than that, but I need to see if you're on board before I tell you the rest." BB set his mug down on the table. "He's offering four times the normal rate if we can guarantee her privacy."

"Four times?" Ben whistled. Even after the Morgan Ranch took its cut, he'd be rolling in dough, and he needed something different to do to sort his head out. "Okay, I'm in. What's the catch?"

BB's grin was wicked. "Well . . ."

When Ben got home, his head was still buzzing with all the stuff BB had dropped on him—stuff that he couldn't tell anyone without losing the contract. He went into the now-quiet dark kitchen and helped himself to a cup of coffee from the metal pot on the stove his father still preferred while everyone else used the one-cup machine.

"You okay?"

He spun around to see Adam sitting at the table in the dark.

"Jeez, you stalking me or something?" Ben inquired as he got his breath back.

"I just wanted to make sure that you don't want me to talk to Dad."

Ben walked over and took the seat opposite his older brother. "Can you just drop it?"

Adam stared at him, his gaze measuring. "You're the one who seems to be struggling to let it go."

"I need to decide what I want to do with the rest of my life." Ben paused. "Do you still want me working here?"

"Of course I do. What a stupid thing to ask!" Adam said. "You're my goddam *rock*."

"But you're the boss now. You have the power to hire and fire anyone."

"Like Dad's going to roll over and let that happen?" Adam raised an eyebrow. "He might have decided to leave me the place, but he's not going to stop trying to run it just the way he wants."

Ben took a long slug of coffee. "Maybe he'll move to New York to be near Mom."

"Are you kidding, Ben? Dad in New York? He'd hate every second of it." Adam set his cup down on the table. "I figure it's more likely that Leanne will move back here, don't you?"

Ben tried to imagine the mother who'd left them over twenty years ago coming back for good and couldn't get his head around it. She was definitely getting on with their dad, and apparently they'd talked things through and forgiven each other—something Ben found unbelievable, knowing his father's legendary ability to hold a grudge. He didn't like all the changes happening around him; he didn't feel settled anymore. It reminded him way too much of his late teens, and he never wanted to feel like that again.

"I was thinking that maybe I'd look around the valley and see if anyone needs a ranch manager," Ben said, studying his mug as though it held the secrets to the universe.

Silence met his words and eventually he had to look up

at his brother, who was sitting back in his chair, his fingers drumming on the table, his expression unreadable.

"What?" Ben asked, all innocence.

Adam shrugged. "I'm not going to stop you if you really want to leave."

"Good to know," Ben said, even as he wished his brother had put up more of a fight. "In the meantime, I'm going to be working at Morgan Ranch for a couple of weeks doing a trail ride."

"Right now?" For the first time Adam frowned. "What about all the new calves?"

"I'm sure you'll manage without me. It's not the first time I've been away."

"Yeah, we'll manage. Danny's not going to like it much, but he'll come through." Adam abruptly stood and shoved in his chair. "Never thought you'd be the one to let me down, bro."

Ben was aware that he was being unfair, but he needed to get away and sort his head out before he did or said something stupid. Adam had recently found the new love of his life, their father was rekindling some kind of weird relationship with their mother, Leanne, and Ben wasn't dealing well with any of it. Did he want to be the guy who was miserable when everyone else was so fricking cheerful? He was usually the happiest guy on the planet.

When Ben didn't reply, Adam turned on his heel and left the kitchen. Ben considered going after him and apologizing, but what was there left to say? Adam *would* do fine without him, and Ben needed a break.

He grimaced and rubbed his face in his hands. He had to go through with BB Morgan's plan now. He had nothing left to lose.

"What are you doing upsetting your brother like that?"

"God, not you as well." Ben groaned as his father came storming into the kitchen.

"And what's this about you skipping out on us during calving season?"

"I'll be gone for a maximum of ten days, and I'll be right next door," Ben said. "You can get a hold of me if there's a real emergency."

"Maybe I can, but where's your loyalty to this family, eh? We need you here for calving," Jeff said. "Why are you sucking up to the Morgans?"

Ben leaned his chair on its back legs so that he could really glare up at his father. "Because they pay me better?"

"I pay you," Jeff growled. "My dad never gave me a cent!"

Ben had heard that more times than he'd drawn breath and didn't feel the need to respond.

"It's not like you to be difficult, son. I expect that from Kaiden or Danny, but you've always stuck things out and not complained."

"Then maybe it's my turn to stick my neck out and do something for myself? I've been doing these trail rides for a year now, Dad. Why is this one any different, and why are you making such a fuss about nothing?"

Jeff glowered at him. "You're jealous, aren't you?"

"Jealous of what?"

"People being happy. I thought Adam was bad enough, but you take the cake. Maybe if you spent less time moping around the ranch and went out to meet some nice women you'd stop sulking and get a life."

"Gee, Dad, you're such a motivational speaker, you should have your own talk show." Ben stood and faced his father. "I'll be working for BB Morgan for ten days, and then I'll come back, and you can yell at me all you want, okay?"

"Perhaps I won't have a job for you," Jeff snapped. "I let you come back twelve years ago, and maybe once was enough."

"Fine by me." Ben walked past his father. "Have a great week."

He kept walking until he reached the end of the long hall and took a right into his bedroom where he very carefully didn't slam the door. There were enough drama queens at the ranch without him adding to it. The force of his father's last words hit him hard and he sank down on the side of the bed. Had his dad meant it?

If he had . . . what the hell was Ben going to be doing in two weeks' time?

Chapter Two

Silver exited the hired Jeep and stared out over the lush green fields toward the towering bulk of the Sierra Nevada and let out her breath. It looked so empty out here and the sky was enormous. To her right there was the cutest little ranch house, and to the left a big wooden barn just like the one some enterprising kid in a musical would use to hold a show.

"This place has been here for over a hundred and fifty years," her dad said coming to stand beside her. "Run by the same family as well."

"Wow, that's impressive," Silver replied.

A dog barked somewhere, and a guy in a cowboy hat came out of the barn and walked toward them, his spurs jiggling like an old-fashioned gunslinger.

Silver's dad stepped forward. "Hi! I'm Phil Meadows. Are you BB Morgan?"

"Yup." The man shook her dad's hand and then hers. He had such piercing blue eyes Silver wondered if he wore contacts. "Glad you found the place okay." He gestured at the ranch house. "Come on in and meet my family."

"I can't stay long," her dad said. "I'm leaving the Jeep here in case Silver needs it, and I've got a car picking me up in an hour to take me to the local airport."

Silver frowned. "You didn't tell me that you were going back tonight."

"I had no choice, my love. Your sister's got an audition tomorrow, and I promised to take her."

Her dad sounded way too jovial, but Silver didn't want to have an argument with him in front of the Morgan family. The fact that he was willing to leave her by herself for the first time in two years was amazing, and she wasn't willing to sacrifice her freedom over something petty.

When she'd floated the idea of coming out to a ranch to do some research for the indie picture role, she'd expected him to immediately veto the idea like he had all her other attempts to regain her independence. When he'd agreed, on the proviso that he got to approve the place, she'd been thrilled, but suspicious.

It was her first chance to show him that she was more than capable of living her own life and picking acting roles that were serious and required her total commitment. If she got through this, she'd move on to phase two of her campaign to get her life back.

Silver paused at the door of the kitchen and surveyed the huge pine table and the elderly woman cooking at the stove.

"This is my grandma, Ruth Morgan," BB said. "She runs the ranch and feeds the family."

Ruth was as small-boned as Silver, and about the same height. She had the same bright blue eyes as BB and a very welcoming smile.

"My, you're a little bitty thing, aren't you?" She pointed at the table. "Now, sit yourself down and I'll get you something to eat."

"Just coffee for me, thanks," her dad piped up. "I've got to go soon."

Ruth Morgan placed mugs, cream, and sugar on the table while BB wrangled the coffeepot.

"Silver's really looking forward to her adventure." Her dad sipped his coffee. "She loves getting into a part and this will mean the world to her. When are you planning on 'moving out'?"

BB sat at the table next to Silver who was wincing at her dad's joke. "I'm not the guy who will be taking her; that's my buddy Ben Miller. He'll be here tomorrow morning to sort things out." He looked at Silver. "You'll like him. He's really capable."

Silver wanted to ask capable of what, but her attention was diverted to the huge peach pie Mrs. Morgan had placed on the table. She hadn't seen anything like it since she was a kid at her grandparents' house.

"Please help yourself." Mrs. Morgan handed over plates and spoons. "I made it myself. Would you like a piece, Silver?"

Silver glanced warily at her father who was almost salivating at the fragrant sugary-spicy scent wafting from the pie. Like everyone in her personal team, he kept an app on his phone of the calories she consumed, and was usually quick to tell her everything she wasn't allowed to touch, let alone eat.

Mrs. Morgan slid a plate over to her and then one to her father. For a moment, they shared a guilty look, and then he exhaled.

"One little bit won't hurt us, will it, Silver?"

Silver woke up early to the god-awful sound of a rooster crowing outside her window. Even as she stuck her pillow over her head, the noise got worse as a truck pulled into the circular driveway and someone started whistling to the dogs. She'd met a whole houseful of Morgans at dinner last night, and still wasn't sure of all the names. To her relief, after initially staring at her like she was some kind of exhibit in the zoo, they'd all gotten over themselves and treated her just like a regular person. She hadn't even caught any of them trying to sneak a picture of her on their phone.

It had been weird to be surrounded by so much noise and laughter, which wasn't directed at her. She tried to remember the last time she'd been out without her bodyguards, her publicist, at least one member of her family, and her personal assistant beside her. Here, she was just a guest on a ranch in the middle of nowhere, and, although she'd been included in all the discussions, no one had made them all about her.

As she sat up against her pillows, she realized she'd forgotten to close the drapes and that the sun was rising over the mountains to cover the pasture in soft, golden light. A group of horses ran past her window, like in a movie, tails and manes blowing in the breeze as they goofed off with each other. It was going to be a beautiful day.

She grabbed her phone and took a quick picture of the scene before remembering that she wasn't supposed to let anyone know where she was so she couldn't post it to her social media accounts. There were several texts from her siblings, her mom, and her PA, all asking how she was settling in. She was just about to start answering them when she remembered that her bedroom had no attached bathroom and that she'd have to run down the hall to pee and shower.

Normally, when she traveled, she had a huge suite to herself, and didn't share anything with anyone, but she had to pee and that had to come first. She opened the door and looked cautiously out into the hallway. Most of the doors were ajar, indicating that everyone else had already gotten up. She ran down to the bathroom and locked the door, took a quick shower, and spent half an hour on her makeup.

Someone tapped on the door and she went to open it, her gaze dropping to the level of the small boy smiling up at her through the escaping steam.

"Hey, you." She couldn't remember his name, although from his bright blue eyes he was definitely a Morgan.

"Granny wants to know if you're coming down for breakfast. Ben's already here."

"Can you tell her that I'll be down in five minutes?"

"Sure thing."

She went back to her bedroom and lay flat on the floor to wriggle into her jeans, added an off-one-shoulder knitted top, and left her hair loose. She slipped her bare feet into some high-heeled sandals and made her way down the stairs. When she entered the kitchen, there was a man sitting at the table she was fairly certain she hadn't met before.

"Good morning, Mrs. Morgan. Sorry I'm so late coming down."

Ruth smiled at her. "There's no rush, my dear. Ben and I have been catching up on family news while he waited for you."

The man at the table rose slowly to his feet and looked down at her from his considerable height. "Ma'am."

He had a tight beard with a hint of red in it, warm brown eyes, and the tanned face of a man who earned his living working outside. All in all, he lived up to what BB Morgan had promised—capable, if capable meant average.

"Hi, Ben." She held out her hand and looked up at him through her lashes. "I'm Silver. It's so nice to meet you."

"Yeah, likewise." He took her hand in his big, callused one and gently shook it like he thought she might break.

He waited until she seated herself opposite him and then sat back down again. "You ready to go?"

He obviously wasn't the chatty type, which was perfectly fine with her. "Well, I'll need to sort out my baggage, but sure!"

Ben couldn't quite believe he was sitting opposite Silver Meadows, the girl who had starred in his favorite TV show when he was a kid. She was older now, obviously, but she was still petite, and so fricking perfect that it almost hurt to look at her. When BB had told him about her "problems" and that her family was really worried about her, he'd been skeptical. Seeing her face-to-face literally glowing with health made him doubt them even more, but he'd seen drug addiction up close and personal, and he wasn't going to make any snap decisions just yet.

Mrs. Morgan slid a plate piled high with bacon, eggs, and skillet potatoes that he hadn't asked for in front of him.

"Eat it while it's hot, Ben." She turned to Silver. "Now, what can I get you, my dear? The same as Ben?"

Silver looked from Ben's plate to her hostess, her expression horrified. "That's about a week's worth of calories for me. Do you have any grain-free granola or acai berries?"

Ruth and Ben shared an equally puzzled look.

"Or an avocado, or some fresh fruit?" Silver looked down at her phone. "That's what I usually have after my morning workout with my trainer."

"I can go over to the guest dining room and get you some fruit," Ben offered. "We thought you'd prefer to stay here away from the other guests."

"I don't want to put you out." Silver put her phone away. "Can I just have one piece of bacon and an egg and save my carb allowance for later?"

Ben frowned. "That's not going to keep you full until we make our first stop."

She smiled at him and he almost swallowed his tongue. "I think I'll be fine, Ben. I know my own body."

Ben did his best not to look at her body to confirm that fact, and merely dug into his plateful of food while Ruth made small talk with Silver and fed her what she'd asked for. He finished his second breakfast and had another mug of coffee while his companion chewed every dainty mouthful a hundred times.

Ben stood and took the plate over to the sink.

"Thanks, Mrs. Morgan."

"You're welcome, Ben." She patted his arm. "I'm packing you some lunch to take with you and a few extra treats to keep you going."

"I appreciate it." He put his rinsed plate in the dishwasher and turned back to the table. "You can ride, right, Ms. Meadows?"

"Please call me Silver." Her smile lit up the kitchen. "I've done a bit, but I wouldn't say I was good or anything."

"I'll get you to try out a couple of horses before we leave so I can match you up right." He nodded at her plate. "When you're done and you're all packed and ready to go, come and find me down at the new barn."

He retrieved his hat and boots from the mudroom and walked to the gleaming metal-roofed barn down the slope from the house. He'd always loved the old Victorian ranch house with its deep oak planked verandas and delicate lace trim. It was much nicer than his home, although he'd never say that in front of his dad.

His first impression of Silver Meadows was that she was okay. He cracked a smile at his own expense. Yeah, she was the most beautiful woman he had ever seen in the flesh, and she seemed nice, which he hadn't been expecting. He wasn't one to notice online gossip, but he had paid attention when she'd been mentioned because she'd been his first crush, and he kind of foolishly wished the best for her.

"Hey!" BB Morgan stuck his head out from a stall. "Calder and the mules are ready to go. Did you decide which horse you were going to give our guest?"

"She's coming down for some tryouts." Ben patted Calder's nose. He'd brought him over the night before and BB had given him a ride back home. "She's got some riding experience, so who do you suggest?"

"Ladybug or Marilyn would be my best guesses. They're both easygoing and should get on great with Calder." He pointed at the mare he was about to lead out. "This is Marilyn."

"She's as pretty as her namesake," Ben remarked as the honey-colored horse with a white mane and tail sashayed past him.

"So, she'll suit Silver Meadows very well." BB winked at him as he walked the horse out and tied her up. "Ladybug is smaller and a paint."

"A paint what?"

Both men turned to see their ranch guest coming toward them. She still wore her jeans and off-the-shoulder top but had added cowboy boots to replace the sandals and tied back her blond hair.

BB was the first to recover his manners. "It's a type of horse." He opened up one of the stalls and went inside. "In this case, it's a white horse that looks like someone threw cans of black or brown paint at it. This is Ladybug."

Silver stood back as BB brought the black and white mare out into the paddock and tied her up. "She's adorable. And who's this?"

"Marilyn." Ben stepped up his game. "I want to see you ride both of them, and then we'll decide which one suits you best."

Silver went back to the rented Jeep, opened up the rear, and started to take out her bags. Everyone at the ranch had been so nice that the prospect of her trip deep into the unknown was becoming more exciting by the minute. She found her heavy coat and cowboy hat and set them on top of her luggage. Ben might not talk much, but he seemed pleasant, and he wasn't all over her, which she appreciated.

Ben appeared leading Ladybug and his own horse, which towered above the little mare. BB brought up two mules, tipped his hat Silver's way, and wished her a good day before disappearing back toward the barn.

Eventually, Ben turned her way and looked at the pile of luggage.

"You can't take all that with you."

She glanced back at her five suitcases. "Why not?"

"Because we're doing this on horseback." He pointed at the two mules. "Bill and Ted have to carry everything we can't get into our saddlebags. Typically, I put a seventy-pound pack on each side of the mule, and that has to include our camping gear, clothes, food, and fuel."

Silver studied the mules. One of them was already carrying a full load, and the other had one side completely packed.

"So how much space do I have?"

He shrugged. "About seventy pounds max."

"But that's only about one big suitcase! Can't they carry more?"

"They could, but deadweight is hard on their backs, so I prefer to keep it down to the minimum."

"Then could we take the Jeep?" Silver asked hopefully.

"There's no one here to drive it." He raised his eyebrows. "I thought you wanted the 'authentic ranch experience'?"

"I do, but"—she cast a harried glance over her baggage, which was the standard stuff her PA usually packed for her—"I *need* all this stuff."

"Why?" Ben asked simply.

"Because I do!" For the first time, she glared at him. "I'm not used to traveling without my things around me."

He held her gaze. "You're going on a trail ride. You need basic clothing, a tent, a sleeping bag, some food, and a horse."

She folded her arms over her chest. "Well, what are you bringing clothingwise, and where are you going to stash everything?"

"My stuff is already on board." He gestured toward his horse. "I've got a clean pair of jeans, five T-shirts, three shirts, a rain slicker, and this jacket, and that's about it."

"No underwear?"

His slow smile came as a surprise. "Maybe I don't wear any."

Before she thought it through, her gaze slid down to his jeans and then back to his face. His smile had gone and now he wore a patient look she hated when it was directed at her. Just because she was blond didn't mean she was a complete idiot. She pointed at her smallest case.

"I have a ten-step Korean face care regime in there that I *cannot* do without."

His lips twitched. "You've got space in two saddlebags and a maximum of seventy pounds to put on the mule." He turned toward the guest center. "I'm going to speak to BB about the radio system. If you want to leave today, I'll expect you to be ready when I get back."

"But—" Silver watched in dismay as he turned around and walked away. "I don't know how to pack! Someone always does it for me!"

He didn't slow down or appear to have heard her, which was unlikely seeing as she was definitely yelling. She surveyed the two open saddlebags, noted that Ben had tied his rain slicker to the back of his saddle and started with that. To be fair, she didn't have any idea what was in the majority of her bags because Ayla, her personal assistant, had packed them for her.

Jeans . . . she needed jeans. Silver set the biggest case on its side and opened the lock. To her everlasting gratitude, Ayla had placed a list of contents on the top of the carefully folded tissue paper. Silver read through the contents and extracted what she needed before turning to the next bag and then the next. By the time Ben returned, she had all the bags open and a pile of things to take stacked haphazardly on one side.

He hunkered down beside her and surveyed her work. He smelled like leather, hay, and sun-warmed man. "Looking good."

She offered him a haughty stare as she added ten pairs of socks to her pile.

"Would you like me to help you load it onto the mule?"

She wanted to refuse, but she wasn't that stupid. "That would be very kind of you."

He efficiently sorted, rolled, and packed her clothing, and stored it inside the pack. "Weight's okay." He paused.

"You got any sunscreen in that ten-step Korean foot care thing?"

"*Face* care. I have sunscreen." She held it up. "And I'm only taking steps one and ten with me."

"Great. Don't forget your toothbrush."

There was a suspicion of a smile in his voice that made her want to stamp her foot. She sat back, collected her now-minimalist skin and makeup collection, and put everything in her saddlebag. Ben stood, murmuring to the mule, his capable fingers buckling straps and settling the pack.

Silver rammed her hat on her head and marched over to him.

"I'm ready to go when you are."

He cast a long look back over his shoulder at the open bags and then studied her from under the brim of his Stetson.

"What's wrong now?" Silver asked.

"Who do you think is going to put your stuff away?"

Silver looked vaguely around the deserted yard and flung out a hand. "Someone will. . . ."

"You want Mrs. Morgan cleaning up after you?"

"No, of course not!" Silver said hotly and then grimaced. He must think she was a completely spoiled brat. "Okay, I get it. I'll clean up."

She rushed around, randomly stuffing clothes and shoes back into the cases, and loaded them back into the Jeep while Ben continued checking the horses and mules. She finally shut the rear door and turned to face him, only to find he was staring down at his phone, his brow creased as if she didn't even exist.

"Are we good to go now?" She advanced toward him.

He put his phone away and considered her. "If you're

okay with having a bra hanging off the back of your hat, then sure."

She snatched at the pink lacy bra, threw it on the ground, and stamped hard on it.

"Satisfied?"

"Seems like the waste of a perfectly good bra to me, but it's not my call." He nodded toward her horse. "Can you mount by yourself?"

She stalked over to Ladybug, who seemed to get bigger and bigger the closer she got. When she'd tried the two horses out earlier, she'd used the mounting block and BB had settled her on the back of each horse. Silver tried to remember how the heck to get up from the ground, and almost jumped when Ben's calm voice sounded right by her ear.

"Left foot in the stirrup, reach up and grab the pommel or a handful of mane, bounce off your right foot, swing your leg over, and you're good to go."

"Why can't I use the mounting block?" Silver asked.

"Because there won't be any where we're going. I need to know that you can mount up from the ground if we have to move fast."

She tried, she really tried, but ended up looking like a demented, one-legged grasshopper. She had paused for breath, her face pressed against the side of the horse when Ben spoke again.

"Can I help you?"

For a second, she wished the ground would just open up and swallow him, but she wasn't a quitter, and she wanted to be on that horse.

"Sure, thanks."

Before she could get another word out, his hands came around her waist and she was airborne. He lifted her like she weighed nothing and settled her gently on the saddle.

"Put your feet in the stirrups and then stand up for me so I can check the length, okay?"

He fussed around by her leg, shortening the leather straps; his head was lowered so that she couldn't even see his face. She wiggled her toes experimentally. She'd asked Ayla to buy her new cowboy boots and this was the first time she'd worn them.

Eventually, Ben stepped back and looked at her appraisingly. "Do you remember how to hold the reins?"

Seeing as he'd already watched her ride around the paddock, she gave him a haughty stare. "Weirdly, I haven't forgotten how to do that in the last hour."

He passed them over to her. "Like an ice cream cone, right?"

"I *know*."

He nodded and set off for his own horse, mounting with such fluid grace and power that Silver actually gawped at him.

"What's up?" He straightened and met her stare, his brown gaze steady.

"Nothing." She found a smile. "How far are we going this morning?"

He glanced at his steel-faced watch. "Seeing as it's almost lunchtime, not as far as I'd hoped. We'll be lucky to make it to Morgansville."

"I suppose that's my fault." Silver sighed sweetly and waited for him to contradict her.

Instead, he nodded and picked up his reins.

"Yeah, you're right. It absolutely one hundred percent is."

Chapter Three

She certainly wasn't used to picking up after herself. . . . Ben checked that Silver was still following along behind him. She wasn't exactly moving fast, her hat pushed back on her head as she took in the amazing view of the Sierras and the foothills leading up to them. Seeing as they weren't going that far now, he was happy to let her get used to the horse and settle in.

If he'd been famous since the age of five, he guessed he wouldn't be much better. Sharing a room with Kaiden had drummed tidiness into his bones. If he didn't keep things nice, Kaiden would dump all his stuff in the cow barn. Even though they now had separate rooms, he still complained when Ben didn't leave the bathroom quite how he liked it. Silver Meadows was obviously used to being waited on hand and foot.

There had been a moment when she'd looked around the yard like some haughty princess, and he'd almost gone and put her stuff away for her himself. But he couldn't let her think that was the way things were going to be. She might look like some modern-day version of Doris Day, whom his auntie Rae loved to pieces, but when they were out on the trail, they'd have to rely on each other. If she wanted the real experience, he was more than willing to give it to her.

The turnoff to the ghost town of Morgansville appeared on his right, and he waited for Silver to catch up with him. "We're going this way, so take it slow, okay?"

She paused beside him, her blue eyes direct as she inspected the narrow cutout. "This looks man-made."

"It is." He pointed up the straight line of the slope. "There used to be some kind of rail system up to the mine, and this is all that's left of it."

"Mine?" She sat up straight. "Like a gold mine?"

"Silver. We can check it out on the way if you like. It's scheduled for being filled in after someone nearly got trapped in there, but you can still see the main entrance and where the buildings used to stand."

In the last year, he'd taken a dozen trail rides out past the mine and up to the ghost town of Morgansville, and he'd yet to meet someone who wasn't interested in the history of the place. Even though the trail rides went from the Morgans to the Lymonds and beyond, all the best places in his opinion were right here.

He led the way up the rapidly narrowing path, aware of the gradually encroaching silence as the vegetation was stripped away, leaving an unrelenting dusty whiteness that sometimes hurt the eyes. He took another turn off the road and finally came to a stop at the flattened piece of land where all that remained of the once-prolific Morgansville silver mine remained.

"That's it?" Silver asked. She sounded just as disappointed as everyone else who got to visit.

"Yeah." He pointed past the sealed-up door of the mine and the fluttering yellow tape around the cave-in. "The mine buildings used to stand to the right, but they took out the machinery and anything useful years ago."

"It's kind of sad," she said, her gaze fixed on the DANGER DO NOT ENTER sign. "Is it really dangerous in there?"

"Nearly came down on Rachel Morgan and Cauy Lymond last year when they were trying to locate some drunken dude ranch guests."

She shivered slightly. "Well, don't worry about me going down there. I hate small spaces."

"So does Cauy," Ben said dryly. "I'm surprised he made it out."

"I used to be in this kids' cowboy show—"

"—*The Crazy Catsby Cowgirls*, yeah." Ben completed the sentence for her.

She gave him a curious glance. "Most people who watched that show were girls."

He shrugged. "I used to mind my baby sister, Daisy, and she loved it so I somehow ended up watching reruns with her every day." He hastened to add, "I don't normally keep up with all that celebrity stuff, though."

"Well, in that show there was an episode where me and my big sister Cookie got stuck down a mine." Silver blew out a breath. "The thing was, I really did get trapped on the set because Dylan Palmer locked me in. It was terrifying. If my mom hadn't realized I was missing, and hadn't come back to look for me, I would've been stuck there all night."

"That sucks. I never liked that Dylan guy much."

"You had good taste, because most of the fans went crazy over him, and he was the vilest, most awful person imaginable. . . ." She shuddered. "I was so glad when he left the show."

"Can't say I blame you." Ben gathered his reins. "Seen enough?"

"Yes, let's keep going." She waited for him to ride off

in front of her and followed him out, with one last glance back over her shoulder at the abandoned mine. "I can't wait to see what's next."

Silver raised her arm and coughed into her elbow as the dust kicked up by Calder and Ted the mule swirled around her. She eased back on the reins and contemplated the high walls crowding in on them. It felt like she was in a different silent world and it was getting way too narrow for her liking. The sun was right above the gully and beating down on her head, which didn't help. She contemplated calling out to Ben and asking how much farther they had to go, but he was probably too far ahead of her.

Not that he'd answer her anyway. He'd already shown a distinct lack of interest in jumping when she snapped her fingers. She tried to tell herself that it was refreshing to be treated like a normal person, but she wasn't really convinced. Being a star, being on show all the time, was almost as natural to her as breathing, and she wasn't used to being ignored.

Just as the silence was beginning to get to her, the path widened out into a level plane with the sign PARKING FOR MORGANSVILLE. NO UNAUTHORIZED VEHICLES BEYOND THIS POINT.

Ben had stopped ahead, and was already dismounting and tying up the horses on the hitching post. She aimed Ladybug toward him and he caught hold of the bridle.

"We'll have lunch here, and then you can take a walk through the ghost town if you'd like," Ben offered.

Silver nodded and swung her leg over the horse to dismount. When she reached the ground, her knees buckled and Ben reached for her elbow to steady her. Her feet felt like they were made of lead and she had no idea how she was going to move them.

"Muscles locked up?" Ben crouched beside her and dug his fingers into the back of her knee. "Hang in there."

She grabbed for his shoulder as he massaged her leg and groaned somewhere between delight and agony as he expertly stretched out her cramped muscles.

"Better?" He looked up at her, his brown gaze totally professional.

"Much."

"It happens all the time." He rose to his feet. "There are a couple of picnic benches over here so we don't need to unpack more than the lunch Mrs. Morgan made for us."

"Great." Silver managed to take a step and then another one and suddenly everything started working again. For the first time in her life she was glad of the strenuous workouts her personal trainer made her go through every day. "Can I help?"

He was doing something with her horse and spoke without turning around. "Sure. Look in Calder's left saddlebag and grab the food while I check the table out."

Silver approached the huge horse somewhat warily, but he paid no attention to her as she unbuckled the saddlebag, only to reveal a medical kit, three pairs of hand-knitted socks, and four pairs of black boxers. She hurriedly shut the flap and went around to the other left side where she found the packs of sandwiches and a flask of what she hoped was coffee.

She brought everything up to the table where Ben was sitting staring out at the ghost town and placed it in front of him.

"You do wear underwear." The words fell out of her mouth before she considered their impact.

His head jerked up. "Were you checking?"

"No, I opened the wrong saddlebag." Silver sat opposite him. "Although I would think that not wearing underwear when you are riding long distances could cause all kinds of issues."

He studied her cautiously. "Yeah, I guess so. How are your calves now?"

"Much better, thanks." She opened the container of food and her stomach growled. "Oh my God, my dietitian and trainer would kill me if they knew what I was just about to eat."

"It's just a sandwich." Ben waited until she'd made her selection and then helped himself. "What's wrong with that?"

"It's white flour, full-fat mayonnaise, and salted chicken." Silver studied the bread. "If I was going to be good, I'd just eat the chicken and lettuce."

"Then it would be a salad and not a sandwich," Ben commented as he poured them both some coffee. "Are you really not allowed to eat whatever you want?"

"If I want to continue to get film roles, then yes."

He snorted and helped himself to his second sandwich. "I wouldn't last five minutes."

"You wouldn't have to," she pointed out. "Guys get away with a lot of things that girls can't."

"Double standards, right?" He chewed for a while. "My sister, Daisy, who works in tech, says it's hard for her to be taken as seriously as her male colleagues."

"Daisy, the one you watched my TV show with?"

"Yeah, my one and only sister." His smile was fond. "For some reason she liked me looking after her the best, so I'd get my homework done while she watched her TV shows and Auntie Rae made dinner for the rest of us."

"Do you have a big family?"

"There are six of us, so I suppose that's a lot. I'm the second son. My older brother, Adam, basically runs the ranch—"

"Your older brother is Adam and you're Benjamin?" She interrupted him. "Don't tell me you have a Caleb next?"

"Nope, a Kaiden." She grinned at him and his brow creased. "What's so funny about that?"

She set down her sandwich and shook her head. "And then?"

"Danny and Evan."

"Was your mom by any chance a Howard Keel fan?"

Ben frowned. "I've no idea. Why does it matter?"

"Have you ever seen *Seven Brides for Seven Brothers*?"

"Can't say I have."

"It's a musical which came out in the fifties about seven brothers looking for seven brides. The boys are named alphabetically from the Bible, starting with Adam and Benjamin."

She looked at him expectantly.

"I doubt there's a Kaiden in the Bible," Ben said. "What do these guys do?"

"Well, it's all a bit politically incorrect these days because they decide to follow the advice of the Romans and steal their brides from the local town just like the Romans took the Sabine women."

"That's not good." Ben paused to consider what she'd told him. "I can't see us galloping down to Morgantown and kidnapping women somehow. Not that any of them would let us, since BB started those female-only self-defense classes. We'd probably get our asses kicked all the way back to the ranch."

He finished his second sandwich while she still nibbled at her first.

"Did the women in the movie get away?"

"No, they end up falling in love with the brothers."

Ben shook his head. "That's whacked."

"Stockholm syndrome at its finest." She nodded. "But you should ask your mom whether she named you guys after the movie."

"I'm not sure I want to know if she did."

"It is a great movie for its time." She sipped her coffee. "You should still watch it."

"I hate musicals." Ben topped off her coffee. "I can't dance, and I sing like a bullfrog."

"Which is funny because the guy they cast in the movie as Benjamin couldn't dance or sing either."

"Then why the heck was he in it?" Ben asked.

"Back in the day, if you were on contract with a studio they could pretty much put you in whatever they wanted, and you had to make the best of it." She grimaced. "Actually, that hasn't changed much now. Poor old Ben was stuck at the back or sitting down while everyone else was dancing up a storm."

Ben smiled. "Now *that* I can relate to, seeing as I was always stuck at the back in school and church stuff." He eyed the remaining three sandwiches. "You okay if I have another one?"

"Sure! Have them all if you like." She gestured at the sandwich in her hand. "This is plenty for me."

"We'll eat again after we set up camp tonight."

"How far are you planning on going?" Silver asked as she finished up her sandwich.

"About five miles. I don't want to push you too hard." He watched her face fall. "Do you think you can make it?"

She grimaced. "I'm not sure. How far have we come already?"

"Three miles, give or take."

"Is that all?" She gawped at him. "I thought it was at least ten."

"Well, we are traveling very slowly. An average horse can easily put in fifteen to twenty miles a day." He finished off his coffee. "How about you let me know if you can't make it, and if we can stop, we'll do it."

"Thanks for being so nice," Silver said softly.

He shrugged and tried not to smile back at her. He normally had no problem keeping things professional, but Silver wasn't anything like his normal clients. He'd never ended up in a crazy conversation about musicals, and his mother's reasons for giving them alphabetical names. He had no idea why his mother did anything anyway, and in his current mood, was unlikely to ask her.

"We're going to be out here for over a week," Ben reminded Silver. "There's no point in ruining the experience for you on day one, is there?"

She reached over and squeezed his hand, and he fought the impulse to close his much-larger fingers over hers. "Thank you, though."

"Yeah, well, let's get moving, shall we?" Ben eased out of her grasp and stood up, brushing crumbs from his clothing. "We don't want to be stuck up here when it gets dark. It's not called a ghost town for nothing."

Ben wasn't what she'd expected. Silver glanced over at him as he guided her down what she guessed had once been the main street of the once-thriving town of Morgansville. Getting him to talk required a lot of effort, but when he did open up, he had a dry sense of humor that appealed to her, and he was far from stupid.

Due to the higher altitude, a lot of the buildings looked as if they had only just been abandoned, although Ben had told her it had happened a long time ago. Something was bugging her. "Why is it so quiet and barren?" She turned a slow circle, listening in vain for any sounds of life beyond her and Ben. "It looks like someone dumped these buildings on the moon."

"The settlers cut down all the trees to build the houses and the stamping mill, pulled up all the bushes and stuff to plow the fields, and caused the equivalent of a mini dust bowl." He pointed out toward the barren hillside. "That used to be covered in sequoias."

"Is that why the settlers eventually moved down the road?" Silver asked.

"The creek dried up, they couldn't power the stamping mill, and the mine stopped producing enough silver to make it worth the effort anymore. They had a town meeting and they decided to move down the valley to what we now call Morgantown."

"I can't say I blame them." Silver gazed into the broken window of one of the wooden houses where strips of wallpaper were swaying in the breeze. "This would make a great film set."

"I bet—except I don't think the Morgantown Historical Society would be happy about letting a film crew tromp all over the place. These building aren't as sturdy as they look."

"I'm auditioning for a role in a Western next month," Silver said. "I really want to get the part, and I thought this might help me get a sense of how it might have been back then."

"So I heard."

He shifted his booted feet, making his spurs jangle. Since their unexpected bonding over lunch he'd retreated back into the shortest sentences possible. But maybe they hadn't bonded, and he'd just been polite listening to her chat away like a fool. That was his job after all.

She frowned. "My dad *told* you?"

"Yeah." He started moving again, his gaze at the building at the end of the street. "Do you want to see the bank? The vault's still there. I guess they couldn't figure out how to remove something so heavy."

"Sure."

Seeing as her dad was super overprotective, she had to wonder what else he'd said to Ben. Had he warned him off? Silver smiled at her own arrogance. Maybe it was way simpler than that and Ben Miller simply wasn't interested in getting to know her. She rarely got the opportunity to talk to someone outside her tight circle and she'd enjoyed talking to him and stupidly wanted him to like her back.

But how would she know if him liking her was genuine? Being around famous people could distort the most basic of interactions. She'd done her first commercial as a baby, and never had what could be considered a normal life. Maybe she wasn't even capable of being liked for herself—maybe she didn't know who she was after all.

"You okay?" Ben had halted in front of a brick building and was looking back at her.

"Yes, sorry, I was just thinking."

"About this place as a movie set?"

"No, about my inability to know how to act like a normal person."

He looked her up and down. "You're doing okay."

"Thanks." She frowned at him. "Every time I start a conversation, you look at me as if I'm nuts."

He took so long to answer that she'd almost given up hope.

"You're . . . different than the people I normally take out on a trail ride."

"In a good way or a bad way?" Silver advanced toward him.

"Neither. Just different." He pointed in through the open doorway. "If you look right through the back you can just about see the open vault."

Chapter Four

God, she was tired. The sun was setting, and there were no other lights around them as Ben finally called a halt. In the gathering darkness, she could just about hear the sound of running water and make out a copse of trees. For some reason, she'd been expecting a lot more than that.

She managed to dismount and just stood there holding Ladybug's reins as Ben started to unload the mules.

"Where's the backup staff?" Silver asked.

"The what?" Ben looked over at her, his face barely visible in the gloom.

"The people who set up the campsite."

"That would be us." He set two of the packs on the ground and started on the second mule. "Everything we need is in here. Which would you rather do first, start the campfire, or put up your tent?"

She slowly closed her mouth. "I was kind of expecting those things would be done for me."

His teeth flashed white in the darkness. "If you want to eat and sleep safely tonight, then you might have to manage your expectations."

He walked over and took Ladybug's reins out of her unresisting fingers. "I'm going to release the horses and mules into the enclosure. Do you want to help?"

Aware that if he went away too far from her, she'd be alone in the dark, she nodded. "Sure."

"Come on, then."

She stumbled after him, leading Ladybug and Ted toward the dense group of trees. "Do we have food for them?"

He glanced back at her. "Nope, they'll be having beans and singing Kumbaya with us around the fire."

Silver took a moment to respond. "I hope they sing better than you do."

Ben chuckled. "I've got hay, and if there's not enough grass for them to graze on, I have alfalfa pellets, which we'll also be eating if we don't get our camp set up."

He removed Calder's saddle and placed it on the sturdy fence. Silver tried to do the same with Ladybug's and staggered at the weight before she managed to right herself and just get it on the fence.

"Good job," Ben said as he took off Calder's saddle blanket and bridle, replacing it with a halter before he turned to the mules.

He spent a few minutes checking each animal over, picking up their feet to inspect their hooves and generally making sure they were in good shape. While he worked, he offered Silver a running commentary of what he was doing and encouraged her to get involved.

After securing the gate of the enclosure and checking the animals had access to water, he turned back to the campsite. "Come on."

Silver didn't even mind when he grabbed her hand and towed her up the slope.

"Can we start with the tents?" Silver asked plaintively. "I don't think I want anything to eat. I'd just like to go to sleep."

"Sure." He knelt down and unrolled one of the packs.

"Here's yours. There are instructions on the top." He glanced over at her, a challenge in his eyes, and she stiffened. "While you do that, I'm going to start the fire."

When he came back with some wood, Ben tried not to look directly at Silver who was sitting on the ground puzzling over a pile of poles, a ground sheet, and the tent fabric. Usually, he helped the guests with their tents, but her expectation that they would have a support staff setting everything up for them had made him think that she needed to understand that her participation in all events was not only required, but essential.

He hunkered down beside the two flat stones in the center of the circle and carefully stacked his wood before adding some dried grass to act as an accelerant. The wood was quite dry, so he was confident he'd soon have a decent fire going. He always carried cured wood with sap, which burned easily and kept burning long enough to start a good fire.

"Ouch," Silver muttered. "This is way more complicated than it looks."

After making sure that the fire was taking, he went to take a look at what she'd accomplished so far.

"Push that left side pole in further and you've got the basic shape," Ben said. "Then all you have to do is build the sides and the roof structure and you're good to go."

She looked over at him. "You don't think I'm going to be able to do it, do you?"

"No shame if you can't," Ben said provocatively. "You can always share mine. It's also bigger."

The glare she gave him made his lips twitch, so he turned away, opened up his own tent, and started construction. He set a lantern between them so that she'd be able to get a good look at what he was doing. He also slowed down so that she wouldn't miss anything.

"I did it!" She squealed and jumped up and down like she'd won a medal or something.

"Go, you." Ben handed her a canvas bedroll, a pillow, and a sleeping bag. "You can put those inside and then come out and get something to eat."

She disappeared inside the tent and reversed out, giving Ben a fine view of her jeans-clad ass. She sat back on her knees and looked up at him, her hair in disarray and her cheeks flushed.

"There is one thing . . ."

"What's that?" Ben asked.

"Where's the bathroom?"

He extended his hand wide. "Pretty much wherever you want it."

"You're kidding, right?"

"Nope." He turned back to his pack and handed her the camp trowel. "Stay two hundred feet from the creek and the camp, and you're golden."

While she stomped off with her torch in something of a huff, he set a tripod over the fire with a pot and boiled some of the water from his flask. There were a couple of sandwiches left over from lunch, but they'd definitely need something else.

He pulled out a couple random packs of freeze-dried food and placed them close to the fire. Silver might not be hungry, but he certainly was.

When she came back, he held out a roll of recyclable toilet paper. "I forgot to mention we have all the luxuries."

She sniffed. "I used my tissues, thanks."

She definitely wasn't happy with him, but there wasn't much he could do about it. Either she worked out that things were different out here or she gave up and went home. He'd only had one family bail on him on a trail ride before and that was because the kids had been so obnoxious that the parents had given in to their constant whining and gone back. If it had been up to Ben, he would've ignored the complaints and made them follow through, but that was probably because he'd been brought up by a father who didn't suffer fools gladly and had never let any of his sons slack off or complain about anything.

Silver hunkered down on one of the logs set around the now-blazing campfire, her gaze fixed on the flames. She yawned so hard, Ben heard her jaw crack.

"You should eat something before you turn in," Ben said. He picked up the packs of freeze-dried food and squinted at the labels. "I've got beef stew or sweet and sour rice. Either of those grab you?"

She shuddered. "If that's anything like the astronaut food I've tasted, it'll be disgusting."

"It's not the same thing, and just remember that unless we catch or shoot our own food, this is all we have."

She didn't look convinced and Ben didn't push it. "There *are* a couple of sandwiches left from lunch, and Mrs. Morgan made some brownies and snuck them in."

"Brownies?" Silver's head came up like one of his dogs chasing a chicken. "Where?"

He pushed the container over to her. "I'm surprised you didn't see them. They were right next to my boxers." She grabbed the box like he'd handed her a lifeline. "You should eat a sandwich as well."

She was already on that, devouring the white bread and mayo sandwich she'd reluctantly nibbled on at lunch in five bites. Ben hid a smile as she started on the brownies.

"Shouldn't you be consulting your diet app?" Ben asked. She literally growled at him and he held up his hands. "Remember, we'll be out here for over a week, so don't eat them all at once."

Silver ate her second brownie, almost moaning at the glorious chocolatey feel of it sliding down her throat. She couldn't remember being quite so hungry before in her life, and yet she'd done nothing more strenuous than sit on a horse and listen to Ben Miller lecture her about stuff. Getting the tent up by herself had felt like some kind of victory, but she had to give him credit for letting her crow.

She glanced over at him as he tended to the fire and then carefully tipped boiling water from the pot into one of the foil pouches. He stirred it with a spoon and then set it to one side.

"Which one is that?" She spoke through a mouthful of brownie.

"I'm not sure. I like to live dangerously." He mock-frowned. "Not as good as Mrs. Morgan's home cooking, but it'll have to do."

"Does your mom cook?"

"Occasionally, but it's mainly Adam because she doesn't live with us." He shrugged. "He finds it relaxing for some reason."

She withheld her curiosity about his offhand comment about his mom and held out the container. "Do you want this sandwich?"

"You have it if you need it." He returned his attention to the pouch.

Silver didn't think that she'd ever met a man who was so contained in himself and yet so comfortable in his environment. She'd already established that he didn't shout, had a dry sense of humor, and that he wasn't willing to take any shit even from her. He spoke the words he wanted to say, and then shut up. He was so completely alien to her, that she didn't know what to make of him or how to charm him into liking her.

Why she wanted him to like her was another issue entirely, and one she wasn't sure she needed to examine right now. Her therapist said she had a compulsive need to be liked, and not in a good way. Did she assume everyone would love her? Was she really that conceited? Maybe she needed to make more of an effort to get to know him.

"So your sister Daisy is the only girl," Silver asked.

"Yeah." For the first time he smiled with real warmth. "And the youngest and definitely the smartest of the bunch."

"She's in tech?"

He nodded, stirring the contents of his meal and then set it down again. "She's in a start-up that's looking like making her a millionaire in a couple of years."

"That's awesome." Silver resisted the lure of the brownies and firmly resealed the lid. "Does she look like you?"

"A little bit, but her hair has less red in it, and she's petite."

"Is she pretty?"

"How would I know? The guy she's engaged to seems to think so." Ben opened his meal, stirred it again, and sat down on one of the logs opposite her. "I think Daisy is more interested in being smart than in being pretty."

Silver raised her chin. "There's nothing wrong in being both."

"True." He ate a spoonful of his meal and chewed slowly. "I think it's beef stew."

"People often think I'm dumb just because I'm blond," Silver added.

"I don't think you're dumb."

"But do you think I'm pretty?"

Ben turned fully toward her, his considering gaze on her face. "Not really."

"Beautiful?"

"I don't judge people on what they look like on the outside."

"Everyone does that whether they mean to or not," Silver countered. "That's why women and men who look a certain way become famous."

"Maybe I don't care about the being famous part." He ate another spoonful of stew. "Why does it matter what I think of you anyway?"

"Because . . ." Silver was beginning to regret starting such a stupid conversation. "You said you loved my cowboy show."

"I liked the show, yeah, but that wasn't *you,* was it? That was just a character you played on TV twenty years ago." He met her gaze. "I don't know the real you, do I?"

"You know more than most fans," she said, all the while wondering why she was being so obstinate about nothing. "You've spent a whole day with me."

"Whoop-de-woo, like I won a contest or something?" His smile didn't reach his eyes. "The thing is, Ms. Meadows, for the next week you're in *my* world, and whether I think you're pretty or not is secondary to whether you have the intelligence to stay alive, learn something, and not fall apart on me."

She put down the brownie box with something of a thump. "We've already established that I'm not stupid, and I'm pretty certain I can manage the rest of it."

He sighed. "Look, I don't want to fight with you. You're a guest on this ranch, and I'll make sure that you get the best trail riding experience of your life, okay?"

"Don't worry. I'm not going to complain to your employers if you actually engage with me as if I am a real person," Silver shot back. "I can take criticism and I do want to learn."

"Then we're good." He focused his attention on the fire. "Are you sure you don't want some of this?"

Aware that he'd dismissed her again, Silver considered what to do. "I think I'm full." She faked a yawn. "Is it okay to use water directly from the creek?"

"I've got drinking water if that's what you need." He nodded over at the pack set up against one of the rocks.

"What about washing myself?" She'd already given up on the notion of having a proper shower.

"You can use it for that, too. I'll fill up the bottles again tonight and add purification tablets so we're good to go tomorrow."

"I think I might turn in, then." Silver stood up and stretched. "Do I need to set an alarm?"

"I'll wake you." He abandoned the fire, walked over to the pack, rummaged around for a few moments, and offered her a small plastic basin, a mirror, and a bottle of hand sanitizer. "I figured you'd need these."

"Don't most people?"

He grinned. "Not our guests. They tend to just jump in the creek, splash around a bit, and call it good."

She considered calling his bluff and then took the proffered items. "Thank you."

He followed her over to her tent. "Take one of the small lanterns, the water, and a torch in case you need to get up during the night."

"I can use my phone if I need a light." She looked up at him. "Speaking of which, where do I plug my adaptor in?"

Ben made sure he was well clear of their campground before he allowed himself to laugh out loud. Her face when he'd had to point out that there was no electricity had been priceless, like he'd offered to murder her first-born child or something. She'd rallied fast and inquired about the availability of the Internet, and had taken the fact that it didn't exist out here very well, considering . . .

Ben sighed and looked up at the stars. She wasn't the first guest to have a complete freak-out when deprived of their daily barrage of social media. If she'd bothered to read through the package of information from Morgan Ranch, she would have seen that it clearly stated that Internet coverage was spotty on the trails and electricity hard to come by.

He continued to walk up the slope to the top of the hill and took out his radio to check in with BB who was acting as his base camp buddy. He'd set up a series of talk windows every evening to share information about his current position. If he missed the half hour check-in time, BB would assume something was wrong and attempt to get to him as soon as possible.

For his part, BB would relate current weather conditions, any fire risks, and anything else that might cause problems along the way. It was a system that worked well, and so far, apart from the bratty family insisting on returning to the ranch early, they hadn't had any major issues.

Ben paused to look up at the sky, seeking out the familiar constellations his father had shown him when he was a kid. After their mother left, at his sister's urging, Jeff had made the occasional effort to do stuff with them that wasn't directly related to work on the ranch. He'd been really bad at it, but looking back, Ben appreciated that he'd made the effort.

His radio crackled and BB's voice came over loud and clear. Seeing as they were still on Morgan Ranch land, there wasn't much to talk about after Ben updated BB with his position and the route he intended to take the next day. He ended the exchange and leaned back against the rock wall, his keen gaze sweeping the land below him. In the distance, a pack of coyotes howled, and he decided he'd better get back in case Silver woke up and wondered why the hell it sounded like babies screaming into the void.

After telling her there was no electricity, he'd braced himself for her demanding to go back to civilization, but she'd surprised him by laughing and going into her tent. She was a mass of contradictions. Sometimes, he felt like she was trying on different roles waiting to see which one worked on him, and then occasionally she'd laugh at something and he'd get a glimpse of what he thought of as the real woman.

She'd asked him if she was pretty. . . .

He thought about that as he walked down the slope. She wasn't conventionally pretty, but when she smiled she was so damn beautiful he couldn't look away. And somehow, when she was on screen, that ability to hold his attention was magnified a thousandfold. She had that "it" thing that made you want to keep looking even when you knew you were way out of your league, and she was your client, and you had to remain professional.

Ben stopped walking on the edge of the camp. When the hell had his musings become so personal? She was a famous actress; he was a professional trail guide, and that was how it was going to be until he delivered her safely back to her father, happy and healthy in less than two weeks.

Chapter Five

"Did you say coffee?" Silver croaked as she crawled out of her tent on her hands and knees and headed for the fire, not caring what she looked like or what Ben might think of her.

"Way ahead of you." Ben, who was looking remarkably bright-eyed and bushy-tailed, pointed at the metal pot sitting over the fire. It was already sunny and the birds were singing so loudly they hurt her head. "It's cowboy coffee, nothing fancy."

She used the thick cloth to lift the pot and poured the dark brew into the cup Ben had left for her, almost salivating at the aroma. She clutched her mug hard and looked over at him.

"This morning I think I might love you."

"For my coffee?" He chuckled. "You'd better taste it first."

She took her first sip and felt the caffeine shudder through her veins. "Perfect."

"I'm impressed." He threw the coffee grounds from the bottom of his cup onto the ground and checked the fire. "I've got high-protein pancakes and maple syrup coming up for breakfast."

"Gluten-free?" Silver said hopefully.

He gave her a pitying glance and slid a plate over to her before turning to eat his own.

"Did you sleep okay?"

"Yes." Silver couldn't actually believe it herself. "I'm not used to all this fresh air."

"Your dad said you hadn't been well." Ben cut into his second pancake.

"Did he?" Her goodwill toward him over the coffee dissipated slightly and her stomach tightened. "I wonder why he told you that?"

"Was he not being truthful?" Ben met her gaze. "If you do get sick, or need medical assistance, tell me as soon as possible."

"I'm perfectly fine." She faced him. "My dad is a terrible worrier."

"Why's that?"

"Ever heard that story about the goose who lays the golden eggs?"

His brow creased. "I'm not following."

"I basically support my whole family. I have since the age of seven when I was cast in my first major film role," Silver said flatly. "They all work for me. If I go down, they go down."

"That's pretty harsh."

"Of me?"

"No, *on* you. That's a hell of a responsibility." His smile wasn't happy. "I have the opposite problem. No one in my family depends on me at all."

Happy to get off the subject of her complicated relationship with her father, Silver pounced on his admission.

"That's not what I heard. My dad had to pay through the nose to get you to be my guide for this trip. You're obviously in demand."

"Maybe BB Morgan's just a shrewd negotiator." Ben

set his plate aside, licked the syrup from his lips, and rubbed a hand over his mouth. "It was expensive because it's calving season and most ranches need all hands on deck."

"Oh." Silver took a bite of one of the pancakes and it wasn't bad at all. "So was your family mad that you took this job?"

"You could say that." He stood up, dusted down his jeans, and put his mug and plate in the center of the circle near the fire.

"So your family *does* depend on you," Silver said triumphantly.

He looked over at her, one eyebrow raised. "I'm here, aren't I?" He nodded at her plate. "Help yourself to more coffee if you need it. I'm going down to the creek to check on the livestock."

She finished her pancakes, had another cup of coffee, and felt better than she had for a long while. Her body was aching in weird places, but the rigorous fitness regime her occupation demanded was definitely paying dividends. Ben obviously had a few issues with his family, and she couldn't say she blamed him. She knew all about being beholden to people yet feeling like they no longer saw you as a person but as a means to an end.

Going back to her tent, she changed out of her jammies and back into her jeans, fleece top, and boots before heading down to the corral.

The horses and mules were eating hay Ben must have put out for them, but there was no sign of him. She turned a slow circle and then walked down toward the edge of the creek where she abruptly stopped.

Her trail guide was just stepping out of his boxers and wading naked into the creek. She took three steps backward until she was in the shadow of the trees, and couldn't take her eyes off his rather nice ass. She doubted he'd ever been near a gym, but he didn't have any surplus fat on his well-muscled physique.

He crouched down and splashed water over his face and body all the while cursing up a storm. She guessed it had to be cold in there.

"I'm going to come out in a second, Silver, so if you don't want to see the rest of me, you might want to get back to camp."

Silver jumped as he spoke directly to her.

"We're really going to have to work on your tracking skills." He started to rise and turned toward the bank. "Last chance to run."

Silver clapped her hands over her eyes like a scandalized maiden aunt, but still got an eyeful of his lightly haired chest, six pack abs and . . .

"I suppose you're going to say that the water was cold." The words slipped out before she could stop them.

He glanced down past his flat stomach to his groin. "I think everything is perfectly in proportion, thanks." He advanced slowly toward her without a hint of shame. But why would he be ashamed, Silver thought feverishly, when his body was everything most men aspired to? "Sure you don't want a dip? I could throw you in, if you like?"

She ran, then, all the way up to the camp, and started packing up her tent. By the time he joined her, she'd managed to stop blushing.

"I'm sorry." She made herself look at his face, which now that she'd seen the rest of him was harder than she'd thought. "It was incredibly rude and insensitive of me to invade your privacy like that."

He waved off her apology. "You didn't know I was bathing when you came down there. I should've told you to keep away."

"But I should've known better," she kept on arguing. "I hate it when people take unauthorized pictures of me when I'm not expecting it."

"I bet." He eyed her curiously. "Maybe I should be glad that you didn't have your phone on you or else I'd be Internet famous right now."

She met his gaze. "I would *never* do that to you. I swear it."

He nodded and turned toward his own tent. "Let's get packed up."

Ben led the way up the slope that looked over the interior of Morgan Valley. There were several ranches out here with land boundaries that met and separated and rejoined like the random outlets of a creek. BB had secured access to most of the valley for the trail rides. In return, Ben, or whoever was leading the ride, would report back on boundary fences, the presence of predators, water issues, or any of the hundreds of problems running a large ranch brought up without having the necessary hands.

Budgets were tight these days even at his own family ranch. If Ben saw a fence that needed mending, he'd get it done with the assistance of his guests who got to support with real-time ranch conservation. He'd even moved a few cows out of a flooded field into a safer one on the Garcia ranch once, which currently needed all the help it could get. If he saw any predators, he also had permission to hunt them. It was an arrangement that had worked well so far.

Somehow, despite not having bathed in the creek or had a proper shower, Silver still looked good. He guessed carting around that Korean skin cream was worth it. He should've told her that he was going to wash in the creek, but he hadn't thought she'd come looking for him for a while. When he'd heard her footsteps, he should've kept his boxers on and called out a warning. Had he wanted her to see him naked? If that was true, what was wrong with him?

The last time he'd felt so off-kilter was as a stupid teenager who'd done some stuff so out of character that he still didn't understand it himself. Mind you, she could've walked away, and she hadn't. He'd noticed the second she'd stopped retreating and stayed to watch.

At least he'd told her that he was turning around and coming out. That had done the trick, but he'd noticed that she'd still gotten an eyeful. He half smiled to himself. And she hadn't exactly run away screaming; she'd had enough time to make a joke about a certain part of his anatomy. . . .

"Why have we stopped?" Silver asked as she came up alongside him.

"I wanted to show you the valley from up here." He stood in his stirrups and pointed downward. "We're going to make our way to the floor and head out to the right of the canyon where the trees are."

"It doesn't look that far," Silver commented as she shaded her eyes against the glare. There were patches of green, but big stretches of dry barren grassland that in the summer months were a real fire hazard. Morgan Creek ran through the top right corner of the valley and meandered its way down to Morgansville, past Morgan Ranch, and disappeared underground just after the town.

"We're higher than you think, and going down can take twice as long as going up." He turned to look at her. "You know how to shift your body weight to balance out the horse, right?"

"Yes." Silver nodded. "Lean back and let the horse do the work."

"Ladybug's a champ at this so you'll be fine. I'll deal with the mules." He handed her his water flask and waited as she took a sip before handing it back. "Any questions?"

She looked him up and down. "You should use sunscreen."

"I do." He blinked at her.

"Your nose is red." She leaned over and lightly touched it. "Stay right there."

A second later she was slathering his nose and face in something that smelled like a bunch of roses.

"There, that's better." She recapped the lotion and put it back in her pocket.

"Thanks, Mom," Ben quipped, surprising a laugh out of her as she picked up her reins.

"Trust me, Ben Miller, I have no motherly feelings toward you whatsoever."

"Was it something I said?" Ben asked innocently.

"You have the body of a god, and you darn well know it," she said severely. "I'd have to be dead not to appreciate it."

"A god?" Ben echoed and patted his chest. "And it's all natural and homegrown."

"Like your beef?"

"You could say that." Ben studied her. "You had a nose job, didn't you?"

"Where did that come from?" she squeaked.

"Because we're talking about appearances." He paused. "You might as well admit it. I'm not going to tell anyone."

"I broke my nose and had to have it reset." Silver sniffed. "While they were fixing it they might have altered it 'slightly.'"

"Slightly?"

"Oh, come on, it's such a minor thing to do!" Silver

protested. "Lots of girls have it done. At least I didn't do the boob thing."

His attention dropped to her chest and he raised one eyebrow. "You sure about that?"

She grabbed his wrist, pulled off his glove, and pressed his hand to her chest. "Feel it! It's one hundred percent natural!"

He went still, his gaze on his trapped hand, which was now full of warm, squeezable, female boob. His thumb rested right over her nipple, which was rapidly hardening.

"Uh . . . I . . ."

She hurriedly released his hand and threw his glove back at him. "Do you want to untie Bill from the back of my saddle if you're going to take him down the slope?"

"Yeah, *yeah*, I'll do that now." He dismounted and untied the rope, glad that he was out of her view as the fit of his jeans grew way more uncomfortable. "You can start on down. I'll be right behind you."

Silver kept her gaze on the downward slope, which was way less regular than the previous route, with several switchback turns to avoid large boulders or landslides. Why had she put Ben's hand on her boob? What on earth had she been thinking?

Again, it all came down to her inability to have a normal conversation with anyone. She just didn't know how to do it. He must think she was insane. She should never have agreed to come on the trail ride. She'd been so shocked when her dad had agreed she could go by herself that she hadn't thought things through. Being out here without her usual support team was making her look like an ass.

But if she wanted to break out of her light comedy, blond girl roles and appear in the gritty Western, she needed this kind of experience on her resume. She wanted to *act,* to show the world that she wasn't just a pretty face, and was more than willing to take a huge pay cut to do the independent film if they'd have her.

Silver stared off over the valley. Had her father just been humoring her all along? Did he think that ten days stuck out here would be enough to make her give up her dreams and return to the kind of roles that had made her famous and her family rich? The more she thought about it, the more likely it seemed. Maybe he'd told Ben Miller to make things as difficult as possible for her. . . .

A shadow loomed over her and both she and Ladybug jumped a little to the side as a turkey vulture flew low over their heads. Silver banged her elbow on the protruding rock wall and muttered a curse as her mare righted herself.

"You okay?" Ben called out to her from behind.

"Yup." She wasn't in the mood to turn around and talk to him right now—what with the boob incident, and her gathering suspicions that Ben and her father were somehow in cahoots.

She focused her attention on the path ahead. It had taken way longer than she had anticipated getting down. She hadn't reached the valley floor yet, and the sun was already overhead. She was so hot that rivulets of sweat were running down her back. When she was on solid ground, she would take off her fleece and leave just her T-shirt on. The thought of jumping into the creek with or without a naked Ben in it was really appealing.

She took the last angled corner and walked Ladybug out onto the sparse grass, turning in a circle to watch Ben complete the descent. Despite the fact that he was managing his horse and Bill and Ted, he still looked more competent than she ever would. He barely moved in the saddle yet was so in tune with Calder that it was like watching poetry in motion. He clicked to the mules, took the last turn with a dexterity that impressed her, and came down in a cloud of dust that briefly obscured him.

He pulled up beside her and silently offered her his water bottle. She showed him her own, and drank from that, still unwilling to share more than she had to with him.

He took off his Stetson and knocked the dust off it. "Jeez, it's hot. Let's find some shade, check the time, and have something to eat."

She was more than willing to get out of the sun. When Ben suggested they pick up the pace and kicked his horse into a smooth sitting trot, she ended up bobbing along behind him like a demented whack-a-mole. She didn't care. Gaining the shelter of the trees was such a welcome relief after the unforgiving glare of the sun. Ben had already stopped and was busy tying up the mules and his horse, his movements efficient with long practice. She dismounted and led Ladybug over to stand beside Calder.

"Give me five," Ben said as he loosened Ladybug's girth. "And I'll get the fire started."

"Fire?" Silver shuddered. "Like we need more heat?"

"We have to eat something." He glanced over at her as he checked her horse, all business again. "And, until we reach the creek, we can't catch any fish, so we'll need to boil some water."

The wall to the right of the wooded area was a mixture of crumbling red clay and rock through which a trickle of water made its way down to the valley floor.

Silver's stomach gurgled as if to agree with him. "What can I do?" She was determined not to sit around and watch him work. If he and her dad thought she was a quitter, she would prove them wrong. This was part one of her independence campaign and nothing was going to stop her achieving her goals.

"Gather some wood for the fire while I set a bucket under the water to give to the horses and mules."

"Okay." Silver took off her fleece, wiped her brow, and went off into the wooded area gathering the plentiful dry, fallen wood as she went. It was peaceful within the shadowed shelter of the trees and, when a slight breeze picked up that ruffled her hair, almost pleasant.

She came back to find that Ben had unpacked the food and the pot and was lining a small indentation away from the trees and within the shelter of the wall with stones.

"Thanks." He inspected her offerings, picked the ones he wanted, and arranged them in a neat interconnected pile over the stones. He added some grass and hunkered down beside the fire beckoning for her to join him. "When you light a fire, pay attention to where the wind is coming from so you don't accidentally set the dry grass alight."

"Good thinking."

"If it's high summer, always have a bucket of water or a fire blanket close by to douse the flames if they get whipped up by the wind." He set the tripod over the flames and waited until the wood caught before setting the pan of water to boil. "Shouldn't take long. The water in my flask is already warm."

"Shall I check the horses?" Silver asked, getting to her feet.

"Yeah, sure, thanks." He looked up at her, his brown eyes narrowed against the sun. "If the bucket is empty, fill it up again, and make sure the mules get their fair share. Calder's a pig and too much water is bad for him."

"Will do."

By the time she'd completed her tasks, the water was boiling, and Ben was digging into the container of freeze-dried food. "Beef, chicken, or sweet and sour rice?" he called out.

"Chicken." Silver sat down next to him, her back against the canyon wall. "You are going to put that fire out as soon as you can, right?"

"Absolutely." He poured water into the two packs and handed her one. "Stir it and then leave it for a couple of minutes before you eat."

Silver instinctively got out her phone while she waited for the meal and made a sad face at the screen. "The battery's almost gone."

"Good." Ben met her gaze. "You know what really bugs me? When people come out here and spend their whole time looking at the view through their phones instead of experiencing it in real time."

Silver hastily put her phone away. "That's great, but now you're going to have to talk to me for the next eight days, and that's been going *so* well."

"I'd rather talk than touch your boob again."

"What was wrong with my boob?" Silver demanded. "Most men would give a million dollars to get to do what you did."

"But I didn't do it." He raised his eyebrows. "You made me."

"What are you, *nine?* I was trying to prove a point!"

He shrugged. "Seeing as I wouldn't know what a fake boob felt like anyway, I'm not sure what you proved."

"None of your girlfriends have had breast implants?" Silver asked.

"Nope, or nose jobs, or any other kind of stuff you celebrities get up to."

"So trying to look your best is a bad thing?"

"Of course not, but morphing into a totally different person is just weird." Ben mimicked a frozen face.

"I'm not planning on doing that," Silver assured him. "But when your face *is* your business, you do have to take care of it. Even the male stars get work done these days."

"Work." Ben chuckled. "Like it's hard to do or something."

Silver opened her food pouch and vigorously stirred the contents. She didn't know a single person who hadn't had some kind of plastic surgery. Even her mom who tended to stay out of the limelight had had a tummy tuck and endured the occasional injection of Botox.

"Must be nice to be so perfect that you don't have to worry about the lines on your face," Silver muttered between mouthfuls.

"Lines build character," Ben said. "Look at Mrs. Morgan. She's going on seventy, and she's still beautiful."

"That's a different kind of beauty altogether," Silver argued. "And she doesn't have to see her face magnified five hundred times bigger on a screen where everyone can tell if you have a pimple or a booger up your nose."

He snorted a mouthful of food and started to wheeze. She couldn't help but grin even as she passed him his water bottle and helpfully thumped him on the back.

"See? You've never thought about these things, have you?" Silver finished off her meal. "We live in very different worlds."

"But yours is totally fake," Ben protested.

"That's very judgmental of you." Silver wasn't buying it. "Are you saying that my family aren't real people with real problems just like anyone else?"

He studied her for a long moment. "No, I'm not saying that. I have no right to judge you whatsoever." He sighed.

"Jeez . . . I'm beginning to sound as bad as my father, so just kill me now."

"Your dad runs the ranch with you and your brothers, correct?"

"Technically, it's just my dad, Adam, and me who work full-time at the place."

"So what exactly do you do?" Silver asked as he handed her an apple.

"It's a cattle ranch." His smile dimmed. "I do all the stuff that no one else has the time or energy for. I'm basically the clean-up guy."

"Or the guy everyone depends on?"

"Yeah." He slowly raised his head to meet her gaze. "You could say that."

"So they'll probably miss you more than they thought," Silver added encouragingly. "And when you go back, they'll be nice and grateful to you."

"I'm not sure I'm going back." His smile was wry. "My dad wasn't happy at me taking off to do this trail ride during calving season. He said he might not have a job for me when I return."

"Did he mean it?" Silver felt instant guilt.

"Maybe." Ben set his food pouch down and started on his apple. "He's got something of a temper. When my mom left him, he threw all her stuff out in the yard and had a big bonfire."

Silver pressed her hand to her mouth, aware that even though Ben was acting like they were discussing the weather, there were storm clouds gathering in his eyes.

"My parents never fight."

"Lucky you." Ben crunched down on his apple. "Mine were awful."

"Did they divorce?"

"Yeah, when I was around ten or eleven." He finished his apple and set the core on the ground.

"How long did you have to go to therapy to get over *that?*" Silver asked.

"Therapy?" He raised his eyebrows. "What I had was my auntie Rae coming to save the day, and a miserable bastard of a father who decided that hard labor was the best way to stop us having time to miss our mother. It kind of worked, too. Do you want coffee?"

Silver just stared at him.

"What?"

"You poor little boy," she blurted out.

"Nothing poor or little about me." He stood up and held out his hand. "Do you want to give the apple cores to the horses while I clean up?"

The fact that Silver felt sorry for him was still bugging Ben as they cut through the copse of trees and followed the line of the canyon wall around to the right. Sure, he'd cried himself to sleep a few times after his mother had left, but only because he was exhausted after completing the long list of chores his father laid on him every day after school. Ben was fairly certain there were laws about child labor, but Jeff hadn't cared about such niceties.

Silver was supposed to be the one with the issues, not him, but he'd let himself be railroaded into a discussion about his father, which would never end well because as much as he loved his old man, Jeff definitely had a few issues of his own. . . .

Ben was supposed to be keeping an eye on Silver, not the other way around. He'd gone through her saddlebags the first night when she was sleeping, feeling bad about it, but aware that he'd promised her father that she wouldn't be smoking anything on his watch except jerky. He'd found nothing but makeup, skin care products, and silky underwear that had given him some great dreams.

She didn't seem jittery or anxious, and he was beginning to wonder exactly why Mr. Meadows had been so insistent that his daughter was using drugs. He'd promised the man that he wouldn't mention the subject directly to Silver, which should probably have been his first warning. There was obviously a lot going on that he didn't understand. Ben didn't appreciate being stuck in the middle of another family's drama. He'd had enough trouble dealing with his own.

"Ben!"

He turned his head sharply as Silver yelled from behind him. She was pointing at the sky. "What's up?"

"Look at that bird!"

He grinned as a raptor flew by with a still-wriggling snake hanging from its beak.

"Let's hope he doesn't drop it." He squinted into the sun. "That's a red-tailed hawk."

"How do you know?"

"Because it's my job to know," Ben replied, glad to be back talking about something he could handle. "I've got a set of binoculars in my saddlebag if you want them."

"Maybe later." Silver smiled at him. "I suspect I'd get nauseous if I tried to ride and stare upward at the same time. Are there a lot of raptors around here?"

"Yeah, there's even a pair of nesting condors on the canyon wall we're heading toward."

"They're rare, right?"

"Very." He shortened his reins. "You ready to move on? We're going to camp by Morgan Creek for the night, and I want to get there before it's too late."

He heard the sound of the water well before they reached

the edge of the creek. They'd had a lot of rain recently and the creek level was rising, which would be good for the drier months ahead. There was still snow on the peaks of the Sierras, and one of the mountain passes wouldn't be open until at least June, if not July. If the snowpack was good, the melted ice flow would eventually work its way down to their level and keep the valley blooming.

He dismounted, tied up the mules and Calder, and beckoned for Silver to follow him. He led her through the trees to the rocky wall of the canyon and stood back. The ground was trembling beneath their feet and there was a peculiar muted booming sound.

Ben pointed upward. "It's cool, isn't it?"

Silver gasped as she looked up at the water pouring over the rocky, top ridge of the canyon and crashing down to the base with an almighty roar.

"It's incredible." She had to raise her voice to be heard.

"This is where we start calling it Morgan Creek," Ben said. "It feeds the whole valley."

There was a deep pool of water under the fall and then a wide rock-filled riverbed along which the water meandered at varying speeds, swirling and crashing and reforming in an endless dance.

"Is it safe to walk into?" Silver asked.

Ben grinned down at her. "It's safe enough to walk behind the waterfall. Wanna try it?"

"Really?"

"That's why I wanted us to get here before it got dark." He pointed at the bank. "Take off your boots, socks, and anything else you don't want getting wet, and we'll get going."

While Ben stripped down to his black T-shirt and jeans, Silver hurried to do as he suggested and then rolled up her jeans to her knees.

"It's going to be slippery," Ben warned. "If you think you're going to lose your balance, feel free to grab on to me."

She glanced at his muscled biceps and figured he'd probably be able to hold her up if he had to. He led the way along the path toward the waterfall and Silver was quickly enveloped in a damp mist that felt like she was in the middle of a cloud.

He stopped on the edge of the creek and leaned down to talk directly in her ear.

"We're going to walk out along the flat piece of rock and then head toward the canyon wall, okay?"

Silver nodded, and as he smiled down at her she noticed the absence of his cowboy hat, which now looked wrong.

"Come on." He reached for her hand. "It's worth it."

He didn't tow her along, but allowed her to pick her way through the boulders and slippery flat rocks at her own pace. The noise got louder and louder and the power of the water more immense the closer she got. She risked one more look up before she took a deep breath, gripped Ben's fingers hard, and followed him into darkness.

The water this close up sounded like the roar of a jet engine. She closed her eyes and trusted that Ben would lead her safely through. Her feet hit drier, pebbled ground and she went still.

"Move in a bit more," Ben said, "and open your eyes."

She did as he suggested, and just stared in stunned silence at the curtain of water rushing downward in front of her while she remained relatively dry and safe. Ben maneuvered her backward, pressed on her shoulder, and she sank down onto the bench someone had thoughtfully provided for visitors. The diffused light that managed to filter into the cave flickered and danced like a lace curtain billowing in the breeze.

Ben sat beside her, his hard thigh aligned with hers, and she reached for his hand and just held it tight. He made no effort to speak or rush her out the other side. She again got that sense of how much a part of him this valley was, and how comfortable he was with its wonders.

If it weren't for Ben she would be completely by herself. How often was she ever alone like this? Silver wondered. Just sitting and observing rather than being observed? Her breathing slowed, and her shoulders dropped in a way that all her yoga and meditation classes had never achieved. If it weren't for Ben she would never have known that such an amazing space existed. Part of her wanted to stay there forever to experience the power of nature and suck that energy into her own spine.

She shivered and Ben put his arm around her. "You ready to go?"

"Not really," she confessed. "It's blowing my mind."

He chuckled; the warm sound reverberated around the rock cave and settled somewhere in her stomach.

"I'm glad you like it. Some people get freaked out by the lack of space."

She finally tore her gaze away from the waterfall and looked around the small cave. "It's okay. I don't feel trapped in here at all."

"I did have second thoughts about your claustrophobia just before I stepped through," he confessed. "But I thought you'd let me know real quick if you wanted to get out."

She shivered again and made herself stand up. "It's definitely damp, but I'm really glad you brought me here." She looked up at him, noticing the droplets of water caught on his eyelashes and his beard and couldn't look away. "Thank you. I really mean it." She went on tiptoe and kissed his cheek.

He stared at her for a long moment and then slid his hand under her chin. "I know I'm going to regret this, but what the hell."

He kissed her with such urgency that she kissed him back, letting him inside her mouth, curling her tongue around his and giving as good as she got. He wrapped one arm around her hips, bringing her entire body in contact with his. With a convulsive shudder, she pressed closer, just as he wrenched his mouth away from hers and stepped back, breathing hard.

"Jeez, I'm sorry. That was way out of bounds."

Reaching forward, she grabbed hold of his damp T-shirt and hauled him back in. "*That* was going really well until you had to spoil it."

He stared down at her. "How about we get out of this cave and go and set up camp?"

"Coward." She let go of his shirt and pushed him back on his heels. "Fine. Why don't we do *that?*"

Chapter Six

Silver put up her tent with far more ease than she had the night before and placed her bedding inside. She changed into her jammies rather than putting on a clean pair of jeans, and brushed out her hair, which was a mass of frizz. When she crawled out, Ben was already lighting a fire and had set a lantern next to him. He glanced over at her but didn't turn around.

"You can dry out your clothes on the bushes or set them near the fire."

Silver stalked past him and spent a few minutes spreading out her jeans and T-shirt next to Ben's. She could hear the horses munching on something, and the distant roar of the waterfall. She wanted to hold on to the feelings she'd had and how it felt to be kissed by Ben Miller.

"What's for dinner?" Silver wasn't one to dodge a fight, and as Ben was her only companion for the next few days, he could hardly avoid her. "Didn't you say something about fish?"

"It's too dark to fish now. We can have a go in the morning if you like?" he offered, his tone back to professional guide, and not the husky-voiced seducer who had kissed her apparently despite himself.

"What was that about regretting kissing me even before you did it?" Silver asked.

Ben winced. "Jeez, you do have a good memory."

"Were you hoping that your sheer amazingness would make me forget what you said?"

"Maybe." Ben patted the log next to him. "Can we get started on dinner and talk about this afterward?"

"Do you think I'll be nicer if you feed me?" Silver demanded.

"I know I will be. I'm a grump when I'm hungry." He pointed at the log. "Will you at least sit down and stop towering over me?"

Silver sat. "You tower over me all the damn time," she grumbled.

"Can't help that." He handed her the container of meals. "Pick something."

She rifled through the packs, aware that she was really hungry and that her mother also believed that you should never go to a grocery store or argue on an empty stomach. "Next time I do something like this, I'm going to have my personal chef cater it for me."

He fought a smile as she handed him two packets. "Can I have both?"

"Sure. I brought plenty because they are so light to carry." He took two himself. "I found some cookies today Mrs. Morgan snuck into my saddlebag."

"The one with your boxers?"

"Yeah. I took out a clean pair of socks and there they were. You can help yourself after your dinner."

She rolled her eyes at him. "You're not the boss of me. If I want one now, I'll darn well have one."

For a moment their gazes locked, and then he smiled. "Technically, I *am* the boss of you because you signed an agreement to do what I said on this trail ride, but if you want cookies, I'm not going to stop you."

"Thanks." Silver took possession of the cookie box while Ben sorted out the meals. Perhaps she was crankier than she'd thought. She waited until he set the two pouches in front of her. "Can I have a plate?"

"They're in the pack that's open. Help yourself."

Silver was hungry enough to stop talking long enough to basically inhale her meal. Something about the combination of the great outdoors and sparring with Ben Miller was inspiring all her appetites. She opened up the cookies and smiled when she saw they were cow and horse shaped with frosting eyes, manes, and tails.

"Mrs. Morgan is a genius." Silver slowly chewed the buttery cookie. "These are delicious."

"May I have one, please?" Ben reached out a hand.

"I'm not sure you deserve one," Silver said, whipping the box behind her back. "Do you go around kissing all your clients?"

"No, I don't." He winced and rubbed a hand over his bearded chin. "It was unprofessional of me. If you want to lodge a complaint and go back, I'll totally understand and accept the consequences of my action."

"It was just a kiss," Silver reminded him. "My beef with you is why did you do it when you knew it was wrong?"

"Because I couldn't help myself? Because I'm in a weird place in my life right now when I just want to crash through all the safe boundaries I've erected and destroy things?"

Silver blinked at him. "Wow, that was a way heavier answer than I thought you'd go with."

He grimaced. "I'm sorry. I don't know where that came from either."

"Do you want to talk about it?" Silver asked cautiously.

He made a revolted expression. "Hell, *no*."

"Why not?"

He shoved a hand through his hair. "Because talking just makes things worse."

"Because you have to deal with stuff you don't want to deal with?" Silver pointed her fork at him. "Because pushing it all down inside you has obviously worked *so* well."

He glared at her. "Look, I don't know why I said it, and I have no obligation to explain myself to you, okay?"

Silver held his gaze and then nodded. "Fine." Even though she'd only been trying to help, she wasn't his therapist, and he didn't owe her an explanation.

She ate another cookie, and solemnly handed him the box, and they crunched away together in silence.

"I don't want to go back yet," Silver eventually said when she realized he hadn't been joking about clamming up completely. "It really was just a kiss because we'd shared that awesome moment in the cave." She brushed crumbs off her lap. "It's not like either of us meant anything by it or are in other relationships where we would have to feel guilty."

He didn't say anything, and she kept fishing. "Obviously, I can only speak for myself."

"I'm not going out with anyone." Ben met her gaze. "I wouldn't have kissed you otherwise."

"Then can we just move on?" Silver suggested.

"Sure." He nodded. "Like you'd be interested in a guy like me when you could go out with someone like Zac Efron."

"Zac Efron?" Silver glared at him. "You think that's the kind of guy I like?"

"Hell, I only know his name because Daisy watched all those stupid *High School Musical* movies to death. I have no idea who's hot at the moment. I'm just saying that you're beautiful enough to date any guy you want."

"You think it's that easy? That I just snap my fingers and *kaboom*, someone takes me out? Have you any idea how *hard* it is to get a date in Hollywood?" Silver demanded.

"You're out all the time!" he protested. "I see you in the news wearing some new dress or just out shopping practically every day!"

"I thought you didn't do trashy gossip," Silver reminded him sweetly. "I thought you were above that kind of stuff."

"Can't help it if I see you sometimes. That stuff gets everywhere. I can't even go into Maureen's in town without seeing your face plastered on the cover of some magazine at the checkout," Ben replied. "And you're always with some guy."

"Because usually I'm in a movie with him, and we're both legally and contractually obliged to turn up, pretend we like each other, and smile for the press. If there are rumors that I might be dating another actor, they usually come from the publicity department."

"Who wouldn't want to date you?" Ben repeated.

"Ben, the guys I meet are usually starstruck and babbling, already a star and unwilling to date me in case I upstage them, afraid that I'm prettier than they are, or controlling assholes who want to tell me what to do with my life and my money."

"That's . . . not good."

"No, it is not good at all. I'm twenty-five and I've never had a real boyfriend." She sighed. "That's just sad."

He handed her back the box of cookies. "I definitely think you need these more than I do."

"Thanks, but let's save them for tomorrow." She smiled

at him, aware that he now knew more about her than almost anyone else in the world outside her private circle. "You won't go and tell the press any of this, will you?"

He looked offended. "Who the hell cares what I think?"

"What if they offered you fifty thousand dollars?" Silver asked as she stood and gathered up the plates. "How about a million for a tell-all exclusive?"

"Hmmm." He got to his feet, rubbing his jaw. "I gotta be honest with you here, Silver, and say that if it was a million, I might have to think about it."

She marched over to him, one finger already raised to poke him in the chest, and he grinned at her. "Just kidding. I already signed a nondisclosure agreement. I promise you that in the unlikely event that I get hounded by the paparazzi, I'll keep our secrets, okay?"

"We'll see, won't we?" Silver replied. He obviously had no idea how much the press loved to turn up dirt. "If they do contact you after I've left, will you at least talk to me before you say anything?"

"Jeez, you're serious about this, aren't you?" Ben was staring at her now, her expression concerned.

"Very serious." She grabbed his plate. "I'll use the rest of the water to rinse off these plates and pack everything away while you deal with the horses."

By the fourth morning, Ben had worked out that just brewing a pot of coffee was enough to get Silver up and ready to face the day. Her phone had died completely the night before and she'd taken it way better than he'd anticipated. Despite her stardom, she had a determined streak that he had to respect, and a practicality that sometimes surprised him.

He'd taken her with him when he went to higher ground

to check in with BB so that she'd know how the radio system worked. They'd stayed up there for a while watching the sun go down, and she'd held his hand when they walked back to camp in the gathering darkness. He liked her. She gave as good as she got, and despite her complaining, she usually completed the tasks he asked her to finish. He'd dealt with way less competent guests than she had turned out to be.

And, then sometimes she casually said something that was so out of his ballpark that he didn't even know how to respond. Twenty-four-hour security against the nuts who tried to get to her or get in her house, never being able to drive herself anywhere in case some overly enthusiastic fan crashed into her or tried to get in her car. She talked about these things as if they were just daily inconveniences, like him getting stepped on by a horse, rather than a terrifying look at the downside of being famous.

"Cat got your tongue?"

Ben brought his attention back to Silver who was eating granola and sitting opposite him at the campfire. She hadn't put on her makeup yet and her hair needed brushing, which made her look way more approachable.

"Just thinking about how different our lives are." Ben finished his coffee. "I bet it's going to feel weird going back after ten quiet days."

"Yes, it will. It's the first time my dad has let me out of his sight for the last two years and I'm really enjoying the freedom." She looked down at her bowl. "I did some stupid stuff a while back, and he kind of took over everything until I got my head on straight."

Ben desperately wanted to ask her to elaborate, but concluded he'd be as bad as the worst gossip reader if he did. If she revealed what her dad had already told Ben, would he have to come clean about that? He had a sense that it wouldn't sit well with her.

"Sounds like my dad," Ben said. "I did some 'stupid stuff' in my late teens and my dad had to bail me out. He never let me forget it." He nodded at her coffee mug. "Do you want more, or are you ready to move out?"

"I'm good, thanks." She shook off whatever thoughtful mood had settled on her shoulders and tipped out the dregs of her coffee onto the ground. "Where are we headed today?"

"To the outer reaches of the canyon, which is right in amongst the Sierra Nevada foothills. It'll take us most of the day because even though it's not that far, the terrain becomes very rocky, and we'll have to pick our way through."

"Okay." She looked him over. "Don't forget your sun-screen."

"Already done."

She picked up the bowl and poured the remaining hot water into it before adding the mugs and plates. Without turning around, she started speaking again. "Thanks for not asking about all the stuff that went down with my dad. I appreciate it."

"Nothing to do with me." Ben shrugged and immediately felt guilty. "What happens on a Morgan Ranch trail ride, stays on a Morgan Ranch trail ride."

She snorted. He was still smiling as he walked down to get the horses and mules. Being with Silver out in the valley was helping him get his head together. Something about the quietness, the open spaces, and the lack of interruptions was calming for the soul, but it did give him way too much time to think.

Within an hour, they were packed up and on the move, Ben leading the way while Silver followed along behind, chatting away whenever something caught her eye. Her delight in the things that were so familiar to him made him appreciate what he had so much more. He couldn't ever manage living in a city, having a desk job or commuting. Why would he want those things when he had everything he could possibly want right here on his doorstep?

Except there was something missing . . . something that disturbed his sleep and made him want to break free of all the restrictions he'd placed on himself. Recently he'd felt it within him like a restless, prowling entity that demanded release, and he didn't know what to do about it. He was the sensible, easygoing Miller, the one everyone relied on to sort things out and keep the peace. Except he hadn't always been like that. Long ago, he'd been the rebel. . . .

He slowed his horse and waited for Silver to catch up with him. "We're going to ford Morgan Creek again and make camp on the other side, okay?"

"Sure." She smiled at him. "It's been a long day and I'm starving."

His gaze fastened on her mouth, and it took him a moment to remember how words worked. There was no point denying it. He wanted to kiss her again.

"Let's get going, then." He turned Calder's head and focused on the route ahead rather than anything to do with Silver.

Halfway across the creek, Silver was fairly certain she was about to take an early bath. The rocky surface was so slippery and uneven that she was struggling to keep her balance as her horse rocked and rolled through the upright boulders. Ben watched her from the middle of the water where the current ran more smoothly.

"Don't pull on her reins so hard."

She gave him a distracted glare. "I'm trying not to fall off!"

"If you're worried about that, tie the reins on the pommel and hang on to it. There's no need to direct Ladybug right now. She knows what she's doing, and she's got four-wheel drive."

His infuriatingly calm voice was really annoying.

"I wish I had four-wheel drive, like a Jeep or something."

"You specified that you wanted to do it like this," Ben reminded her.

"I *know!*" So much for liking him. At the moment, she wished a huge tidal wave would engulf him and take him far away. "Next time I won't be so stupid."

He chuckled. "I'm flattered that you're contemplating a next time."

"Not with you." She breathed out hard as Ladybug reached the more level ground and splashed through the water to meet Ben. "I'll hire a veritable army of people to make sure I get the full five-star treatment."

"Where's the fun in that? You're doing great." He met her gaze, his brown eyes dancing with amusement. "And you'd be bored silly, and you'd learn nothing."

"Maybe that's how I like it."

He leaned back in the saddle, making the leather creak, and studied her carefully. "You okay?"

"I'm great! Why?"

"Because you seem a bit salty today."

"Maybe that's because I'm in the middle of a creek with an infuriating know-it-all cowboy!"

He nodded. "Fair enough." He clicked to his horse and the two mules. "Come on, Calder. We'll stop bothering the lady and see her on the other side."

He turned and headed for the far bank, leaving Silver behind. Now she had to get herself out of the creek without any helpful suggestions from Ben about her route, or how to keep her balance. If she could just stop fixating on the absolutely ridiculous idea her brain had come up with just before she'd gone to sleep last night, she'd be out in no time.

But then again, shouting at the only man who could keep her safe in the middle of nowhere was probably not a wise move, even though her stupid idea involved him big-time. She should keep well away and let him be all professional and annoying as hell.

"Come on, Ladybug. You've got this."

Silver looped the reins around the pommel and hung on for dear life as her little mare navigated her way out of the creek. Ben, of course, had been right. Letting Ladybug find her own path was way quicker without Silver interfering and confusing her.

When they reached the bank, Silver reached down and hugged Ladybug around the neck. "Thank you, girl. You rocked the rocks!"

She triumphantly looked around to see where Ben might be and couldn't see any sign of him or the other animals. How far had she traveled downstream without checking her position? It couldn't be that far. She took off her sunglasses and searched the tree line, which looked exactly the same all along the ridge and bank. She swiveled in the saddle and looked back across the creek trying to pinpoint where they had entered the water, and where Ben had ended up. Had she exited upstream or downstream from where he was?

Apart from her hectic breathing, the thump of her heart, and the rush of the water behind her, there was no other sound. The scrappy pine forest that covered the upward slope of the Sierra foothill directly behind the creek was ominously quiet. She wished her phone was working so she could text Ben and ask him where he was.

"I'm all alone. . . ." Silver whispered to herself. Ladybug snorted and pawed the ground as if even she thought her rider was being far too dramatic. Perhaps she shouldn't have been so keen to get rid of Ben after all.

"Yo! Silver!" A piercing whistle echoed down the creek toward her. "Wrong way!"

Silver headed back upstream toward where Ben was standing on the slope looking out over the land. She'd never been so pleased to see anyone before in her life.

"There's no need to shout," Silver commented as she rode up. "I was just admiring the view."

"Sure you were. I could see you panicking from all the way up here." He came down from the stone platform and turned to his left. "You can bring Ladybug over here and dry her off if she needs it, okay?"

Silver gave her mare a good rubdown, and then went to find Ben who had established their camp close to the water's edge. He viewed her cautiously as she sat down beside him on one of the large, flat rocks, but didn't speak.

She scowled at him. "I was fine! If you'd just waited a second, I would've found you all by myself."

He held up his hands. "Whatever you say. Are you ready to fish for your supper?"

"As in catch my own food?" Silver blinked and looked around. "I don't see any fishing rods."

"That's because we're going to catch them by hand." He pointed at her boots. "Take them and your socks off, and roll up your jeans to your knees."

"Can't you do it? I just got out of the water." Silver waved a languid hand at him. "I'm exhausted."

"Sure I can, but I'll only catch enough for myself." He shrugged.

"And leave me to starve?" Silver asked plaintively.

"There's plenty of food. If you don't want fish, boil some water, and make yourself something." He stood. "I'll be back in a while."

Silver let him go, filled the pan with water, and set it over the fire before sorting through the packs of food. The thought of eating the same thing again wasn't inspiring. With a resigned sigh, she took off her boots and socks and walked down to the edge of the creek where Ben had gone.

She found him lying flat out on his stomach on one of the spare horse blankets wearing only his boxers. He really did have a nice ass. . . .

"I thought you were catching fish, not sunbathing," Silver remarked.

His head shot up and he frowned at her over his shoulder. "Shh."

She tried to remember the last time someone had told her to shut up and couldn't. Then, with a martyred sigh, she crouched down next to him and listened to what he had to say. . . .

Two fish of her own now, and she was proving just as good at getting them as Ben until she leaned out too far, and almost face-planted the rocks surrounding the small pools.

"Careful." Ben grabbed hold of her elbow and hauled her back, grinning as she spat out a mouthful of water. "Who knew you were so competitive?"

"Why do you think I've been so successful?" Silver asked. "By sitting on my ass looking pretty?"

He glanced down at her. "You are good at that, though."

"What? Ass sitting?"

"Nope. Looking pretty." He smoothed the wet hair away from her face, his brown eyes narrowed. "Damn pretty."

She raised her head to be kissed just as he lowered his, and their mouths met in the middle. She grabbed hold of his bare shoulders and held on for dear life as the kiss consumed her. He drew her tight against him until she was straddling his lap and continued to kiss her, one hand now on her ass, rocking her into the hardness contained in his now-soaked boxers.

"Ben"—she eased her mouth away—"can we talk about something important?"

"Right now?" he breathed. "Like, can't it wait five minutes?"

She pressed the flat of her palms against his muscled chest. "You know I told you that I hadn't had a proper boyfriend?"

"Yeah." He looked confused.

"I wasn't joking." She looked at him expectantly.

"Okay."

"Like as in never, which means I've never had sex."

His mouth opened and closed at least twice as he stared at her.

"Which is something that I'd like to change—like with you—if that's okay," Silver added just to make sure things were absolutely clear.

"That's . . . one hell of a thing to say, Silver." Ben frowned. "We've only known each other for four days, and I'm not the kind of guy who—"

She pressed a finger to his lips. "I know you aren't, which is why I'm suggesting it. You were the one who gave me the idea when you said that anything that happens here, stays here."

"This wasn't what I meant." Ben put his hands around her waist like she was made of china and set her carefully away from him. "It's great that you can be open about this, and I really appreciate the fact that you consider me worthy, but—"

"You're not interested." Silver felt her cheeks heat up. "It's okay. It was just a stupid idea, and I'm sorry that I even said it out loud." She paused. "You won't tell my dad, will you?"

"Hell, *no*. I don't have a death wish."

"Okay, then, can we just forget it?" Silver asked brightly. "And eat our fish and move on?"

She scrambled to her feet. He stayed where he was looking up at her, his brow furrowed, his expression concerned.

"I'm really sorry, Silver."

"It's all good."

She made her way back to the camp, aware that she felt like crying and determined not to let him see her tears. He hadn't asked her to come on to him, and he'd been very sweet about letting her down. If anyone should be embarrassed, it should be her.

When she reached the camp, the water in the pot had almost burned dry. She hastily took the pan off the heat, aware that she could've started a fire, and that Ben would kill her if he knew she'd been so careless. She wiggled out of her now-wet jeans, laid them on a rock to dry, and focused on finding a frying pan and whatever else Ben might need for the fish.

Keeping busy, doing stuff, had always been a way to keep her emotions at bay. When you were in the middle of a big budget movie, no one cared if you were having a bad day. Even if you were a kid, you were paid to turn up and act, and if you didn't do that you were fired. Maybe if she acted like nothing was wrong, Ben would go along with her, and they could move past this. She hoped so with all her heart.

Chapter Seven

Ben stared at the pile of dead fish until his vision blurred and the blood thumping in his dick subsided. Silver Meadows was a virgin and she wanted him to take care of that for her. . . . He had a sudden urge to pinch himself just to make sure he wasn't in the middle of one of his more lurid dreams about Silver smiling at him as he made love with her.

He shivered, suddenly aware that he was half-naked, and that the sun had disappeared behind the clouds. He needed to get back to camp, deal with the fish, and work out how to look Silver in the eye without imagining he had accepted her invitation.

He was an honorable man, the voice of reason in Miller family arguments, and the kind of boyfriend who was invited to his exes' weddings because he always stayed friends with them. He raised his gaze to the creek. And yet he wanted Silver like he needed to breathe, and the wildness he'd caged deep within himself was howling to get out.

No one would know, his inner demon whispered. *You could help her out, have a great week exploring sex, wave good-bye, and never have to see her again. . . .*

"I'd know." Ben spoke the words out loud as if to make sure he heard them.

He wasn't like that. Since his lost year, he'd never had sex outside a relationship, and he certainly wasn't about to start now. He *liked* Silver, he *respected* her—and she'd asked him if he'd mind having sex with her like he'd be doing her a favor. . . .

Ben shot to his feet, picked up the fish and the blanket, and started back the way he had come. One thing he wasn't was a coward, and skulking around not doing everything in his power to make his valued client feel okay about what had just happened wasn't an option.

He walked into the camp and then stopped, his attention riveted to the fire as he slowly inhaled.

"What's burning?"

Silver sat back on the log, dusting off her hands. "I left a pot of water over the fire. It almost burned dry."

"That was really stupid. You could've burned down the whole camp," Ben snapped, almost glad to be able to shout about something.

"I know." She faced him, her expression contrite. "I'm sorry."

He marched over and checked the pan, which looked a bit scorched on the bottom and was still radiating heat.

"I'll buy you a new one when we get back," Silver offered.

"That's not the issue, and you know it." Ben held her gaze. "Just because we're beside the creek doesn't mean that you can't start a fire." He bent down, picked up a handful of pine needles, and tossed them in her direction. "These things are as dry as a bone and would act as an accelerant."

She stood and faced him, her hands on her hips. "I get it! I messed up! Can you stop yelling at me now?"

He set the pan down, laid the fish on a flat-topped rock, and tried to rein in his temper. The fact that he'd even let it fly was a good indicator of how far off-kilter he was.

"And maybe you could put some clothes on?" Silver demanded.

He set his jaw and pointed at the fish. "I'll get dressed after I deal with the fish—unless you want to do it?"

She folded her arms over her chest and glared at him. "I don't know how."

"Then you'd better learn quick if you want to eat tonight." Ben pointed at the spot opposite him. "Sit here."

She made a huffing sound as she joined him. "You'd better cut the heads off because I'm not having those eyes staring at me while I'm eating."

"You can do what the hell you like with yours." Ben got out his knife, efficiently slit the first fish's belly, and shoved his fingers inside. "You've got to clean out the guts like this."

Silver made a gagging sound as he threw the innards into the creek. "I can't do that. It's disgusting."

"Sure you can if you want to eat." Ben wasn't in the mood to be helpful. "Watch me and then do the next one yourself."

Eventually, he handed her the knife, his fingers slippery with gore.

"I . . . can't," Silver whispered. "I'm really sorry, but I'm going to barf." She scrambled away from him and ran toward the creek.

Ben briefly closed his eyes. Way to channel his father right at the wrong moment. What exactly had he been hoping to achieve by making her puke? He finished the rest of the fish and retrieved the cast-iron frying pan, setting it over the fire to heat up.

He washed his hands thoroughly and took a quick

splash in the creek to get the fish smell off the rest of him before getting dressed and going to look for Silver. He found her sitting slightly upstream on a rock, her legs crossed under her and her expression unreadable.

He halted beside her and she didn't look his way, which kind of hurt.

"I'm sorry. I behaved like a jerk," Ben said. "I've finished the fish and I'm about to cook them. Will you come back and eat?"

She didn't reply, and he stood there like a fool waiting for direction.

"I'm sorry about *all* of it," Ben continued. "The way I reacted to your suggestion, the fish, the—"

"I'll be there in a minute, okay?"

"Sure, I just wanted to make sure you were all right." He half turned and then swung back around. "The thing is, I'm not behaving like myself, and part of me wants to take you up on your offer, and the other part of me is horrified that I'd even go there."

"Because I'm so objectionable?" She finally turned toward him.

"No! Because I'm such a mess." Ben tried to get through to her. "I'm the problem here—not you." He held out his hand. "Come and eat with me, please? We can talk all you like after that."

Silver slowly unfolded her legs and stood up, ignoring his proffered hand. She might be capitulating about having dinner with him, but that was as far as she was willing to go right now and that was only because she was starving. "We can't have another burned pan, so I suppose I'd better eat. Thank you for doing the fish."

"I shouldn't have insisted you had to help." He grimaced. "My dad made me do it even when I puked."

"He sounds like a bully."

"He . . . means well." Ben hesitated. "He was left with six kids to bring up, and he believed in the value of hard work and no coddling—he left that to his sister."

Silver entered the camp and noticed that the appalling smell of gutted fish had disappeared. She concentrated on acting like she didn't have a care in the world and that she hadn't just offered up her virginity to a cowboy she'd only known for four days.

"Do you want me to find plates and silverware?"

"That'd be great." Ben set the fish in the pan and the sizzle of the skin hitting the hot metal made Silver lick her lips. "These won't take a minute. I kept some rice from last night, so I'll stick it in the pan and warm it through when the fish comes out."

"Sounds good."

Jeez, for an actress who'd won her fair share of awards, she sure was sounding wooden right now. Why did she care what Ben Miller thought of her anyway? She wasn't going to see him ever again after the trail ride, and she was fairly certain that he'd never mention what she'd suggested to anyone, because he was that kind of guy.

But he'd said part of him wanted to say yes. . . . She had a fairly good idea which part of him, but did she want to go there? Find out if she could change his mind because kissing him had been a revelation? Shouting at him was pretty cool, too. She'd never met anyone who didn't pander to her every need, or who had the balls to tell her off and expect better of her. He made her *want* to be better.

But because she'd finally found an honorable man who treated her like an equal, her chances of getting him to do something so out of character were amazingly slim. And, if he did do what she wanted, would she be damaging him? Would he be the same man?

"Fish is ready."

Silver brought the plates over, and almost moaned with greed when Ben placed the two fish on her plate with the fried rice.

"I cut the heads off."

"Thank you, but I'm so hungry I bet I wouldn't have cared much if they'd still been attached."

"It was no trouble." Ben avoided her gaze as he served himself. "I usually take them off for our guests."

He was back into professional mode, which suited her just fine as she gathered the ragged threads of her self-esteem back together again. She'd asked him to forget her stupid suggestion, and it looked as if he was going to follow through. If so, she was more than willing to play her part.

"Do you need to speak to BB again tonight?" Silver asked as they settled down beside the fire.

"Yeah, I talk to him every night between six-thirty and seven. If he doesn't hear from me, he knows something might be up."

"Makes sense." Silver ate some of the fish and actually moaned. "Oh my God, this is *so good*."

"Yeah, isn't it?" He finally cracked a smile. "Well worth getting splashed for."

"Better than anything I've ever tasted in a five-star restaurant." She savored every mouthful, making it last. "I feel bad for the fish, but not that bad, because it's their fault for tasting so good."

Ben ate his fish and then insisted they divide the fifth one between them. They finished the meal with a couple of the remaining cookies and a cup of strong coffee.

Silver gave a discreet burp. "That was the best meal ever."

"Caught and cooked by us." Ben handed her a napkin. "You've got frosting on your cheek."

"Thanks." She dabbed at a sticky patch. "Can I come with you when you go to speak to BB?"

"Sure." He nodded. "Let's clean up, and pitch the tents, and then we can go."

He didn't offer her his hand this time as they walked up the slope into the pine forest to find higher ground. He'd brought his compass with him, just to make sure they didn't get lost, which Silver appreciated, because as far as she was concerned all the trees looked the same.

BB's voice was fainter than last time, but still clear enough to hear.

"There's a big storm approaching Morgan Valley. It's coming in over the mountains, so watch out for that," BB said.

"Will do," Ben replied. "Any other news?"

"Well, your dad cornered my dad in Maureen's this morning, and asked when the hell you were coming back." BB chuckled. "He wasn't happy."

"He never is. Did he say if there was a problem at home?" Ben asked.

"He didn't mention anything specific. But you know Jeff. He just likes complaining about stuff."

"Yeah." Ben grimaced. "Apologize to Billy for me, won't you?"

"Sure will. Anything else?"

"No, we're good."

"Tell Silver her dad called, and said he'd be coming by to pick her up in five days."

"She's standing right here beside me." Ben looked over at her, eyebrows raised. "Anything you want to say to him?"

Silver shook her head. In five days' time she'd never

see Ben Miller again. For some reason that was way more concerning than having to deal with her father.

"Nope. Over and out, BB."

"Have a good one." BB's voice faded, leaving them in the silence of the pine trees.

"Ready to go back?" Ben asked.

"Yes." Silver hesitated and glanced around the trees. "If I knew which way that was."

He took her gently by the shoulders and rotated her ninety degrees. "You see that red glow down there? That's our campfire. If we just head for that, we'll be fine."

Walking in front of him in the darkness gave her the opportunity to talk to him again without having to look directly into his sweet, brown eyes.

"I just want to tell you why I asked."

"Do you have to?" His sigh was so fervent that it made the hairs on the back of her neck rise.

"Yes, because I think it's important." She kept moving, organizing her thoughts as she went. "I've never met a man like you before."

He took a while to answer her.

"I'm pretty damn ordinary, Silver."

"Not in my world. You're honest, smart, and confident without being a real prick about it."

"Gee, thanks."

"I know you're going to say that we've only spent four days together, but that's almost a hundred hours, which means we've had at least thirty dates already, which is almost a *year's* worth."

He snorted. "Your math sucks."

"I trust you." She reached the level ground and turned toward him. His face was a shadow beneath the brim of his Stetson. "And I don't trust any men except my father and brother."

"That's sad."

"That's a fact. And if I don't trust a man, how could I possibly sleep with him?"

"You're only twenty-five, you'll meet someone, you're a star, you're *beautiful*," Ben said with some emphasis. "Any man would be lucky to have you in his bed, or in his life."

"Except you?"

He reached out and cupped her chin. "I'm not . . . that guy. I've done some stupid shit. I don't deserve someone like you."

She'd done enough therapy to hear the pain in his voice and instinctively turned her head until her lips met his thumb.

"Don't do that," Ben said quietly.

"Why not?"

"Because it makes me want what I can't have."

He went to move his hand away and she grabbed his wrist. "But you *can* have me. I've already told you that." He went to speak, and she rushed on. "I want you, just for the next few days. I'd never ask for more. I know you wouldn't accept that, but please? Here in this beautiful place, with just the two of us, can't you just help me out?"

He groaned and leaned in to kiss her, and she melted into his arms.

"Please, Ben."

He framed her face in his hands and drew back, his gaze devouring her, his indecision plain to see.

"I promised your father I'd look after you and bring you home safely."

Silver stamped her booted foot. "I'm twenty-five and I am not an extension of my damn father! He's controlled everything in my life for years; he is not going to decide whom I sleep with!"

"That's not quite what I meant, but I'm not going to argue about what you said," Ben replied. "You're in control of you." He cleared his throat. "You ready to move on?"

"No!" Tears gathered in Silver's eyes and she spoke fast. "I know what I'm asking you is stupid and ridiculous, but I've never felt like this about a man before. I'm afraid I might never feel like this again."

"I'm not—" Ben attempted to interrupt, and she was having none of it.

"I don't care if you think you're not perfect! You're what I want!"

"Maybe that's the real problem, Silver," Ben said slowly as he took a step away from her. "That for the first time in your life you're not *getting* what you want, and what you feel about me isn't actually the point at all."

"That's"—she breathed out hard—"not *fair*."

He shrugged. "As my dad often says, 'Life's not fair.'"

She stuck her finger in his face. "Don't you *dare* quote that big bully to me."

"Because just for once he's right?"

She gave him a withering stare, turned on her heel, and stomped back to camp. Damn him and all the Millers. She couldn't wait to get back home to L.A. where people treated her with the respect she deserved.

A boom of thunder woke Ben up from a troubled sleep, and he opened one eye just in time to see a truly spectacular flash of lightning brighten the sky. The air had that restless feel to it, like a horse about to explode from the bucking chute—like he felt right now about Silver Meadows.

He'd given her a five-minute head start and then had taken a roundabout route back to camp, checking on the livestock, cleaning up the remains of their meal, and making sure everything was undercover or packed away in case it rained. He was glad he'd taken the time to do so now as he guessed the mother of all storms was about to break over their heads. She'd disappeared inside her tent by the time he'd gotten back, and he was kind of glad about that. Her wounded expression when he'd suggested that she just wanted what she couldn't have had unsettled him more than he'd anticipated.

He shifted uneasily in his sleeping bag. Had he totally misjudged her? Or had he hit on the truth, which had finally made her angry enough to walk away from him? There was another crash of thunder and Ben reluctantly sat up. He'd better check that the horses and mules were safe in their temporary shelter, and that everything in the campsite was nailed down.

The lightning was coming so frequently now that he barely needed the torch he'd brought with him. He made sure the livestock wasn't going anywhere, repacked almost everything under tarps, and hid it in the sheltering trees. He whistled in silent appreciation as a huge fork of lightning lit up the sky followed by a rumble of rolling thunder that sounded like someone bowling a rock down the mouth of the canyon. The air was hot and dense and there was a sense of anticipation, like static shock.

The tents were built to withstand a large amount of rain, and they were well above the line of the creek on solid rock so he didn't think the campsite would be overwhelmed. He started back, pausing outside Silver's tent. Should he wake her up? He didn't want her to panic if the storm suddenly worsened. Knowing that he was probably the last person she wanted to see right now, Ben decided to let her sleep, and retired to his tent to sit and monitor the situation. He switched on his lantern, got a book out of his travel pack, and settled down to read.

Silver sat bolt upright, her whole body shaking. What the hell was going on? It sounded like she was in the middle of a war zone. Gathering her courage, she crawled toward the sealed opening of her tent and slowly unzipped the door. Lightning flashed right in her eyes and she blinked. It must be the storm that BB had mentioned coming through.

She didn't like thunderstorms at the best of times, and being stuck in the middle of nowhere with only a flimsy bit of nylon between her and the elements was not reassuring. Thunder rumbled overhead, pinging off the rock walls of the canyon like the rattle of an automatic weapon.

Silver swallowed hard and looked over toward Ben's tent where she could see a light shining through the side. He was obviously up and aware of what was going on. If he thought they were in any danger, he'd definitely let her know. Even though he might not like her much at the moment, he was too much of a professional not to do his job.

She'd cried when she'd gotten into her sleeping bag, her anger with Ben disappearing as quickly as it had come. Was that really who she was? Someone who was so used to getting her own way that she couldn't actually believe she couldn't make it happen? The thing was, if that were the truth, why would she be feeling so hurt? She'd tried to let him see the real her and somehow all he'd seen was the big, demanding, selfish movie star?

She was trying to become a better, more independent person, and she'd already learned so much about herself on the ride—that she was capable, that she could be resourceful, that maybe she would do okay on her own. Maybe her two personas were so intertwined that she could no longer separate them. Maybe Ben was both right and wrong at the same time.

She found her fleece and put it on over her pajamas. There was no way she was going back to sleep now. She unzipped her tent flap, stared out at the black, star-encrusted sky, and tried to pretend she was at a fireworks display rather than watching Mother Nature throw a massive hissy fit.

She counted the short seconds between the lightning and thunder and guessed the storm must be directly overhead. The air was still as if all the motion had been sucked up into the gathering clouds. The only sound was the reassuring roar of the waterfall and the busy rush of the creek. She had no idea where all the birds and wildlife went when a storm passed through. She'd have to ask Ben.

The gap between the lightning and the thunder was down to a couple of seconds when a particularly jagged fork of lightning crashed into the pine trees above them and there was a horrendous tearing sound. Silver crawled out of her tent on all fours and headed at rapid speed for Ben's.

"Let me in!"

He was there in a second, pulling her inside and inadvertently into his arms when she bowled him over onto his back. He patted her shoulder in soothing circles.

"It's all good. We're perfectly safe in here."

She breathed in the now-familiar scent of him, warm man, leather, and horse and it felt like home.

"I hate storms," she confessed in a muffled voice against his chest. "I got stuck in the middle of one when we were filming in the Nevada desert once. One of the cameramen was struck by lightning."

"That must have been terrifying."

Since he didn't seem to mind holding her, she allowed herself to enjoy the moment. Another flash of light illuminated the tent and he looked up.

"It's right overhead now. This is the worst it will get. I guarantee it." He hesitated. "Do you want to stay here until it ends?"

"If that's okay," Silver asked. "I promise I won't jump you or anything."

His soft chuckle reverberated in his chest. "Same here." He eased her out of his arms. "I'm going to get your sleeping bag, and other stuff, so you'll be comfortable."

He turned around and she grabbed the back of his blue T-shirt. "Are you sure it's safe to go out there?"

He raised an eyebrow. "You made it across, so I think I'm good."

She moved to the back of the small tent and settled herself in the warmth of his sleeping bag, her gaze falling on the book he'd placed facedown on his pillow.

When he came back in, his arms full of her things, she helped him line up her sleeping bag and pillow with his and scooted over to her side. Desperate to steer the conversation in a nonconfrontational direction, she pointed to the book.

"You like fantasy novels?"

"Yeah." He set the lantern to one side so that the light fell over both of them. "This series is pretty good."

"There are plans to make it into a movie," Silver said. "I'm up for a part."

He looked her up and down. "Let me guess. Gelliflower."

"How did you know?"

He shrugged. "Seems like a slam dunk to me. A petite, fairy monster hybrid is so you."

"Thanks." She smiled at him, proud that she was still able to look him in the eye after what had happened earlier. "I think I'll probably take it if it's offered to me."

"Awesome." He picked up the book, creased the corner of the page down, and set it to one side. Silver winced.

"What?"

"Don't you have a bookmark?"

He looked at her oddly. "It's my book. I paid for it. I'm not damaging anyone else's property."

"Still . . ." She shook her head and cringed as the thunder went on and on. "Why is it so loud out there?"

"The rock acts like an amphitheater," Ben said. "Unless there is a massive landslide, we're perfectly safe."

As if to mock his words, the tent suddenly swayed back and forth, and it started to rain with all the intensity of a pressure shower.

"Looks like we're stuck in here for a while." Ben didn't sound at all worried and Silver tried to relax as well. "Might as well try and get some sleep."

"Sleep? With that racket going on?" Silver asked.

He gestured at her sleeping bag. "You set for the night? This is a two-person tent so we should have enough space."

"Fine," she grumbled, and unzipped her bag before she took off her fleece. "You sleep. I'll just stare up at the tent and hope it doesn't spring any leaks."

"It won't. I checked." Ben got into his own sleeping bag and lay back on his pillow, one arm bent behind his head. Sometimes his quiet competency was infuriating; at other times it was downright reassuring. "Can you switch off the lantern?"

"But it'll be dark," Silver protested.

"Yeah, that's usually what we call the absence of light."

She leaned over and poked him in the ribs. "You're not

funny, and just so you know, I'm still mad at you about everything else."

"You're a woman. Of course you're still mad," he murmured, his eyes remaining closed. "As long as you don't strangle me in my sleep, I'm good with it."

Silver switched off the lamp and lay down, her gaze on the vibrating roof of the tent. How the fabric withstood the onslaught of the pounding rain she had no idea. She just hoped it kept doing it and she didn't wake up in the morning floating down the creek.

Chapter Eight

Ben woke up thinking one of his dogs had climbed onto his bed and automatically went to push it away, only to tangle his hand in Silver's hair. He opened his eyes and stared down at the top of her head, which was buried against his shoulder. She lay on her side, her knee riding against his hip and one of her hands flattened on his chest.

At some point in the night, she must have unzipped her sleeping bag and climbed all over him. As he lay there appreciating her tiny snores and the soft warmth of her body pressed against him, he couldn't say he minded. It was a long time since he'd slept with anyone and he'd forgotten how much he liked it. The rain was still falling and he grimaced. He was going to have to leave the warmth of the tent and take a look at the damage the storm had caused on its way through the valley.

He gently rolled Silver onto her back, and after some complaining noises, she went back to sleep leaving him free to get up, get dressed, and get out. He'd brought his rain slicker in with him last night and put it on over his T-shirt and fleece. Jeans, socks, and boots completed his outfit and he braced himself to leave.

Everything was gray, and the rain was still hammering

down. He zipped the tent back up, rammed his hat down low on his head, and set off toward the trees. It was hard to see ahead of him and he almost tripped over a downed pine tree that now bisected their camp.

"Shit," Ben murmured, risking a glance up the hill to note how close the tree had been to coming down on top of their tents. "*Way* too near."

It was too heavy for him to move out of the way, so he hopped over the trunk and set off toward the corral. To his relief, both the mules and the horses were standing quietly under the shelter and appeared damp, but unhurt. He left them some alfalfa pellets and checked the water trough and buckets, which were well filled.

As he turned back, a gust of wind nearly blew him off his feet, and he grabbed hold of one of the trees. Unless the rain stopped, it didn't look as if they'd be going anywhere today. The creek level was high and the water was seething and boiling, making it impossible to cross. He wasn't in a rush to get anywhere, so waiting until things calmed down was definitely the best solution.

He glanced over and considered what he needed to get to make sure he and Silver could survive a day together without killing each other, and grinned.

Probably a bigger tent.

He recoiled as the rain blew into his face and made some quick calculations. He'd have to build a fire before he could do anything else, and in these conditions, it wasn't going to be easy. For the first time ever, he wished Silver's imaginary support staff were standing by ready to make everything right for them. Unfortunately, it was down to him.

* * *

When Ben appeared at the tent entrance, Silver bolted upright.

"Where have you *been?* I thought you'd disappeared on me, you were out so long."

"Give me a sec, okay?" He was breathing hard, his head down, and his arms full of stuff. He'd obviously taken his rain slicker off outside, but his fleece and jeans were soaked through. "I had to get a few chores done."

"Oh God, I'm sorry I shouted! I was just so worried about you!" Silver crawled toward him. "You need to get those things off as soon as possible!"

"Yeah, I'm trying." He pointed to his pillow. "There are two micro absorbent towels under there. Can you grab them for me?"

He was shaking so hard his teeth were chattering. He took off his hat and started on his boots and socks.

Silver brought over the towels and watched him for a second before diving in to help. "Your fingers are too cold. Let me do it."

The fact that he didn't argue was really worrying. She eased off his second sock and knelt up to deal with his fleece and T-shirt. The fabric was so wet that it clung to him like a second skin.

"Can you put your arms up?" Silver asked him.

He did as she asked, and using all her strength, she managed to get both items off over his head. His skin felt clammy to the touch, and she rushed to put one of the towels around his shoulders.

"I'll get the rest." Ben started on the button of his jeans and eased down the zipper. "Jeez, these things stick like glue."

"Push them down over your hips, sit on your ass, and I'll pull them off you," Silver advised.

"Wow, you're bossy," Ben murmured, but he did as he

suggested, the exhaustion on his face clearly visible as she tugged and cajoled his jeans off.

"And your boxers," Silver said.

"I think I'll keep those on if you don't mind."

Silver snapped the elastic. "They're soaked through. You'll get a chill. Take them off." She handed him the second towel. "For your modesty."

"Thanks."

He removed the boxers, tied the towel around his waist. and used the other one to vigorously dry the rest of his body and hair.

"What shall I do with all this wet stuff?" Silver asked as she piled it all up by the entrance.

"Except for my hat and boots, put the rest outside."

She opened the tent momentarily to push everything out and got a blast of cold air that made her hurry up. By the time she turned back, Ben had crawled over to his sleeping bag and had wrapped it around his shoulders.

"I'll sort out the rest of it when I've warmed up." He shivered convulsively.

"How about you tell me what's what, and I can sort everything out?" Silver asked. "For a start, you need something warm to drink."

"Way ahead of you." He nodded at the smaller of the two containers he'd brought in. "Two containers of hot coffee, two of hot water for food later, and some creamer."

"How did you manage that?" Silver gaped at him as she opened the icebox that also contained the freeze-dried food packs and protein bars.

"I lit a fire." He shrugged. "That's one of the reasons why I was out there so long."

She gazed at him with new respect.

There was an amused glint in his eye as he looked

back at her. "I knew you wouldn't survive long without your coffee."

She opened one of the flasks and poured him the first cup, happily inhaling the aroma.

"Thanks." He held the cup with both hands. "I definitely need this." He nodded at her. "Don't forget to help yourself."

Silver worried her lip. "The thing is . . . I'm not sure if I should drink anything else because I haven't peed since last night."

He sipped his coffee. "Well, you have two choices. One, go outside, or two, use the funnel."

"The what?"

He pointed at the second container, which was marked with a red cross and an EMERGENCY sticker.

"In there, among other things, you'll find a funnel and a big plastic jar. If you don't want to go outside you can use that."

Fairly certain that he was joking, Silver opened the lid and surveyed the neatly laid out interior.

"This?" She held up the funnel, which was attached to a bottle. "*Really?*"

"It works," Ben assured her. "We had a couple of female scientists from MIT out here a few months ago and they came up with the idea. You can do it in the corner behind me. I won't watch."

"I think I'd rather go out," Silver said. "This is bizarre."

"Up to you." Ben finished his coffee. He was still shivering, and Silver topped up his cup. "You can use my rain slicker. It's hanging up right outside."

When Silver staggered back in, Ben had put on a clean T-shirt and was sitting with his lower body inside his sleeping bag. He glanced up at her and threw her one of the towels.

"It's wet out there, isn't it?"

"Duh." Silver mopped her face and hair. "The wind blew the hood down at a crucial moment and my hair got soaked."

"Should've used the funnel."

She balled up the towel and threw it at his head before climbing into her own sleeping bag and setting her pillow in the small of her back.

"It looked pretty bad out there."

"Yeah, the creek isn't crossable for sure. We'll have to wait and see if it settles down. I'm not risking the horses or you in there."

"You'd be fine then?" She gave him the eye.

"Probably." He shrugged. "I'm a way better rider than you are."

"Please, go ahead." Silver made an extravagant gesture toward the exit. "Don't let me stop you."

"Like I'd leave you here," Ben scoffed. "BB Morgan would kill me."

Silver helped herself to some coffee and a protein bar and returned to sit next to Ben who had taken out his book.

"Which one is that?"

He glanced over at her. "Book three. *The Cave of Sighs*."

"That's a good one, especially when—"

He put his finger to his lips. "Don't spoil it."

She sighed. "Fine."

He returned to his book and Silver sipped her coffee and slowly ate her protein bar, which had the texture of thick toothpaste.

"You don't read very fast," Silver commented.

He looked up again, placing his finger in the crease of the book. "Maybe that's because someone keeps interrupting me, and I keep having to go back and find my place."

"I've got nothing to do," she confessed. "When I'm bored I usually play games on my phone or online."

He set the book to one side and regarded her. "So, I'm supposed to entertain you?"

"Well, considering my actual job is entertaining millions of people, not having to do it for a change is quite nice, so yes."

"Okay, so can I ask you something?"

"Sure," Silver said encouragingly. "Go ahead."

"Why did your dad take over your life for two years?"

She stared at him for a long moment. "You said that deliberately to shut me up, didn't you? Maybe you *should* go back to your book."

He'd already turned to pick it up before she spoke again.

"I got into drugs."

Ben went still. "I suspect that's quite easy to do in the world you live in."

"I didn't start snorting cocaine or anything. I had a bad fall on a movie set and I hurt my back. The doctor prescribed me some pretty strong painkillers, and I gradually became addicted to them."

"I take it back." He nodded. "That can happen to anyone."

"The problem was that there were lots of people who were more than willing to keep getting them *for* me after my doctor cut me off, because everyone wanted me to be happy." Silver exhaled. "But they didn't make me happy. I became irritable, overanxious, paranoid, and so desperate to get my next fix that it became a priority in my life."

"Didn't your parents notice anything?"

"They knew there was something wrong, but I lied to them a lot." She grimaced. "I even manufactured a fight with them, moved out of our house, and saw them as little as possible."

Silver folded the wrapper of her protein bar into a set of precise triangles.

"Eventually, my best friend, Carla, went to my dad and told him how bad things had gotten. I was so angry that I cut her out of my life, but even that loss didn't make any difference because by then I was convinced that everyone else was the problem. My dad literally kidnapped me and took me to rehab."

Ben reached over and took her clenched fist in his hand.

"I complained for the whole of the first month that I wasn't like the 'other people' in there—that they had serious issues, and that I could stop whenever I liked. . . ." Her voice trailed off, her thoughts fixed in the past. "But eventually, I worked it out. The problem was me, and I had to deal with it."

She looked directly at Ben to find his brown gaze waiting for her.

"So I've been fine since, but my dad . . ." She sighed. "He's terrified that I'm going to go off the rails again. For the last two years, he's been grudgingly handing me back control of my finances, career decisions, and general life. Coming out here to the ranch was the first time he's trusted me to go somewhere on my own since rehab."

"He wasn't there for you though, was he?" Ben commented, his fingers drumming on the cover of his book.

"You don't get it, do you?" Silver said. "I lied and stole

and pretended everything was fine. I really am a very good actress, you know."

"He should've noticed sooner." Ben wasn't giving up. "Even my dad—"

Silver pounced on his words. "Your dad noticed what?"

Ben stopped talking and just stared at her.

"Seeing as we're sharing our darkest secrets, how about you confess the stupid shit you got involved in when you were a teen?" Silver asked sweetly.

Ben held up the book like a shield. "You can borrow this if you like. I don't mind."

Silver choosing to answer his question about her dad had been quite unexpected, but her answer had lined up pretty accurately with what Mr. Meadows had told Ben after he'd agreed to take the job. The only difference was that Silver's dad seemed convinced she'd gone back on drugs, and that a ten-day trail ride would act like some kind of mini-rehab. Ben was looking forward to reporting back to Phil Meadows and giving his daughter a clean bill of health.

"That's very kind of you, but I'd rather you answered the question." Silver was speaking again, and Ben forced himself to pay attention. Her damp, blond hair was piled up on top of her head and she wasn't wearing any makeup, but she still looked formidable. "I promise I won't tell anyone a single word you say."

He put the book down.

"It's only fair, Ben." She crossed her arms over her chest and stared at him expectantly. "What did you do that was so bad it made you believe you're not worthy of being loved?"

Her words hit him hard and he resisted the urge to run out into the rain and never come back.

"That's a bit deep," Ben commented, playing for time. "I didn't know you had a degree in psychology."

"I've seen enough therapists to play one, and you're just prevaricating. Answer the question."

"How about you ask another one?" He met her gaze. "We could revisit the idea of me helping you out with that virginity thing if you like."

"Wow." She shook her head. "You must be really desperate not to talk about it to go *there*."

"We're stuck in this tent together for a few hours; we could work on your foreplay skills." Ben was improvising now, but what the hell. "Because when you do find the right man, you should expect him to be good with his hands and his mouth before he even gets to the penetration part."

Silver's gaze fixed on his mouth and then she flopped back onto her sleeping bag. "I can't believe you're saying this out loud."

He followed her down and leaned over her, his elbow parked near her shoulder, his hand supporting his head. "I'm good at foreplay. I love going down on a woman."

She briefly closed her eyes. "Now you're just being silly. All my girlfriends say that getting a man to give as good as he gets is impossible."

"Not this man." He picked up her hand and pressed her fingers to his bearded chin. "Just imagine how this is going to feel against your skin."

She shuddered as he gently sucked her fingers into his mouth. "Come on, Silver, we've got a couple of hours before I need to go and check on the horses again. We might as well put it to good use."

"You'd really rather go through with this than answer a single question about your past?"

"Hell, yeah. This is much more fun." He lowered his head and kissed her slowly and lavishly. "Have I convinced you yet?"

She licked her lips as if she tasted him and his cock woke up big-time.

"I'm so confused."

"Why?" He kissed her again until she made that desperate humming noise in her throat that drove him wild.

"Because I want both things." She looked up at him and grimaced. "And don't tell me I always want everything. I get it."

"You'll have to choose." He nipped her lip and then sucked the tender spot into his mouth. "I'm a man. You know I can't multitask."

Silver's hand came up of its own volition to caress Ben's neck and keep him exactly where she wanted him. Unfortunately, all he was proving was that her physical desire was stronger than her blatant curiosity about his early life. She could always ask him about that later, whereas she feared the opportunity for a lesson in foreplay would never come up again.

She took a deep breath. "Okay, then this had better be good."

"It will be." Ben's slow smile made everything inside her perk up. "The first woman I dated long-term was a lot older than me, and she had . . . high expectations."

"As to what exactly?"

"How to properly please a woman. She was a damn fine teacher. She said she considered it her mission in life to send well-educated men out into the world who women would appreciate."

"Was she right?"

"Damn straight." He smoothed his thumb over her mouth. "Because the important thing to remember is that some women can take longer to reach their sexual pleasure and that getting them there is worth the time."

"Okay, well, that explains a lot," Silver said. "Because when I have dated guys, they've always rushed me, like sticking their tongue down my throat, their hands in my panties, making me grab their dick . . ." She shuddered. "I felt so used."

"Then they were all doing it wrong." Ben kissed her lips. "Are you willing to take your fleece off?"

"Sure." Silver removed it and lay back down again, watching him watching her.

"You got a bra on under that bunny top?"

"No, because these are my pajamas, and I don't sleep in a bra." She pointed at her chest. "And this is another way to tell that these are my real boobs, because they don't stay sticking out when I lie down."

"May I?" He gestured at her chest.

Silver nodded as he gently cupped her breast, his fingers warm and strong.

"Nice." His thumb grazed her nipple and she jumped.

"Thanks."

He bent his head to kiss her mouth, his hand remaining on her breast, his thumb slowing circling her hardening nipple. She grabbed hold of his shoulder bracing herself against the stirrings of pleasure as he transferred his attention to the other breast.

"You okay with this so far?" he breathed against her lips.

"Definitely," she reassured him. "You can even speed up a little if you like."

"Nah." He kissed her again, learning and exploring her mouth with his usual slow efficiency.

Just about when she thought she might die of frustration, he eased his mouth free of hers.

"Can I take your top off?"

"Are you going to ask permission for every little thing you do?" Silver demanded.

"Yeah, it's called active consent." His mouth kicked up at the corner. "Ever heard of it?"

"I'm a woman. Of course I have, but I've never met a man before who knows what it means. I've been on movie sets where I've had to deal with a lot of unnecessary and uninvited dicks."

He actually looked angry. "What kind of jerk does that?"

"Sometimes it's an accident, and I get an apology, but sometimes the bastard knows exactly what he's doing, and I just have to grin and bear it." She stroked his chest. "Wow, talk about ruining the mood. No wonder no one ever wants to have sex with me."

"Don't worry," he assured her. "I'm very focused on your pleasure right now."

"Only because you're scared I'll ask you questions you don't want to answer."

He pulled her top off and stared down at her breasts like a man who'd been struck dumb, which was highly gratifying. She knew she was in good shape. She put in hours at the gym to maintain her body because otherwise she wouldn't get cast, but she was used to being examined like a piece of meat. For the first time in her life she had someone gazing at her with uncritical adoration, and it was really something.

He leaned in and placed a deliberate kiss between her

breasts. "You're so beautiful. I can't believe I'm here with you like this."

He licked a path to her nipple and sucked it into his mouth. Silver gasped and shoved her hand into his hair, her nails scratching his scalp as he licked and teased her tender flesh. Just when she thought she might scream, he transferred his attention to her other breast, and gave it the same amount of intense interest. By the time he finally sat back, she was breathing hard, all her attention focused on the physical sensations he had aroused in her.

"Still okay?"

She nodded, her gaze falling to his boxers where the thick outline of his cock pressed against the cotton. There was a damp spot at the top and she reached out to touch it with her finger.

He shuddered and took hold of her wrist. "You'll make me come."

"I've done that for men before." She tried to sound nonchalant. "It's no big deal."

"Are you trying to tell me that the kind of guy you go out with expects you to get him off, and gives nothing in return?"

His outrage on her behalf was so sweet that she patted his cheek. "Sometimes they tried to reciprocate, but it always felt awkward and rushed." She bit her lip. "A couple of them said I was frigid."

"Bastards," Ben growled. "Look at you! You're so hot, you're making me burn." He held her gaze. "You ready for the next lesson?"

She pointed at his groin. "Is it my turn?"

"Hell, no, this is all for you." He stroked her thigh. "Will you take off your jammies?"

She wriggled out of them and lay there feeling rather self-conscious in just her panties.

"Are you scared?" Ben asked gently.

She met his brown gaze. "Not with you. I'm just trembling with excitement."

"Right." He climbed over her leg and eased his thigh between hers. "Let me get comfortable, and I'll make you forget anything except how to scream my name."

"So conceited," Silver murmured, and got a flash of his teeth in response as he lowered his head and kissed his way down from her breasts to her most private flesh. She had to agree that his beard against her skin was the most exquisite sensation she had ever experienced. His fingers hooked into the side of her panties and he drew them off her.

His mouth covered her, his tongue seeking her already-needy bud, tending it like the most dedicated of gardeners. She'd never had a man go down on her before in real life, and she wasn't quite sure how to deal with the intensity of her physical reaction. Each leisurely flick of his tongue sent a thread of pleasure deep inside her, making her press up against him in unconscious appeal.

"It's okay," he murmured against her thigh. "Don't be shy. Do whatever feels right. I can take it."

"I'm scared I'll suffocate you," Silver croaked.

He raised his head to grin at her, his mouth wet with her need. "But what a way to go." He hesitated. "You okay if I use my fingers as well? I won't go deep."

"I might die of pleasure, but please, go ahead." Silver reached down and patted his broad shoulder. "Maybe neither of us will come out of this alive."

Damn, she tasted so fine he could stay right where he was for the rest of his life—except maybe he'd like more. He reminded himself that full-on sex wasn't on the agenda, and that this was all about giving Silver pleasure. The fact that he was the first man to go down on her was doing all kinds of crazy things to his libido. He'd promised he was going to make her come, and he was a man of his word.

He slid just the tip of his finger inside her and continued to lavish attention on her clit until she was rocking up into his touch, her breathing uneven, and the bite of her nails in his shoulder painful.

"I can't . . ." she gasped.

He grazed her with his teeth and she came apart in his hands, screaming his name just as planned, and filling him with an immense sense of satisfaction. He continued to pet and soothe her until she gave a shuddering sigh and relaxed back against the pillows.

He wiped his face on the sheet and raised himself up to look at Silver who had one hand over her eyes. He wanted more. He wanted all of it. His dick throbbed in agreement and he frowned down at his groin.

"That was . . . amazing." Silver's voice was a mere thread.

"Glad you enjoyed it." Ben kissed her mouth and she opened her eyes to study him wonderingly.

"I've never had an orgasm with a real live man before."

He wanted to beat his chest and roar like a caveman but settled for a modest smile. "You're welcome."

She pointed at his still-hard and very hopeful dick.

"Can I help you with that?"

He made the mistake of checking the time, and regretfully shook his head. "I've got to go look in on the horses and the state of the creek." Five minutes out in the rain would take care of any lingering problems.

"But it doesn't seem fair."

Ben forced himself to move away from her. "Think of

it as payback for all the men who have left you unsatisfied over the years."

She smiled, but still looked worried as she sat up, her hair around her shoulders, which made him want to get right back into bed with her. "I'll get up and come with you."

"Would you mind if I go by myself this time?" Ben asked. "It's not really safe out there yet." He wanted to be by himself for a moment to get his head around what had just happened.

"Okay." She put a brave face on it. "How about I start lunch?"

"Great idea."

He grabbed his clean pair of jeans and his fleece. Getting his jeans zipped was going to be a problem, but he could always leave them undone and let the weather shrink him down to size. He put on clean socks and glanced at his soaked boots and hat. They would have to do. Getting out of that tent and away from Silver Meadows before he gave in and made love to her was absolutely imperative.

Chapter Nine

By the time Ben came back, Silver had put on proper clothes and set out some of the freeze-dried meals and protein bars. Part of her wanted to stay right where she was, naked in Ben's sleeping bag, preferably with him wrapped around her. If she really got in his face about his past, would he finish the job and actually make love to her?

But that wasn't fair, was it? And he'd know what she was trying to do, and call her out again. She didn't want to destroy the fragile trust they'd built between them while her body was still purring like a well-petted cat.

"It's still raining, the animals are fine, and the creek's even higher." Ben came in and stripped off his boots, his expression grim. "We're not going anywhere."

"Should we move up the slope?" Silver asked, handing him one of the towels to dry his hair. "Is it possible that the water will reach here?"

"I've never seen it happen before." He spread the towel out to dry. "BB wouldn't be letting his ranch guests come up here if there was even a chance of it being unsafe. If we settle in for the rest of the day, and make plans for tomorrow, we'll probably be fine."

Silver frowned. "You don't sound very convinced."

"I've never seen the water so high and so dangerous up here." He shoved a hand through his still-damp hair. "I'm going to try and contact BB tonight and see if he has any more up-to-date information on the state of the valley."

"Let's have something to eat," Silver suggested. "Maybe that will cheer you up. You must be hungry after all your exertions."

He winked at her. "Honey, that wasn't work."

"I meant all the work you've been doing outside the tent, not in it!" Silver protested, and then laughed when he grinned at her. Why had she ever thought he was stern looking and average? "Okay, maybe I could've put that better."

She turned to the icebox. "What would you like for lunch?"

"You?"

Silver clutched the freeze-dried packet to her chest and felt herself blushing. "I thought our lesson was over."

"You don't want part two?"

She handed him the container of hot water. "There's a part two?"

"Sure there is." He took a pack at random and opened it up. "If you're interested."

"Does it have something to do with reciprocal pleasure?"

His brow creased. "I'm not sure what that means, but if you want to learn a few things to drive a man wild, I'm more than willing to teach you."

"Don't try and play the dumb cowboy with me. I bet you went to college."

He rubbed a hand over the back of his neck, something she'd noticed he did when he didn't want to talk about something. "Yeah, I got a football scholarship."

"Where to?"

"Stanford."

She slowly closed her mouth. "So why aren't you in the NFL right now?"

"I wasn't good enough." His smile was wry. "And I crashed out of college after two years, so I'm definitely not as smart as you think."

"What did you do?" Silver asked.

"Failed my academic classes." He looked down at his hands. "Didn't live up to expectations, so they were delighted when I screwed up my finals."

It didn't sound like him at all, but one look at his closed-in expression made Silver realize he was unlikely to elaborate on what he'd already said, or appreciate her asking him about it.

"I didn't get the chance to go to college." Silver filled the tense silence. "I barely got schooling because I was on set so much." She sighed, aware of the tension leaching from his frame as she didn't ask him any more questions about himself. "We had tutors, but sometimes they were having such a great time being on a movie shoot, they forgot they were supposed to be teaching us stuff. I suspect I only graduated high school because my dad paid off the one I had in senior year."

He stirred his food and sat down on his bedding while she poured two cups of coffee and shook the empty pot.

"Maybe we should start rationing this if we aren't going anywhere until tomorrow."

"I can always boil more water."

"And get soaked to the skin again? We have nowhere to dry all the wet clothes already." She stirred up her food and started eating. "I just had an idea. We could put them in my tent."

"You're staying here then, are you?" Ben finally looked up at her.

Her smile faltered. "No, of course not, if you need your space." She chewed determinedly on her beef stew and took sips of her precious coffee. "I can move my stuff back right after lunch."

"Silver . . . I'm not telling you to go," Ben said quietly. "I just wanted to give you the option to leave." He set down his meal. "I'm treading on dangerous ground here. I'm supposed to be your professional trail guide."

"And you are very good at that," Silver agreed cautiously.

"But touching you like this? Wanting to keep touching you? That's hardly fair when you're depending on me to get you safely out of here."

"This is a fine time to get cold feet, Ben." She met his gaze. "If I felt like you were taking advantage of me, I would tell you. I'm an expert in detecting all kinds of bullshit, flattery, and downright creepiness. In fact, I've spent my whole life dealing with it." She took in a quick breath. "I *like* you touching me. I was the one who suggested it in the first place, remember? You made me feel . . . special. But, if that's all you want to give me, that's also okay. I'm a big girl, and we're both adults. You've already given me much more from a man than I've ever had before."

She reached over to get his cup and he caught her hand and dragged her over to sit in his lap.

"What—" She stopped talking as his mouth crashed into hers and concentrated on kissing him back.

"This isn't about not wanting you." He looked right into her eyes. "I know it's wrong, and I know you're probably sick of me dicking you around, but I can't deny how I feel." He smoothed her hair out of her face. "But you should also know that I'm not behaving like myself, and that when I get wild, I usually crash and burn."

"We've got four days before we have to return to the ranch," Silver said. "How about we just forget about the real world and just make our own here? Then, when we get back, we'll shake hands, say good-bye, and both have fond memories of each other, and our experience together."

"That sounds great, but—" He hesitated. "Sex *complicates* things, you know?"

"I don't know," Silver replied evenly. "Do you think I expect you to marry me if you're my first lover?"

He visibly recoiled. "Jeez, no."

She stared at him, one eyebrow raised, and he groaned. "That came out wrong."

"I'm not sure I'm ready for a long-term relationship with anyone at the moment," Silver reassured him. "And I can't imagine you thriving in the middle of L.A. anyway."

"I hate big cities." Ben shuddered. "Even Palo Alto was too busy for me."

"Then as we know that neither of us wants more than this, can we just get on with it?" Silver asked.

"If you're sure." Ben still looked worried. "I'm older than you are; I shouldn't be making stupid decisions."

"Which proves that this decision isn't stupid," Silver repeated. "We're both going in with our eyes open. Do you have protection?"

"Yeah." He patted the side of the first-aid box. "We get a lot of couples on our trail rides, and occasionally they get caught short, so we always carry condoms."

Silver climbed off his lap, lay back on her sleeping bag, and looked expectantly up at him. "Come on then, cowboy. You were going to teach me how to please a man, remember?"

Ben stared at her beautiful face. Every part of him wanted to follow her down and make love to her. She was right—if they were careful, no one would ever know except the two of them. The thought of her meeting someone who wouldn't treat her right, and who would ruin sex for her, didn't sit well with him. The responsible Ben, the guy he usually was, took a step back, hands held high, and disappeared behind the Ben who wanted to feel something intensely—to live a little—to show Silver that sex was the most amazing thing in the world with the right person.

And he was the right person, right now for her. He knew it in his soul.

Holding her gaze, he shrugged out of his T-shirt and crawled over to her.

"I'll make it good for you, I promise." He kissed her and she kissed him back. "I'll make you come so hard you forget your own name."

"Promises, promises," she murmured against his lips. "And all talk, and no action."

He eased her out of her clothing, kissing each newly discovered piece of skin, enjoying each catch of her breath as he learned her and what she liked. Her hands wandered freely over his body as well, making him feel more alive than he had in years. This was what he'd been missing—this closeness, this rawness, and this sense that he was truly living.

He cupped her breast and drew her nipple into his mouth, making her gasp and clutch his shoulder. He hummed his appreciation against her hardening flesh, sliding one muscled thigh between hers. Within seconds she was arching up against him rubbing herself to the rhythm of his sucking. He slid his hand down over her stomach and spread his fingers over her mound, aware that she was wet for him, and that she was already sensitive from his earlier attentions.

Her fingers slid under the elastic of his boxers. "Will you take them off?" Silver asked. "I'd like to see you."

"Last time you saw me, you ran away," Ben reminded her.

"Only because I was enjoying looking at you too much," Silver confessed, making him smile. "It's okay, really. I've seen a naked man before."

He sat back on his heels, shoved his boxers down, and then he was bare-ass naked.

"Oh," Silver said, and he was amused to see her blush.

"That's all you've got?" Ben asked. "A guy could feel insulted right now."

"Maybe it's because I'm lying down, and you're not, that you look way bigger than I remembered."

Ben ran a hand along his shaft. "Keep talking like that, and it'll get even bigger. How about we do this? I'll lie down and you can tower over me."

He reversed their positions and put one hand behind his head so that she could look her fill without him touching her. He knew her well enough by now to guess that she needed time to work things out to her own satisfaction.

"You wanna touch anything?" Ben asked.

"Yes." She reached out, wrapped her hand around the base of his shaft, and squeezed hard enough to make his eyes pop out. "Was that too much?"

He let out his breath. "A little."

"I'm more nervous than I thought," Silver confessed.

"Which is why if you want to change your mind at any point, you just speak up, and we stop, okay?"

"More of your informed consent stuff?" Silver asked, her whole body relaxing.

Ben shrugged. "Daisy made me learn it by heart, so yeah, I suppose it is." He closed his fingers over Silver's. "And I mean it. You want to stop. We stop."

"I want to learn. I mean, I know how to make you come." She moved her hand up and down his shaft, making his hips roll into her touch. "I even know how to give you a blow job, but what do you like?"

"All of it." He held her gaze. "Whatever you choose to give me, no expectations, no demands."

She bit her lip, and he tensed for rejection, ready to give her whatever she wanted, regardless.

"I didn't realize I'd be so . . . scared."

"Sex is a big deal, Silver," Ben said gently. "Whatever anyone tells you, it's a powerful thing, and it changes everything."

She leaned over him, her hair tickling his skin, and kissed his mouth. "Can you just . . . lie there, and let me explore?"

"Sure." He eased his other hand behind his head like he was about to take a nap. "Be my guest."

Silver ran her fingers through his short beard, noticing that it grew in redder than she had expected, paused to run her thumb over his lower lip, and then trailed her hand down over his lightly furred chest. He sighed but didn't do anything more threatening than suck his stomach in as she ventured lower. Not that he had much gut to suck in, but it did make his abs look good.

"I have to go to the gym to look like this," she mused as she circled his belly button. "And you just . . . look like this."

"I work hard," he murmured. "And riding is great for your core, apparently."

"So I see."

He spread his legs wide and she knelt between them, one hand braced on the jut of his hip bone. He smelled like hot, sexy man, and she wanted to taste him so badly. She should've known he'd be calm and controlled for her. It was so much a part of who he was, and the reason why she instinctively trusted him. She sensed there was fire there, too, waiting to ignite, but he wasn't going to allow it to consume either of them.

She cupped his balls and kissed the very top of his shaft. He shuddered, his gaze riveted to the tip of her tongue as she licked him like an ice cream. He tasted of himself and, emboldened by his stillness, she sucked him deep into her mouth. Unlike the other two guys she'd tried this with, he didn't immediately start shoving himself down her throat, but let her play and proceed at her own pace.

Only at the end, did he lift his hips and he quickly controlled himself, lying flat again, with a muttered curse. When she felt that she'd teased him enough, and the heaviness between her own thighs was begging for relief, she lifted her head, and found him looking right back at her, his brown gaze steady.

"You okay?" she asked.

He nodded. "You?"

"I'm . . . good." She regarded him seriously. "So, this reverse cowgirl thing? Would that work?"

He blinked at her. "What?"

"The sex thing when I face the other way and wave my arm over my head like a cowboy on a bucking horse."

He stirred. "I was thinking more of good old missionary for your first time, but—"

"Well, thank goodness for that." Silver flopped down beside him. "It looked really complicated to me."

He came up on one elbow and regarded her intently. "If you don't mind me asking, where did you get that idea?"

She felt her skin heat up. "One of my boyfriends made me watch porn. He thought it might inspire me."

His disgusted expression said it all. "How about we do it the old-fashioned way, and when we get good at it you can try anything you like?" Ben suggested.

"Sounds way better to me." She smiled up at him.

"Then stay there while I get some protection."

She waited for him to crawl back to her, cocooned in the warmth of his sleeping bag and surrounded by his scent and the sound of the rain. He set the foil package to one side and spread her thighs wide.

Silver held her breath, but he did nothing more frightening than touch her gently between the legs while he leaned forward and kissed her in the same rhythm. After a while she was pushing up against his fingers, and his thumb was planted firmly over her now-sensitive bud.

"More," she demanded.

"Nope, you're not the only one who gets to take their time."

He nipped her throat, as his other hand found her breast. Everything he was doing was coalescing into a ball of pure sensation that she recognized for what it was.

"Ben . . ." She gasped his name as she climaxed, and he slid his fingers even deeper inside her, rocking them back and forth until she came again.

He raised himself over her, one hand reaching for the foil packet. "Do you still want me? Want this?"

"Yes." Silver held his intense gaze. "Please."

"So polite," he said, his attention on rolling on the

protection and lowering himself over her. "Hold on to me, bite me if it helps, and tell me to stop if you want."

"I will." She stilled at the first thick press of him at her entrance and forced herself not to tense up. He brought his mouth to hers and kissed her so thoroughly that she almost forgot about the gradual rocking intrusion until he stopped moving.

"You good?" he asked through clenched teeth.

"Yes," she said again, her feet instinctively climbing his thighs so that she could cradle him more completely within her body. "Oh *yes* . . ."

Ben woke up with a naked Silver draped over him. She was smiling in her sleep and so beautiful that he wanted to roll her onto her back and make love to her again. He waited for the all-too-familiar guilt to swamp him and felt nothing. Being here with her like this felt right, and he wasn't going to allow anything to spoil that. They'd have to go their separate ways soon, and, for once in his life he damn well wasn't going to destroy anything before he had to.

He checked his watch and grimaced. It was still raining, and he'd have to get up, check the campsite and the horses, and contact BB. He gently rolled Silver over onto her back and her blue eyes opened. He tensed, waiting to see if she was the one who would be swamped with regrets, but she just smiled at him.

"Hey."

He smiled back like a fool. "Hey. I've got to go check the horses."

"I'll come with you." She sat up and immediately winced.

"You okay?" Ben asked.

"Yes, I just used some unfamiliar muscles." She pushed her hair out of her eyes. "And you weigh a ton."

"Which is why next time you can try out your reverse cowgirl move if you like." Ben moved off the sleeping bags to gather his clothes. "I'll wash and get changed in your tent, okay? There's warm water in the flask if you need it."

"Damn . . ." Ben looked at the creek and then back at their camp. "We're going to have to move higher up the bank if the water continues to rise like this."

The rain had eased off slightly, but the volume of water pouring over the waterfall into the valley wasn't letting up. As it stood, there was no way he could see them getting back across the creek and into the safety of the valley beyond.

"What happens if we can't get across?" Silver asked. She was wearing her rain slicker, and every time she looked up at him she had to hold on to the hood to stop it from blowing down.

He pointed upward. "We'll make our way out of the canyon that way, come around the edge, and drop back down into the valley farther along."

"It looks too steep."

"You're right. But if we go downstream, the slope gets easier, and we'll be able to get out. I've done it before."

He'd done it on a sunny day with a group of experienced hunters, not in the middle of a rainstorm with a relative newbie, but he had no intention of mentioning that. It was not a route he'd ever pick voluntarily.

"I need to talk to BB," Ben said abruptly.

"Why don't you do that while I tend to the horses and

mules and watch the fire?" Silver suggested. "We definitely need more hot water and coffee."

"If you're okay with that," Ben said. She was being amazingly calm about everything, and he really appreciated it. "No point in both of us scrambling up there."

She nodded, and went down toward the horses while he trudged up the side of the hill, which wasn't easy when the mud beneath his feet kept sliding away like molasses.

He was amazed that he could actually get a signal in such crazy weather and even more grateful when BB came through loud and clear.

Ben briefly outlined their current situation and then asked the all-important question. "Any chance this rain is stopping soon? I don't want to risk getting out of the valley at this end if I don't have to. But I don't want to get stuck here or cut off by the creek overflowing its banks."

"The forecast is rain and more rain." BB sighed. "Knowing where you are, I think you'd better consider evacuating."

Ben let out his breath. "Do you think Silver will make it out?"

"From what you're telling me, she's soon going to have a choice between fording a creek that might drown her, or climbing out of a valley on a good horse with the best guide possible."

"I hear you."

"Sorry I can't give you better news, Ben, but my advice would be if you can hang in there tonight, to leave as soon as it gets light. It's not only the water you should be worrying about, but the possibility that the whole hillside could come sliding down on you as well."

Ben's first thought was that at least he'd get to spend one more night with Silver, which was when he realized how far from being his normal self he still was.

"You're the boss, and you know this land way better than I do," Ben said. "If you say we should move, then we'll leave in the morning."

"Good man. I'll keep this channel open tomorrow. If you have any problems ping me, okay?"

"Thanks, BB. I'll stay in touch."

He ended the call and headed carefully down the slope, slipping and sliding until he was finally on the rock level. They still had plenty of food. They weren't cut off from help, and he would do anything in his power to make sure that Silver got out of the valley alive.

Chapter Ten

Silver knelt by her pack, folded everything up, even her damp clothes, and secured the ties. Ben had gotten her out of bed in the dark and given her the bad news that they had to leave, and that they'd be going up the outer edge of the valley. Seeing as he'd told her while holding her in his arms, she'd taken it way better than he might have expected.

She didn't regret having sex with him. The only thing she was beginning to regret was that they probably wouldn't get a chance to do it again. They'd made love once more during the night and he'd been so careful and considerate of her that she'd almost ended up in tears. She had a terrible suspicion that finding another man in her world who would ever come close to Ben Miller was already a lost cause.

Made love . . . Silver paused and looked over at an oblivious Ben who was busy dealing with the horses. She wasn't going to pretend. That's what it had felt like and even if she never acknowledged that to Ben, it meant something to her. The trouble was that now she wanted to touch him all the time, to feel his skin against hers, hook her foot over the tight muscles of his ass as he drove into her, and . . .

"You ready?" Ben turned to look at her.

"Almost." She hurried to complete her task. There was barely enough light to see and it was still raining. "I just need to load this up on Bill."

"I'll do it." He strode over, lifted the pack as if it weighed nothing, and took it over to the patient mule. "You can mount up when you're ready. Ladybug's all set."

She walked over to her mare and managed to get up the first time. Ladybug's body heat enveloped her in warmth as she settled into the saddle and took hold of the reins.

Ben brought Ted over and tied his lead rope to the back of Silver's saddle. "We're going to take this real slow. All you have to do is hold on, follow my lead, and by the end of the day, we'll be out of here and back in Morgan Valley." He looked up at her, his brown gaze steady. "I promise I'll keep you safe."

"Okay, then, cowboy." She blew him a kiss. "Let's go."

He set off, following what remained of the bank of the overflowing creek, constantly scanning the steep slope. Silver wondered how far they would have to go before the horses could scramble upward, and whether she'd be able to hang on. She had to hang on. She reminded herself that falling off was not an option. When she got back to civilization, she'd tell the movie producers about her real live adventure on a trail ride, and they'd have to give her the part.

At least amongst the trees the rain was less heavy, which was a good thing, because the clay soil, which was already completely saturated, was falling off in chunks and sliding down the hillside. Eventually, Ben stopped and looked back at her, the rain dripping off the brim of his Stetson. She couldn't come up alongside him because the widening of the creek had narrowed the available path considerably.

"We're going to start up the slope, okay?"

She looked up at the sparse pine forest. "This doesn't look any easier than the last mile or so."

"It is, but we're going to have to take our time." He hesitated. "If it gets too difficult, just shout out, and we'll try another way."

"Don't baby me." She held his gaze. "There isn't another way." She pointed at the creek. "We can't get across that because it's flowing too fast, and there's a lot of debris in there. We have to go up."

"We could just follow the creek and hope it hasn't completely taken out the path at some point," Ben reminded her.

"Which you said it probably has where the canyon narrows." Silver gathered her reins. "Let's just try this, shall we? I'll do my best to stay on Ladybug's back and not slither all the way down into the creek."

He still looked worried, but she also knew his commonsense would prevail.

"Okay, but take your time and be careful."

"Will do." She paused. "Will I get a reward if I make it to the top?"

His smile flashed out. "Maybe. I'll think about that while we're getting there."

"Don't think too hard. We don't want you losing your concentration."

He chuckled and turned Calder's head toward the bank. "Let's go."

It wasn't easy. The ground was so unstable that taking a direct path was impossible. He had to pick his way through the pine trees, making sure that both Calder and the mule could fit through the gaps, and watch out for landslides, exposed roots, and the occasional jut of the underlying rock that the rain had exposed. For every foot they gained it felt like they backtracked three, but slowly and steadily they were getting there.

He stopped again to make sure Silver was following behind him. Her expression was fierce with concentration and she hadn't complained once. He was so proud of her right now. Jeez, how was he going to say good-bye in a few days, when they'd shared some of the most intense days of his life?

He reminded himself that he had no claim on her. If they didn't get up this slope and onto the rim of the valley it wouldn't matter what he thought of her or how he wanted to proceed because they'd both be dead.

"You hanging in there?" he called out.

"Yes, but it's awful." She shuddered. "I know Ladybug is good at this, but every time one of her hooves slips my heart skips a beat."

"Luckily for us, she's got three other legs to stabilize her," Ben reminded her. "We're not far from the top now. Another hour should do it."

He checked his watch. They'd been moving for three hours and should reach the top in time for an early lunch. He set his gaze on the next obstacle to overcome, clicked to Calder, and set off. They were going to do it even if it took all day. There wasn't any other possible outcome.

He whooped like a real cowboy when Calder took the final unsteady step upward and they were on flat ground. He had an absurd desire to fall to his knees and kiss the barren rock. Instead, he moved out of the way to allow Silver to come up behind him.

"We made it." He dismounted and went over to her. "*You* made it."

She was soaked through, her hair had come down, and

there was an ugly welt on her cheek from an unruly branch, but she still managed an exhausted smile.

"Can I die quietly now?"

"I'd rather you stayed alive so that I can kiss you."

He waited until she kicked her feet out of her stirrups and lifted her down, keeping her in his arms until she kissed him back.

"That's it?" She looked up at him, her eyes dancing. "That's my reward? I don't even get laid?"

"Seeing as you look like you're about to fall asleep, I was thinking more about coffee, the last of Mrs. Morgan's cookies, and some lunch," Ben said.

She leaned into him. "I'm good for all of that."

"Then how about you sit down over there while I attend to the horses, and—"

She held up a finger. "How about I sort out the food while you deal with the horses? You're just as tired as I am."

"Yeah, well, you did wear me out last night, so there is that," Ben countered.

"Weakling." She moved toward the mules, each step an obvious effort. "Where's the food?"

"Left side of Bill." Ben forced his cold fingers to loosen the horses' bridles and girths. Calder was trained to stand when Ben dropped the reins, but Bill, Ted, and Ladybug needed tying up.

"Got it."

He was so glad to get some hot coffee inside him that he gulped it down in three mouthfuls and helped himself to more. Silver ate two protein bars, finished the last cookie, and also had a second cup.

"What's next?" She looked down into the valley, but

there was very little to see due to the mist and rain. "We stay up here until we find a safe place to descend?"

"Exactly. The canyon we were in is something of a cul-de-sac, so once we get beyond that and out into the central valley there won't be any need to cross the creek until we're back on Morgan ranch land."

Silver nodded and then yawned so hard, Ben could see her tonsils. "Any chance we could stop and take a nap before we move on?"

He checked the time. "It would have to be short. I don't want to get stuck up here in the dark." He took another look at her exhausted face and got to his feet. "I'll put up the tent."

It seemed like five minutes between lying next to Ben in the tent and him gently shaking her to wake up. She was exhausted, her clothes were damp, and her limbs stiff. She wanted to get down into Morgan Valley because being up so high and on such a narrow path cut into the rock made her feel very vulnerable.

Without the pine trees around them, they were more exposed to the rain and wind, which made seeing where she was going even harder. She tried not to look over the side and kept her gaze on Ted's swishing tail, or the back of Ben's head. It was completely silent up on the ridge and much colder than the valley below. Shadows from the Sierra Nevada foothills sent the trail into patches of gloom, which made Silver shiver even harder.

Eventually, Ben turned his head and shouted back to her.

"We'll be able to go down soon, so hang in there. I'm—"

His words were abruptly cut off as Calder stumbled and lurched to the left sending Ben over the edge. When the horse managed to right itself there was no longer a rider on his back.

"Ben!" Silver screamed and hurriedly dismounted, almost tripping over her own feet as she ran past Ted and caught hold of Calder's flapping reins. Half the path had just crumbled away right in front of her. She fell down onto her knees and forced herself to look down.

To her amazement she could see Ben not too far below her. His rain slicker had caught on the branches of a tree, and he lay flat on his back. His eyes were closed, and there was a trickle of blood running down over his temple.

"Ben!" she shouted again, her voice echoing through the canyon. "Can you hear me?"

It seemed to take forever for him to open his eyes, and even longer for him to focus on her.

"Don't move!" Silver added. "You're stuck in a tree." He closed his eyes again, and her breath caught in her throat. "Don't you dare die on me! You promised!"

"I hear you loud and clear, Silver." He winced, carefully brought his hand down to the side, and gripped one of the tree branches. "I'm lucky this broke my fall, else I'd still be rolling."

"Do you think you can sit up? Is anything broken? Will the tree bear your weight?" Silver was babbling now, but she didn't care. He was alive, and he was talking so it couldn't be bad, could it?

He slowly changed position, his breath hitching as he managed to sit upright. He clutched at his ribs and stayed very still for a long while, his face white with pain.

"I think I might have busted something."

"You think?" Silver's teeth were chattering so hard she could barely get words out. "Any idea how we're going to get you up here again?"

He blinked hard as blood dripped down his face into his

eyes. He sounded so weary. "Move Ladybug and the mules out of the way first."

"Okay." Silver nodded, went to stand, and saw stars herself. She pinched her hand hard and told herself off. "This is not the time for hysterics, Silver! You have to help him!"

She decided to take the mules and Ladybug back the way they'd come, seeing as the path there was stable and wider. She tied them up, messing up the knots twice, and inwardly screamed at herself for her clumsiness. She was terrified that if she took too long, Ben would lose consciousness again and slip out of the tree.

The light was starting to fade, which made her even more anxious. At least it was easy to see where he'd gone over as half the trail had gone with him.

"Okay, I'm back. What next?" Silver tried not to shout too loudly this time.

"There's a rope attached to my saddle." He paused to breathe hard. "I don't suppose you know how to make a lasso?"

"Actually, I do," Silver said. "It's one of the things I learned on set."

"What you're going to do is make a loop, and throw it over me, or get it close enough for me to catch it."

"Got it." Silver found the rope and took a couple of panicked seconds to remember how the hell to make a loop before she turned back to Ben.

"Before you throw it, attach one end to the back of Calder's saddle. There's plenty of rope."

She did as he said, and carefully turned Calder around until he was facing back down the trail where the others were.

Her first attempt to throw the rope was way off, but her second was good enough for Ben to catch hold of. His agonized expression as he attempted to drop the rope over his shoulders and around his ribs made her want to cry.

"Okay, now you're going to get Calder to walk forward real slow. I'll jump toward the face of the slope and climb as best I can as he pulls me up. If I need him to stop I'll yell, so stay at his head, and make him do what I say."

"But won't that hurt your ribs more?" Silver asked.

"It might, but I'm not spending the rest of my life in a tree." Ben held her gaze, his mouth set in a grim line. "Let's just get this over with."

It took forever. At least it felt like that as Ben was slowly winched up the slope, stopping every few seconds to readjust his position or just stay conscious through the pain. His hands and knees were bleeding as he scrabbled for purchase on the unforgiving rock, and breathing had become a white-hot agony. Staying conscious when all he wanted to do was crawl into a hole and sleep became harder every second. The only thing that kept him going was that Silver needed him, and he wasn't going to let her down.

When his searching fingers met the top edge and were swiftly gripped by Silver's, he experienced an overwhelming sense of thankfulness. She helped haul him up, and he rolled onto his back, and just stared up at her anxious, tearstained face.

"Hey," he murmured like a fool.

She swallowed hard. "Hey, right back."

Ben forced his lips to move. "I don't think I'm going to be moving far for the rest of the day. We'll have to set up the tent somewhere and make do."

"There's space where I left Ladybug and the mules." She placed a rolled-up saddle blanket under his head and draped him in her coat. "Stay there, and I'll come back and get you when it's ready."

Like he was going anywhere. . . . He wasn't sure if he drifted back into unconsciousness because it didn't seem more than a second before Silver was beside him again. This time, she had her torch, and he blinked to avoid the brightness of the beam.

"Do you think that if I helped, you could walk a few yards?" Silver asked.

"Don't think I've got any choice," Ben murmured. "I'd rather be undercover than an appetizer for a pack of coyotes."

As if on cue, the howls of a nearby pack echoed through the canyon below. He managed to sit up before the pain hit him, and he had to blink back whirling stars of dizziness. Silver crouched beside him and wrapped her arm around his waist. Seeing as she was almost a foot shorter than he was, and about a hundred and fifty pounds lighter, he immediately felt guilty.

"Put your arm around my shoulders and let's try and stand," Silver suggested.

"I'll crush you."

"I'm stronger than I look." She braced herself. "On three."

He lurched to his feet, aware that she was already bearing far too much of his weight and unable to do shit about it. She didn't rush him; she just stood quietly until he got his balance, could see straight, and contemplate moving. He vaguely registered the shadows of the horses and the campfire ahead. It wasn't that far if he took his time.

"Do you want to try taking a step?" Silver asked.

Ben grimaced. "No, but as I said, we need to get out of the open."

He managed to start moving and she helped him,

standing like a rock as he weaved around like a drunk at a bar. He focused on the horses and made himself keep moving forward. They stumbled into the circle of light thrown by the fire and he sank down onto his knees, one hand clutching his ribs as pain knifed through him. He was pretty sure what he'd done because it wasn't the first time he'd busted a rib.

"Ben?" Silver crouched next to him breathing hard. "Do you think you can get into the tent? I need to check you over."

"Yeah, sure."

He slowly turned his head, saw the opening of the tent, and crawled toward it. His sleeping bag was unzipped, and he lay down with a sigh of relief while Silver fussed around him, removing his boots and easing him out of his coat. He didn't mind what she did. He was just glad to be alive and safe for the night.

"I'm amazed that you somehow managed to keep hold of your hat," she commented dryly, as she continued to help him undress down to his T-shirt and boxers.

"I'm a rancher. I'll probably die with my Stetson on," Ben croaked, tasting his own blood on his lips.

He opened his eyes and winced at the brightness of the light. "Can you shoot a gun?"

"If I have to, yes." Silver was setting out a whole load of medical supplies, he suspected were for him. "I'm not putting you out of your misery quite yet, though."

"There's a weapon in my saddlebag. Seeing as I've been bleeding all the way along the trail and the coyotes are out, we might be getting some late-night visitors. You might need to scare them off."

"Got it," Silver said as she rolled up her sleeves and

washed her hands in the basin of water beside her. "I'm going to check your head, okay?"

He closed his eyes as her fingers gently probed his skull and only hissed out a curse when she hit pay dirt.

She studied him seriously. "Do you think you might have a concussion?"

"Seeing as my head hit the tree first, I have a blinding headache, I want to puke, and I can't see straight, then, yeah."

Her fingers stilled on his shoulder. "There's no need to be sarcastic, Ben. I'm doing my best here, and I *hate* blood, and—"

He raised his hand, which felt like it was made of lead, and put it over hers. "I'm sorry. I'm being a jerk. Thanks for looking after me and setting up camp, and everything."

She sniffed. "You won't be thanking me after I've cleaned out your head wound."

"Good that I got it in now, then."

She slipped one of the towels under his head and started cleaning the matted blood from his hair and face, her expression serious. Her hands were shaking almost as much as he was. He wished he could find the energy to comfort her, or take over, or do anything except lie there and fight to breathe.

"I'm going to snip off some of the hair around the wound so that I can stick some antiseptic cream on it."

He didn't have the strength to reply, and started to drift off again, only to have her gently shaking his arm.

"If you do have a concussion you can't sleep yet."

"Try and stop me," he whispered, his voice constricted with all the pain he was forcing down inside him.

"I will." She gestured at the medical supplies and the first-aid manual. "I've been reading up on what to do.

It says that if you have a suspected concussion you should stay still, have someone watching over you for at least the first twenty-four hours, and take acetaminophen rather than any other painkiller, which could cause bleeding." She sat back and regarded him carefully. "Where else does it hurt?"

"My ribs and my right wrist."

"What would you normally do for those?"

"Tape my wrist and wrap up my ribs." He gestured at the box. "There's tape and bandages in there. If you help me sit up, we can get it done right now."

"Wouldn't you rather wait?" Silver looked conflicted.

"Best to do it now before everything swells up."

"Okay." She delved into the box and brought out several different sizes of tape. "Let's do your wrist first, so I can get the hang of it, and then we'll do your ribs."

After making sure that Ben was propped up securely against his pillows, Silver picked up the bowl of water and left the tent. She just about managed to throw the water away before she threw up herself. She'd never liked the sight or smell of blood, and while tending to Ben, she'd had to clamp her lips tightly together and not stare too long at the grisly two-inch gash on his skull.

She took a few deep breaths and went back to the fire where she'd set another pan of water to boil. It was dark now, and she was so exhausted, she wanted to cry. But there were things that needed doing, and she was the only person capable of doing them right now.

Her clothes were damp, she hadn't eaten for hours, and she couldn't seem to stop shaking. Watching Ben claw his way back up the cliff had been one of the most terrifying moments of her life. She made some fresh coffee and filled up the other flasks with boiling water before checking the food pouches. She was fairly sure she'd seen soup in there somewhere, and she was determined to get some down Ben.

She'd settled the horses in for the night, staggering under the weight of removing Ben's saddle and then her own. But she'd done it and was now glad she'd paid attention to Ben's patient lessons. She'd also fed the horses and checked that they weren't going anywhere. She hoped she'd done everything right. She couldn't rely on Ben to remain lucid enough to tell her whether she had or not.

Gathering the flasks, she made her way back into the tent, pausing at the entrance to check Ben over. His eyes were shut, and she considered leaving him to sleep, and then remembered he had to eat and take some painkillers first.

"Ben?" It took him a while to respond to her. "I'm making some soup. I can feed you, or you can feed yourself depending on how good you are with your left hand."

She wished she could strip off her wet clothing and put on her jammies, but she'd have to go back outside to secure the campsite for the night, and it was still raining.

After adding water to the pack of soup and giving it a good stir, she approached Ben who appeared to be half-asleep again.

"If you eat some of this, I'll give you the painkillers, and you can go to sleep for a while," she said encouragingly.

"Promise?" He opened one eye.

She nodded. "I'll have to wake you up a couple of times tonight, just to make sure you can wake up normally, but other than that, you can definitely sleep as much as you want."

He frowned. "I don't want you staying up all night worrying about me."

"I'd be staying up all night anyway replaying everything that happened in my head like a movie," Silver lied. "I'm way too wired to sleep."

"I don't—"

She stuck a spoonful of soup in his mouth and he stopped talking.

"I can do that myself, you know," he murmured. "I'm not a baby."

"I am well aware of what you are and what you are not, Ben Miller," Silver said tartly. "And at the moment, I'm in charge, and you get to do what you're told, okay?"

For the first time in what felt like forever, a hint of a smile broke through his exhaustion. "Yes, ma'am. You sound just like my auntie Rae." He took more soup. "Don't forget to have something yourself."

"I won't." After he finished the soup, she handed him the packet of acetaminophen. "Dessert."

"Just what I needed." He cracked open the pack. "My head's about to split open."

She offered him some coffee to wash the drugs down and finally let him be. He lay back stiffly against the pillows, a frown on his face, his eyes closed, and his hands folded together on his lap.

It took all her remaining energy to go back outside, make sure the fire was out, and that everything was quiet. She removed Ben's gun from his saddlebag and brought it and a box of ammunition into the tent with her. By the time she zipped up the door, he was fast asleep.

Silver stripped off her wet clothes, put on her thermal jammies and a clean pair of socks, and immediately felt better. She'd used some of the hot water to wash with and took more to make herself something to eat. Despite all the shocks of the day, or perhaps because of them, she was ravenous and ate two packets of what passed for sweet and sour chicken. She wished she'd rationed Mrs. Morgan's brownies more carefully because she really needed some chocolate right now.

After a cup of strong, black coffee, she regained some energy and snuggled down in her sleeping bag beside Ben. If she kept the lamp on she figured she wouldn't sleep too long because according to the first-aid manual she had to wake Ben at least twice during the night.

His skin was hot to the touch, which concerned her, but he'd only just taken the painkillers so hopefully that would resolve itself. If it didn't, and he became seriously ill . . .

Silver opened her eyes again and checked the time on Ben's watch. *Dammit*. She'd missed the window to contact BB on the radio. Would he be worried now? Would he send help? It was possible that no one would be able to get to them until the creek level subsided anyway. There were no roads out here suitable for emergency vehicles. She wasn't even sure a helicopter would be able to fly in such poor conditions.

She sat up and hugged her knees. She had no skills beyond basic first aid, but she did know that if Ben's ribs were severely damaged, any further movement might make them worse. The mere thought of sleeping disappeared in her rising panic. She was a movie star, for God's sake; she wasn't cut out for this. She had *people*. She studied Ben's pale features and heard his strained breathing. She had no choice. She couldn't walk away from him. It was time to woman up and do her best.

Chapter Eleven

Ben glared at Silver as she gently shook his shoulder. "Jeez, woman, can't you let me sleep?"

"No, I can't, and you know why." She handed him a cup of coffee. "Drink this, and I'll get you some breakfast."

"I can get it myself," Ben argued and tried to straighten up.

She gave him a severe look and put her hand on his chest. "You will stay there, have something to eat, and then if I say it's okay, you can try and move a little. Got it?"

The aroma of the coffee drifted up to him and he buried his nose in his cup and inhaled it greedily. His right wrist was throbbing, and his ribs were creaking like they'd become totally detached from his spine.

"Is Calder okay?" Ben sipped his coffee.

"I couldn't see any obvious damage when I checked him over this morning, and he was moving quite freely." She went over to the side of the tent. "I've made you some pancakes."

Ben looked around the neat tent and back at Silver, who was already dressed. She had big purple shadows under her eyes, and yet she was still smiling and taking care of him without a single complaint.

"I'm sorry," Ben said gruffly

"For what?" She handed him a plate, and he noticed she'd already cut his pancakes up like he was three.

"For all the trouble I'm causing you."

She sat down beside him. "To be honest, I'd rather you were here causing trouble than stuck in a tree dying."

"Can't argue with that." Ben managed to get some pancake in his mouth, and realized he was starving.

"I didn't get to speak to BB last night," Silver said. "By the time I thought about it, it was too late. Do you think I should try and contact him this morning?"

"Yeah, because he might be worrying about us by now. Do you remember how to use the radio?"

She nodded. Her blond hair was tied back in a scrappy ponytail and it looked like she hadn't had time to brush it. "After I've cleaned up breakfast, I'll try and contact him."

"You don't have to give him all the details. Just tell him my ribs are busted up, and give him our current position. He'll work it out." He set the plate away and finished his coffee.

"What is our position?" Silver asked.

He fumbled for his compass, silently showed it to her, and she memorized the information.

Ben cleared his throat. "I'm sorry, Silver, but you're going to have to make it clear to BB that I'm not going to be able to ride out of here." He laid it out there straight. "If it was an easy ride back, maybe. But trying to come down the slope with all those twists and turns? Not sure my ribs could take it."

"I understand." She pointed at his cup. "Do you want more coffee?"

"Sure." He watched her carefully as she filled up his cup. "You're taking this really well."

She shrugged. "I did all my freaking out last night while you were asleep, so I'm kind of resigned now."

"You're being amazing." He gently closed his fingers around her wrist. "You saved my goddam life."

"I did not," she protested, her cheeks reddening. "I just helped a little bit. You and Calder did all the hard work."

"And how do you think either of us would've achieved anything if you hadn't been there to hold it all together?" Ben asked, and kissed her palm. "Thank you."

She snatched her hand back, grabbed his plate, and turned toward the exit. "I'll go and call BB right now."

Silver took the radio and walked a little way from the camp to a slightly clearer more elevated spot. The sky was still gray, but it had at least stopped raining. When BB immediately answered, Silver thought she might cry.

"Hey, what's up?"

"Hi, it's me, Silver. Ben's hurt, and he doesn't think he can ride out of here."

There was a slight pause before BB spoke again.

"Okay, can you tell me what happened and exactly where you are?"

Silver relayed the basic details and waited again while BB recited them back to her to make sure he had everything clear. She didn't know what his background was, but he was incredibly concise, and God, she wanted someone to take charge of this mess so badly right now.

"Here's what's going to happen," BB said. "I need to check in with the local emergency services and find out what the best options are for getting you out. I'll get back to you in one hour. If Ben's condition worsens, contact me immediately."

"Okay." Silver nodded even though he couldn't see her. "Thanks so much."

"Hang in there, Ms. Meadows, you're doing great. Speak to you in an hour."

She walked back to the campsite, feeling more positive than she had for the past twenty-four hours. BB Morgan *inspired* confidence. If he couldn't get them out, she was fairly sure no one could.

"How'd it go?" Ben asked as soon as she came into the tent.

"He's going to get back to me in an hour with a rescue plan." Silver sat cross-legged beside him on her sleeping bag.

"That's BB for you," Ben commented. To her relief he looked a little better than he had the previous day, although he was already developing a black eye. "He's got *Semper Fi* tattooed on his ass, or arm, or something, and he still believes in it."

"What does it mean?"

"Always faithful," Ben replied.

"Is that military?"

"Yeah, he's a retired Marine."

"Good." Silver smiled at Ben. "He certainly made me feel like we weren't going to be stuck here forever."

"Oh, he'll get us out. Don't worry about that," Ben assured her. He took some more painkillers and set his cup down. "I want to get moving."

Silver held up her hand. "I'm not sure that's a good idea. The book says—"

He talked over her. "I've had broken ribs before, and I know that if I sit here all hunched over myself, I'll end up feeling worse than if I tried a little gentle exercise."

"If you must." Silver sighed. "But I'm going to keep an eye on you the whole time." She backed out of the tent, giving him space to maneuver. "If it feels really bad, I'm relying on you to use your common sense, Benjamin Miller, and sit right back down again!"

It took him an age to emerge, and by the time he did, his face was bathed in sweat. Silver gave him a disapproving look, but he simply raised his eyebrows at her.

"Can you help me stand?" Ben asked.

"If you're sure." Silver went to his side and offered her shoulder. "Take it slowly."

"I don't have any other choice." His breath hitched every time he straightened another inch. "Jeez . . ."

Silver pressed her lips together to stop herself suggesting he was a fool, and waited until he was completely upright and not swaying on his feet.

"I want to take a look at Calder."

Vaguely insulted that he didn't trust her judgment, Silver helped him limp forward until he was able to prop himself up against one of the trees to observe his horse.

"He does look okay," Ben said.

"I told you so." Silver was fairly certain she sounded snippy, but it had been a long night. She was so tired that all she wanted was to sleep for a week and wake up in L.A. surrounded by her team, her family, and . . .

Ben cupped her cheek. "I wasn't meaning to imply you hadn't done a good job. It's just that I raised Calder from a foal, and he's kind of special to me."

"Fine."

His brown eyes softened. "I'm really sorry about all of this."

"It was hardly your fault that the path gave way, was it?" Silver wasn't in the mood to be humored.

"Silver . . ." His thumb grazed her mouth and she went still, her whole body yearning toward him. "I mean it."

She sighed and let him gather her close and kiss her. Maybe she could be cajoled after all. . . .

"Hey, Ms. Meadows. How's it going?" BB said.

"Well, Ben's not any worse, and it's finally stopped raining, so things are looking up." Silver spoke into the radio. "How about at your end?"

"I spoke to the rescue services. They are going to send the helicopter to get you and Ben out."

Silver looked desperately around the narrow path. "Where will it land?"

"It won't. They'll come down and winch you up."

"What about Ben's ribs?"

"The medics will make sure he's okay and stabilized before they do anything too dangerous."

"What about the horses and Bill and Ted, and all our stuff?" Silver asked.

"When we pick you up, we'll send down two guys who will bring everything down through the valley and back to Morgan Ranch." BB paused as if he was talking to someone else. "The helicopter should be with you in fifteen minutes. Can you make sure the livestock are tied up, and that anything that might get blown away is secured?"

"Yes, of course," Silver said. "Where do you want us to wait?"

"Do you have shelter?"

"We're in a tent."

"Then stay in there and we'll come to you."

"Are you sure you'll find us?" Silver asked dubiously.

BB chuckled. "Seeing as there's nothing else up there, and I've got your coordinates, I think we've got this."

Silver rushed around the camp, packing everything away except what was in the tent, and making sure that all the animals were securely tied up before she went back to Ben. To her dismay, he was looking feverish again, his mouth set in a hard line. She sat beside him and took his uninjured hand.

"They're coming in fifteen minutes. BB said to stay in the tent and the medics will come to us."

"Cool." He swallowed hard. "I knew BB would come through. I just hope he doesn't take the cost of the helicopter out of my wages. Just my luck, my dad's got no job for me, and BB's probably going to fire me, too."

"If it comes to that, I'll pay for the helicopter, and tell them that everything was my fault." Silver gently squeezed his hand. It was disconcerting to see him so down about everything. "I've packed up and secured the horses and mules, so there's nothing else to worry about."

"Are they sending someone to take our stuff down?"

"Yes." She smiled at him. In the distance was the faint whapping sound of a helicopter coming their way. "I'm sure they'll take great care of Calder."

He frowned. "I'm taking people away from the busiest time of the year in ranching."

"I'm sure you'd do the same for them." The sound got louder and louder and she had to raise her voice. "I think they're just about here."

Ben didn't remember much about the two medics who came into the tent and asked him a million questions before strapping him to a board and maneuvering him out into the clearing. To his relief, someone had already taken charge of the livestock because the noise from the helicopter was deafening.

"Don't worry about anything, Ben," Ry Morgan shouted

to him as the medics expertly attached ropes to his gurney. "We'll bring them all home safely."

He managed a wave and then he was airborne, one of the medics hanging on to him like he was a fairground ride. Out of the corner of his eye he saw Silver was already onboard and wrapped in a thin, silver blanket. She smiled at him when he was set down, and he managed a weak thumbs-up.

The female medic loomed over him, mouthed something, and made a jabbing motion with a syringe. He nodded like a fool and a second later was flooded with warmth as his pain receded. He floated away on a cloud of relief.

"I want to stay here until Ben is better." Silver kept repeating the same thing and hoped that eventually someone would listen to her. She was still huddled in her thermal blanket, but at least she was on the ground and sitting in the Morgan family kitchen. Ruth had fed her and fussed over her and she was already feeling a lot better.

"And I don't want you to call my dad. He's busy," Silver said firmly. "He'll be here in a couple of days anyway. I'd rather wait until all my stuff gets back before I leave."

BB glanced at his grandmother who was sitting next to Silver.

"What do you think?"

Ruth studied Silver, her blue gaze shrewd. "I think this young lady should be allowed to make her own decisions. If she wants to stay here with us, that's fine by me."

"Thank you." Silver grabbed hold of one of Mrs. Morgan's hands. "I just want to make sure Ben's okay, because he was so great with me, and—" She turned to BB. "None of this was his fault, he didn't do anything wrong, and he shouldn't lose his job. If there are any costs to be paid, just send the bill to me, okay?"

It was BB's turn to stare at her like she was nuts or something. "It's all good. We're fully insured and, as the helicopter is actually owned by Morgan Ranch, and we lease it to the emergency services, there won't be any additional costs." He paused. "Do you think Ben will be okay if you stick around?"

"I think he'd like to see me before I leave, yes," Silver said definitively. "I'd just like to thank him for everything."

"He's lucky Dr. Tio said he could convalesce at home," Mrs. Morgan commented. "But all these cowboys are the same. They hate going to hospital."

BB shuddered. "There's a reason for that. Hospitals suck."

"Ben's settled in nicely upstairs in your old room, Blue. Why don't you take Silver up to see him?" Mrs. Morgan suggested. "And show her Maria's bedroom right next door. She can sleep there." She patted Silver's hand. "I assumed you'd be staying so I put out some night things for you. The bathroom is at the end of the hallway."

"I remember from last time," Silver said as she rose wearily to her feet. "Thank you for letting me stay."

"You're welcome, my dear." Ruth Morgan smiled at her. "Sleep as long as you need, and I'll make sure you get fed whenever you come down."

At the foot of the stairs, BB paused and looked down at Silver. "If you don't mind me asking, how did Ben come to fall off his horse?"

"The path gave way ahead of him and Calder nearly went over. While Calder managed to regain his footing, Ben had already gone over the side." Silver leaned against the wall. Dr. Tio had checked her over, and said she just needed to sleep and eat, and she would be fine. "He fell into a tree, knocked himself out, and had to climb back up the slope."

"How did he manage that?" BB must have sensed Silver's exhaustion because he grimaced. "I know this is the last thing you want to talk about right now, but I need to know what happened so that I can square things with our insurance company, and get this matter settled as soon as possible."

"I sent over a rope, Ben jumped toward the side of the hill, and Calder pulled him up." She shivered. "It took forever, but Calder was really good at stopping when Ben needed him to. All I had to do was stay by his head and make sure he did what he was asked."

"And then you had to haul Ben's ass back to the tent, set up camp, and keep him alive until we got there." BB's blue eyes gleamed. "You did good, Ms. Meadows. You should be proud of yourself."

Silver shrugged. "I didn't really have any choice, did I?"

"Yeah, sure you did." He smiled. "Believe me, a lot of people would've freaked out and done nothing but run around in circles, making things worse." He nodded at the stairs. "Come on, you should get some rest."

"Can we check in on Ben first?" Silver asked.

"Sure, although I think he's still out of it, which is a good thing because broken ribs hurt like a b—anything." BB led the way up the stairs and down the main hallway. He paused at a door that still had his name on it and went in as quietly as possible.

Silver held her breath as she stared at Ben who was sleeping like the dead, his wrist properly bandaged by the efficient local doctor.

"He's a tough old bird, Ms. Meadows. He'll be fine," BB murmured.

She wanted to smooth Ben's hair away from his forehead and kiss his brow. She wanted to climb in beside him and just breathe him in, knowing they were both safe. But she didn't think BB Morgan needed to see that, and it might get Ben into all kinds of trouble. She reluctantly turned to the door.

"Will he need someone to keep an eye on him overnight?"

"I think we've got that covered." BB paused at the door, his keen gaze assessing her. "You don't need to worry about him anymore. You did a fantastic job, but you're no longer responsible for him, and you can sleep easy."

She reached out to touch his arm. "You won't tell my dad about any of this, will you?"

He hesitated. "That's up to you and Ben, although if it were me, I'd probably tell him."

"Why?"

He shrugged. "Because I'd want him to know how well his daughter reacted in a dangerous situation. Don't you think he'd be proud of you?"

"He'd be horrified," Silver said wryly. "He'd worry that I wouldn't be able to do my next project, and we'd get sued."

"I doubt that." He held her gaze. "From what he told me about your problems, I think he cares about you a lot."

Silver didn't have the energy to explain her complicated relationship with her father to a man she'd probably never see again. "Thanks for the advice. I'll talk to Ben and see how he feels about it." She offered BB a tired smile. "I think I need to sleep for a week. Thanks for rescuing us."

He grinned. "I think you did that all by yourself, but you're welcome."

He escorted her to her door and left her there with another reminder not to worry, before heading down the stairs.

Silver managed to change into the cotton nightdress, drag herself down to the bathroom for her first shower in over a week, and get between the crisply ironed sheets of the bed. Should she check in on Ben again? If she did she might end up in his bed and she didn't even want to imagine how that would go down the next morning. . . . Even as she considered the idea, her eyes closed, and she knew nothing more.

Chapter Twelve

Silver was sitting in the kitchen enjoying both Mrs. Morgan's cooking and her conversation, when a man she hadn't met before came through the door. He was an older guy with silver streaks in his hair, hard gray eyes, and weathered skin.

"Morning, Ruth. Where's Ben?"

Mrs. Morgan turned to regard the intruder, her spatula raised in a rather threatening manner.

"Jeff Miller, where are your manners?"

The man blinked at her. "I said good morning, didn't I?" His gaze fell on Silver and he frowned. "You look familiar. Is this one of your grandson's girlfriends, Ruth?"

"No, I'm not." Silver stood and offered him her hand. He looked nothing like Ben at all. "Hi, I'm Silver."

He shook her hand and continued to stare at her, his brow furrowed. "You sure do look familiar. Do you work in the bank?"

Mrs. Morgan advanced toward them. "Now, you just leave her alone, Jeff, and tell me what you're here for."

His brow creased. "I already said. I've come for Ben."

"Dr. Tio says he's to stay put for the next couple of days."

"And what does that youngster pretending to be a

doctor know about anything? He told me I had high blood pressure, and I'm not fat and I hardly drink!"

"Dr. Tio knows what he is doing, and if he says Ben has to stay here for a couple of days, he's not going anywhere," Mrs. Morgan repeated with some emphasis.

For a second, Silver held her breath as the two of them faced off.

Jeff sighed. "All right. If I can't take him off your hands, can I at least see him?"

Mrs. Morgan turned to Silver. "Why don't you go and see if Ben is ready to receive visitors, and tell him that his father is here."

Silver nodded and hightailed it up the stairs. She'd peeked in on Ben just before she'd come down for her very late breakfast, but he'd been sleeping.

She knocked on his door and went in to find him awake and alert. His slow smile did something funny to her heart.

She smiled foolishly back at him. "We made it."

"Yes, we did."

She went over and sat on the side of the bed. "How are you feeling this morning?"

"Way better than I did two days ago." He slid his left hand into her newly washed hair. "You look clean, and you don't smell of woodsmoke and the great outdoors."

"Does that make me immediately unattractive?" Silver asked.

"Nope." He bent his head and kissed her very thoroughly. "Thanks for getting me out."

The sound of loud throat clearing at the door made them leap apart like guilty teenagers to find Jeff Miller standing there.

"You're obviously not feeling that bad if you've got the energy to canoodle," Jeff remarked as he came into the room.

Canoodle? What did that even mean? Silver leapt to her feet and backed away from the bed.

"Hey, Dad, do you remember knocking? It's something you insisted on us learning when we were kids." Ben looked at his father. "And why are you here, anyway?"

"I had to go into Dr. Tio's office for some silly test, and he asked me how you were doing today." Jeff scowled at his son. "Imagine what a fool I felt when I had no idea what the hell he was talking about!"

Ben eased himself back against his pillows. "I was going to call you when I was ready to come home."

"You should have come home in the first place instead of bothering Ruth Morgan. Don't you think she has enough to do?"

Silver glanced apprehensively from Ben to his father and decided to speak up. "The helicopter landed here and the medical team brought him to the ranch where Dr. Tio was already set up and waiting for him."

Jeff barely spared her a glance as he carried on speaking. "What the hell were you doing out there, son? I told you not to go. I *warned* you—"

Ben slowly closed his eyes and Silver rushed over to the bed and stood protectively in front of him. "He's not well; he has a concussion, broken ribs, and a broken wrist. Will you please stop *shouting* at him?"

"What's it to you?" Jeff demanded. "Are you one of Dr. Tio's nurses? Is that where I've seen you?"

"She's the client I took out on the trail ride, Dad. Now will you please stop shouting at both of us?" Ben's voice was threaded with exhaustion. "I'll keep in touch and let you know how I'm doing, okay?"

Jeff stared down at his son. "I'll come back tomorrow. Make sure you are respectful to Ruth, and don't lie there expecting everyone else to wait on you. I brought you up to be tougher than that."

Silver marched over to the door and held it open. "I'll see you out, Mr. Miller."

She waited as Jeff Miller reached over and squeezed Ben's shoulder before turning toward her, his expression worried, until he noticed her looking at him, raised his chin, and scowled at her instead.

"I'll see myself out, thank you."

Silver watched as he clumped down the stairs. He was still wearing his cowboy boots and spurs and had left a trail of dried mud through the house. She shut the door and rushed back to Ben who still had his eyes shut.

"Are you okay?"

He winced. "After that bracing visit from my parent? Sure, I'm feeling great."

She sat on the side of the bed and held his hand. "He's certainly something."

"He's a pain in the ass, but he means well." He blew out a breath. "In case you missed it, that was him being concerned."

"And I thought my father had problems expressing himself," Silver said. "Is he that loud all the time?"

"Only when he's worried." He attempted a smile. "When he comes back tomorrow, he'll have calmed down enough to ask questions, and that will be a whole 'nother lot of fun."

"Maybe you shouldn't see him," Silver suggested.

"Like I'd be able to stop him," Ben scoffed. "He's something of a force of nature." He hesitated. "Can you get me those painkillers Dr. Tio left me?"

"Sure." She poured him a fresh glass of water. "Do you want some breakfast? Mrs. Morgan is dying to feed you."

"That would be awesome." He took the pills and set the glass back down beside his bed. "How are you feeling?"

"Not as bad as you are." She managed a smile. "I slept for about sixteen hours and that really helped."

"Is your dad coming to get you early?"

"No, I asked BB not to mention what happened if he called." She paused. "He thought I should tell Dad, but I don't want to get you or the Morgans in trouble."

"Hell, we should be in trouble. I could've killed you."

"But you didn't, and we all got back safely," Silver reminded him. "Why does he need to know any more than that?"

"Because he's your father?"

Silver let go of his hand. "You know how your father came in here and immediately started shouting at you to show he cared? *My* father would come in here threatening lawsuits. I don't want the ranch getting that kind of bad publicity, and I don't want anyone to know I was here, full stop."

Ben just watched her, his expression unreadable. "Are you asking me to lie to him, Silver? Because that wouldn't sit well with me."

"I'm asking you not to mention what happened when he turns up here in two days. I'll tell him my version of events when we're back in L.A., and then he won't get all pissy about it with you and the Morgans."

"Don't you think he's going to wonder why I'm all strapped up like this?" He gestured at his wrist.

"If he even notices, and that's not a given, then you can tell him you fell off your horse when we got back or something. He probably won't even ask." She met his gaze. "I'm not asking you to outright lie for me. Just give me some time."

Ben didn't speak for so long, she had to remember to breathe.

"Okay, we'll do it your way."

"Thank you." She leaned in and kissed his cheek. "I'll go and tell Mrs. Morgan you're ready for your breakfast."

She went slowly down the stairs, shutting the screen door that Mr. Miller had left open when he departed, and entered the kitchen. Mrs. Morgan was sitting at the table reading the local newspaper, her glasses perched on her nose.

"You couldn't ever call Jeff Miller a patient man. He was off up those stairs like a rat up a drain pipe before you'd reached Ben's room."

"It's okay." Silver took a seat at the table. "He wasn't very nice to Ben. He basically told him not to be a wimp."

"Jeff brought those boys up hard." Mrs. Morgan sighed. "After Leanne left him, he lost what little softness he had and treated his sons like they were in military school. I always felt sorry for them."

"At least they had Auntie Rae. . . ." Silver mused. "That was something."

"Ben told you about her?" Mrs. Morgan's bright blue eyes fastened on Silver.

Silver felt her cheeks heat. "He might have mentioned it at some point."

"Did he also give you that hickey?"

Silver slapped a hand to her throat. "*What*? He didn't, did he? I—" She stopped and stared at Mrs. Morgan. "Oh crap."

"It's all right, dear. It's barely noticeable now, and I'm not going to mention it to anyone." Mrs. Morgan set her newspaper aside. "That's between you and Ben. I haven't brought up four grandsons without learning to keep their secrets, you know."

"It's not—*we're* not . . ." Silver waved her hands around wildly. "We're just friends, and that's the end of it."

"I have no idea what constitutes courting these days, my dear, so I'm sure you're right. The only thing I *would* say is that Ben isn't the kind of man to run out on a woman, so I do hope you've sorted it out with him."

"I have." Silver nodded like an idiot. "He's good with it. We both are."

"Then that's all anyone needs to know." Mrs. Morgan rose from her seat. "I expect Ben will be wanting some breakfast. Will you take him up a tray?"

Later that afternoon when Silver was sitting reading in Ben's room, the door opened and two men came in.

"Hey, bro, what have you been doing to yourself?" the dark-haired one said. "I know you'd do anything to avoid work, but this seems a little extreme even for you."

The taller, older, sterner one frowned as he studied Ben. "Dad said you got hurt."

Ben looked over at Silver, one eyebrow raised. "Would you like to be introduced to these two idiots, or would you prefer to pretend they don't exist?"

She put down her book. "Hi, I'm Silver."

"The miserable-faced one is Adam, and the way-too-happy one is Kaiden," Ben said. "The one you think should be called Caleb."

Kaiden grinned at her. "*Seven Brides for Seven Brothers,* right?"

Ben frowned. "You know about that?"

"Everyone knows about that." Kaiden sat in the chair next to Ben's bed. "It's a great movie. It was Mom's favorite. That's why we all have these stupid-ass names, although luckily, Dad balked at a couple of them." He touched Ben's arm. "What did you do to yourself?"

"Calder and I nearly fell off the ridge path in the far canyon. Calder righted himself. I didn't, and a tree broke my fall."

Both brothers made identical faces of horror.

"Shit," Kaiden said fervently. "How did you get out of that?"

"With a bit of help from Silver, a rope, and Calder pulling me up the side of the canyon like a champ." Ben nodded at her.

"What's the damage?" Adam asked. He hadn't sat down, but stood looming over them all by the window.

"Broken ribs, broken wrist, and a concussion." Ben's expression was resigned. "I'll be good to go in a few days."

Adam's gray gaze settled on Silver. "I'm glad you were there to help get him out of trouble."

Silver shrugged. For someone who was supposed to be incognito she was meeting a heck of a lot of people. "He got himself out. I just hung around getting in the way."

"She helped haul me up the slope, half carried me to the camp, and looked after me and all the livestock until the medics arrived," Ben said. "Hardly nothing."

"Thank you." Adam smiled at her properly for the first time, which was quite a revelation. "Really."

Kaiden grinned. "If you'd just left him in the tree I wouldn't have to keep sharing a bathroom with him, but I suppose it's all good. He's a hard worker, and if he wasn't at the ranch, Dad would probably make me do all his shit."

Ben's smile was still guarded and Silver wondered why. Did he ever relax around his siblings or was there always that slight tension between them? Or was it because she was there? Was she complicating things just by existing in the same space? She didn't really belong in his world. She never would.

She jumped up out of her seat. "I've got to go and speak to Mrs. Morgan, Ben." She nodded at the two men. "It was great to meet you both."

She slipped out of the room, shutting the door firmly behind her. Mrs. Morgan had offered to show her how to make pastry. Maybe it was a good time to take her up on it.

Ben frowned as Silver disappeared out the door. Something had upset her and he wasn't sure what it was. Adam came to sit on the end of his bed, his expression concerned.

"Are you sure you're doing okay? Falling like that must've been one hell of a shock."

"The falling wasn't the problem." Ben grimaced and gingerly touched his chest. "It was hitting the tree that broke my ribs, but, as it stopped me from ending up in the creek, I can't complain."

"When are you coming home?" Adam asked abruptly.

"In a couple of days." Ben attempted a shrug and then wished he hadn't. "Dr. Tio said to rest up until then." On the doctor's advice he'd removed the wrap this morning and was now just wearing a T-shirt and practicing his deep breathing to avoid pneumonia. His wrist was still taped.

"We could bring you home in the truck," Kaiden suggested. "You could lie in the bed or along the back seat." He gestured at the bag Adam had placed on the end of the bed. "We brought you clean clothes."

"Thanks. Why are you so keen to get me back to mess up our bathroom again?" Ben attempted to joke his way out. "I'm not doing anyone any harm here, and the food is way better."

"Dad wants you home," Adam said. "He's worried about you."

"No, he's not," Ben objected. "He just wants to make

sure I'm up and working the second I'm ready. He's already told me not to get used to lazing around."

"*I'm* worried about you," Adam added. "You could've died, Ben."

"But I didn't. I'm fine, and—"

"And what the hell are you doing taking Silver Meadows, one of the most famous actresses in the world, out on a trail ride?" Kaiden asked. "Did you think we wouldn't notice? I barely managed to keep my jaw off the floor."

"Silver who?" Adam looked inquiringly at both his brothers. "Is she famous?"

"Yeah, Adam." Kaiden shook his head like he was disappointed in his big brother. "Very. She was in that cowgirl show Daisy loved when she was a kid, and that movie last year with the five best friends at the wedding?"

"Oh, right." Adam nodded at Ben. "Lizzie loved that one. I suppose you don't want us telling anyone we've seen her here?"

"That would be appreciated," Ben said, glad for the change of subject. "But you know what a gossip Kaiden is."

"I'll keep it to myself." Kaiden made a cross over his heart. "No wonder you wanted to take this job on. I don't blame you. She's really beautiful and she seems like a nice person as well."

"She is," Ben agreed. "She really did save my life out there. If I'd been alone, I'd still be in that tree."

Adam shuddered. "I don't even want to think about that." He stood up. "I'll tell Dad to hold his fire and remind him that it takes weeks for broken ribs to heal properly, so he shouldn't be expecting too much too soon."

Ben immediately felt guilty. "Tell him I'll be out there working quicker than that, or he'll probably fire me for real this time."

"You'll take all the time you need," Adam said severely. "Danny's working full-time for a while so you can just concentrate on healing, okay?"

Kaiden also stood and offered Ben a pat on the shoulder. "I'll give your best to Danny, Evan, and Daisy, and make sure they know how you're doing. You don't want everyone turning up here."

"Tell them to call me," Ben said.

"Will do." Kaiden grinned at him. "Hang in there, bro."

With a last searching glance at Ben's face, Adam followed Kaiden out of the bedroom. Ben lay back against his pillows and closed his eyes. His dad was right about one thing. He needed to get up and move around before everything seized up permanently.

He carefully reached for the bag of stuff Adam had deposited on his bed, wincing at the pain in his ribs, and unzipped it. There was a clean set of everything he needed along with toiletries and the next book in the series he was currently reading. He smiled as he took out the book and read the sticky note from Daisy. She really was the most thoughtful of his siblings.

Easing his legs over the side of the bed, he contemplated taking a shower. The idea of being clean was surprisingly motivating so he picked up the bag and headed for the door. There was no one in the hallway as he stumbled to the bathroom. The smell of baking apples wafting up the stairs made his mouth water. Whatever Silver was doing down there with Mrs. Morgan, it was all good. He paused at the door and gently knocked just to make sure it was vacant.

It smelled like Silver in there, which wasn't helpful when he'd realized that he still needed to protect her from all the interest his visitors were showing her. She'd asked for her visit to be kept a secret, but the more people who saw her, the harder that secret would be to protect. Kaiden wouldn't be able to keep his mouth shut at home. If he told Daisy, and Daisy told her fiancé, Jackson, who had the biggest mouth in Morgantown, then everyone would know.

He turned the water on and took his time easing his T-shirt over his head and shedding his boxers. His right eye was turning all the colors of the rainbow while the bruises on his ribs were still black and purple. The major issue was his right wrist, which was his dominant hand, slowing him down.

He stepped into the shower and took a long, careful breath. Silver would be gone soon, and he didn't want her to leave. He wanted to look up and see her sitting across from him reading, her expression intent. He wanted her in his bed smiling up at him as they made love. . . .

Which meant that he was going to have to stop being a fool and find a way to let her go with the grace and the thanks she deserved. She didn't want more from him; she'd been very clear on that, and so had he. The fact that he'd changed his mind was irrelevant and stupid. They lived in completely different worlds. She was a global celebrity, and he was a rancher who owned nothing, and never would. What could he offer her? A shared house with his family breathing down his neck arguing about everything under the sun? She'd go crazy. *He'd* go crazy. But he couldn't live in L.A. . . .

He needed to back off. He scrubbed awkwardly at his hair with one hand and the shampoo stung his eyes. She deserved that—she'd *earned* that. If he truly cared about her, and he knew in his soul that he did, he'd let her go with a smile and a kiss on the cheek. She'd forget him in no time. He'd done what she'd asked, and one day some other lucky bastard would fall in love with her and everything would be cool.

He turned the shower off and stood staring at nothing until he started to shiver. Always second best, always the good guy who ended up without the girl . . . Maybe that was his destiny, but sometimes it sure sucked.

Chapter Thirteen

In the early hours of Silver's last day at the ranch, Ladybug and Calder finally turned up with their rescuers. She went down to the barn to be reunited with her horse, and to recover the rest of her possessions. She decided to leave all her damp clothes behind, except for her cowboy hat and boots, and happily reclaimed her skincare and makeup. She'd repacked her cases in the back of the rented Jeep, and was just waiting for her father to turn up.

Ben had gotten out of bed after his brothers' visit the day before, and was determinedly walking around the house and yard, which meant she'd hardly spoken to him. She also had the weird sense that he preferred it that way, which made her feel hurt. Sitting with him in his bedroom, sharing those quiet, intimate moments when they didn't even need to talk much because they were so in tune had meant a lot to her. She'd never had that with anyone in her life, even her siblings who all tended toward dramatics.

The Morgans had joked that she was following Ben around like a mother hen with her chick and she had blushed and laughed along with them. Maybe she was feeling a little overprotective. After meeting his father and two of his brothers, she'd had an overwhelming sense that he *needed* protecting. They didn't seem to value him as much as she did, which was alarming when she was leaving and he had to go back home.

She checked the Jeep one last time and walked back toward the house to find Ben sitting in the swing on the porch watching her, his face hidden in the shadow cast by his Stetson.

"All packed. Just waiting on my dad now."

"Cool." He nodded and offered her a guarded smile.

So he'd gone back to one-word answers. The distance she'd imagined growing between them was actually a real thing. She leaned against one of the posts, arms crossed over her chest, and regarded him carefully. He still looked worn-out and as pale as a man with a permanent outdoor tan could manage.

"How are you feeling today, Ben?"

"Better, thanks."

"Are you looking forward to getting back to work?"

He grimaced. "Sure."

"Promise me that you won't overdo it?"

He met her gaze. "Ranch work isn't like that, Silver. Sometimes you just have to get shit done." He glanced up as a truck drove into the yard. "Jeez, my dad's here. Hide."

Jeff stomped up the steps, talking loudly on his phone. "How the hell would I know how to do that, Leanne? Can't you just talk to him? Why do you need to see his ugly face? He's not dead."

He held out his cell toward Ben who recoiled. "It's your mother. She wants to facepalm with you, or something."

Silver gently took the phone from Jeff, pressed the right buttons, and handed it to Ben. "Here you go."

She retreated back to her post, unwilling to leave Ben alone with his father and admitting to herself that she was curious as to how he had a relationship with the mother who had left his father twenty or so years ago. Ben had never mentioned she was still active in his life. It made her wonder how many other things he'd concealed when she'd been blabbing out her life story.

"Hey, Mom." Ben smiled at the screen. "Yeah, I know I look bad, but I'm doing good, really."

Jeff came over to stand by Silver. "Thanks for sorting that out. I hate technology."

"You're welcome," Silver said. "You do know that Ben's not supposed to do any heavy lifting or excessive physical work for six weeks?"

"You sure you're not a nurse?" Jeff demanded.

"I'm just someone who is very grateful to your son for taking me on a great trail ride," Silver replied evenly. "If you force him back to work too soon, all sorts of bad things could happen."

"He's tougher than he looks," Jeff said. "I raised him. I know what he's capable of." He chuckled. "I once forgot to pick him up after football practice when he was ten and he walked five miles home in the rain because he knew I was busy with the cows."

Silver didn't know what to say to that.

"Will you be coming back?" Jeff inquired. "You and Ben seem to have hit it off."

"I don't think so," Silver hastened to reply.

Jeff frowned. "He doesn't go around kissing just anyone, you know. I brought him up to respect women. If he kissed you, he meant it." He nodded at his son. "You should come back. You make him happy."

Ben looked up at both of them, his gaze fixed inquiringly on Silver's flushed face before he returned his attention to whatever his mom was saying. Had he heard what Jeff had said? Would he want her to come back? The fact that she wanted to wasn't exactly a surprise, but she'd begun to believe that all the attraction was on her side, and that Ben was just fine with leaving things the way they were. . . .

They'd made a deal—one that he'd been originally reluctant to participate in—and he owed her nothing. The fact that he'd been right, and that sex *had* complicated things and made her not want to leave was entirely on her.

"Bye, Mom. Speak to you soon." Ben ended the call and offered the phone back to his father. "She said to tell you to call her when I get home."

"Which will be when exactly?" Jeff demanded.

Ben looked over at Silver. "I've got to see my trail ride guest off, and then I'll come back, okay?"

"Not that there's a lot for you to do right now," Jeff added. "Danny's been doing a great job."

"Good to know," Ben said, his smile dying. "Maybe I'll hang out here and convalesce for a few more weeks then."

Jeff snorted. "Like the Morgans would let you." He turned to Silver. "You have a safe trip home, now, honey, and remember what I said."

"Thanks, I will." Silver nodded.

He tipped his hat to her and went back down the steps to his truck. As he drove away, another car came into the drive and stopped by the steps. Silver's dad got out and waved up at her.

"Silver! You look great!"

She felt Ben come to stand behind her and found a smile somewhere as her father came bounding up to the porch.

"Hi! You made good time!" She turned to Ben. "Dad, this is Ben Miller, my fantastic trail guide."

Ben held out his hand. "Good to meet you in person at last, Mr. Miller."

"Good to meet you, too." Her dad glanced down at Ben's hand. "What did you do to your wrist?"

"Nothing much." He gestured to the door. "Would you like to come in and speak to Mrs. Morgan? I think she's expecting you to stay for lunch."

Ben answered Mr. Meadows's questions as best he could, but happily let Mrs. Morgan and Silver direct the conversation. He had the beginnings of a headache, and he was painfully aware of the minutes ticking down before Silver would be gone, and he'd never see her again. He reminded himself that she wasn't dying, that even if she left him she'd be fine, and that he wouldn't have to feel guilty about anything he'd done.

Eventually, he pushed back his chair and turned to Mrs. Morgan. Maybe he should get out while he could—avoid saying good-bye altogether.

"I've just got to fetch something from the barn. I'll meet you by the Jeep, Silver, okay?"

"You go ahead, Ben, dear." Mrs. Morgan smiled at him, and then turned to Mr. Meadows. "Would you like some more apple pie? Silver made the pastry for it."

Unfortunately, by the time he got back to the house, there was still no sign of Mr. Meadows, but Silver was putting her purse in the passenger side of the Jeep. She looked up when she saw him approaching and smiled so brightly that he had to catch his breath. She came toward him and took his hand in hers.

"Thanks for everything, Ben. I *mean* it."

"Hey, you saved my life, so right back at you."

She held his gaze, and there was a shimmer of tears in her blue eyes, which made his chest tighten.

"Ben . . ."

"Hey"—he cupped her chin—"no tears, remember?

We had a good time together, I like and respect you, and I will *never* tell another soul what happened between us."

She clutched his arm. "I wish I didn't have to go. I want—"

He couldn't let her finish because if he did it would tear him apart.

"Don't you remember our conversation, Silver? You don't always get what you want." He found a smile somewhere. "Let's not spoil it, okay?"

She blinked hard and let go of his arm. "I just want you to know that you're the best man I've ever met, and that I don't think I'll ever find anyone I want to make love with except you."

Jeez, he was going to have to break this connection right now before he caved and did something monumentally stupid like beg her to stay.

He held up his hands. "Look, I'm the first person you had sex with. You're going to think I'm some kind of god because that's the first time you've ever had those particular feelings. But I'm not a god, and there are loads of guys who can give you that feeling and probably better."

"Don't patronize me." She took a step backward, her face white. "Don't trivialize how I feel."

He shrugged. "I'm just trying to be honest here."

"You think I'm infatuated with you because you're the first person I had sex with?"

He winced at the hitch in her voice, but he couldn't back down. Whether she realized it or not, he was offering her a way out. In a few months' time she'd be thanking him for not hanging around and making things difficult.

"Yeah, pretty much."

He leaned in, almost hoping she'd slap his face and walk away, but she was made of sterner stuff.

"Thanks for your input." She glanced toward the ranch, her head held high. "I'm going in to say good-bye to the Morgans. You don't need to be here when I come back out."

"Whatever you want." He turned as the screen door banged. "I need to have a word with Mr. Meadows anyway."

Ben gave his report to Silver's father, who seemed caught between relief that his daughter hadn't used drugs, and suspicion that Ben was too dumb to have noticed if she had.

When Mr. Meadows got into the rental, Ben closed the door for him, and stepped back. Silver came out of the house accompanied by BB and Mrs. Morgan, who gave her a big hug and at least four containers of food for the journey. Ben couldn't stop staring at her, aware that every moment brought him closer to never seeing her again. He wanted to go to her, to tell her that he wanted her to stay, to *beg* her . . .

He stopped after one stumbling step forward. When had begging ever done him any good? He'd begged his mother to stay and she'd still left. He'd told Cassie he'd never leave her whatever she did, and he'd broken that promise. Silver was better off with her own kind, and without him. At least he'd matured enough to understand that even if he hated it.

Silver got into the Jeep without a glance in his direction, rolled down the window, waved at Mrs. Morgan, and that was that. She was gone from Morgan Ranch, and out of his life forever.

Chapter Fourteen

"Silver?" Ayla came into the room with her usual air of efficiency and set a smoothie in front of Silver. "From your chef."

"Thanks." Silver stared gloomily at the green froth. "Great. Just what I needed."

She'd been back home for a month and yet she still found herself reliving those days with Ben and missing the silence, the amazing scenery, and even him. Although she was still pissed off about how he'd ended things.

Her family house sat high in the Hollywood Hills and was protected by twenty-four-hour armed security, a ten-foot-high electric fence, and a complicated security system that included every different camera known to man. Getting into her home took determination and yet some fools still tried. Yesterday they'd caught some guy in a cowboy hat trying to scale the wall, and for one stupid moment, Silver had hoped it was Ben.

She'd have to accept that he wasn't coming to find her. He hated cities and he'd decided that she'd developed a silly crush on him just because they'd had sex.

"Conceited jerk," she muttered as she picked up her smoothie.

"Come again?" Ayla had produced her tablet and looked ready to start their daily meeting.

"Like that's ever going to happen," Silver replied.

"What?"

"Just thinking about someone I used to know," Silver said. "What's on the agenda today?"

"Well, those guys who are casting the Western? They want you to fill out this form." Ayla briefly turned her tablet around so that Silver could see it.

"What is it? A job application?"

"Kind of." Ayla frowned. "I thought I could read the questions out to you, and type in your answers rather than you having to do it all yourself."

"Are they making everyone do this or just me?" Silver grumbled.

"Everyone." Ayla looked at her expectantly. "Ready?"

At Silver's nod, she started reading out the questions. By the time she'd reached question eight, Silver was beginning to feel like she was at her therapist's.

"Have you ever been in real danger like the characters in our script?"

"Yes," Silver said.

Ayla raised an eyebrow. "You have?"

"Well, you know I went on that ten-day trail ride to prepare for the audition?" Silver said. "When we were out there, my guide's horse almost slipped over the edge of a narrow path on a ridge, and my guide went over the side, hit his head, and ended up stuck in a tree."

"I don't remember Mr. Meadows mentioning any of this," Ayla said, typing furiously.

"That's because I didn't tell him," Silver continued. "I

had to throw a rope across to Ben, walk his horse forward so he could get back up the steep slope, and look after him and the rest of the camp until the rescue services could reach us."

"Wow, really?" Ayla pushed her glasses up her nose. "Did he hurt himself?"

"Concussion, broken ribs, and a broken wrist." Silver shuddered. "It was really frightening. I was all on my own, having to make life-or-death decisions."

"They'll love this." Ayla finished typing. "I assume they got the guy out okay?"

"Yes, they picked us up in a helicopter."

"I'm surprised it didn't make the local news." Ayla set down her tablet.

"I hope it didn't because I was trying to avoid the press, remember?"

Silver took a sip from her smoothie and shuddered. She'd put on five pounds when she'd been with the Morgans. The glories of apple pie and a full breakfast had receded to a distant, delicious memory as her team fussed around to make sure she lost the weight.

Ayla tapped her pen against her lips. "It would be better if we could confirm this happened, because it *does* sound slightly made up."

Silver finished her smoothie. "At this point I almost don't care whether I get the part or not since they're making it so hard."

"I think it's because they really want to get it right," Ayla said earnestly. "I've talked to Inola Black Fox, one of the writers, quite a lot over the past months, and she's *super* sincere."

"I get it. I read the script. That's why I want the part. But if I'm not right for it, I wish they'd just let me know." Silver lay back on the couch and flung out her arms. She had another audition for a TV show in two hours, and because of the L.A. traffic she would need to get herself made up, dressed up, and ready to leave soon. She didn't really want the part, but her father had insisted she consider it as a backup plan if she didn't get the independent film.

"I think they are a bit . . . wary," Ayla said carefully. "This isn't your usual kind of project."

"I know." Silver sat up, faced the fantastic view over the Pacific Ocean, and sighed.

"What do you know?" Her father came into the room, cell phone in hand, and a big smile on his face.

"Nothing, apparently." She smiled back at him. "What's up?"

He held up his phone. "We need to go in ten." He studied her workout clothes. "You don't look quite ready yet."

"Maybe I've decided to go like this. The series is about a school, isn't it?"

"I'd prefer it if you dressed nicely, Silver," he said briskly. "You don't know how many paparazzi will be at that studio entrance. You don't want to be on any worst-dressed lists, or look like you don't care about your fans, or that you're going through a crisis, do you?"

"No, Dad, of course I don't." She pasted on a smile. "I'll go and get changed. Where's Mom?"

"Out with Spring at an audition." He paused. "Why, do you need her for something?"

"No, I just . . ." Silver didn't even bother finishing the sentence because he was already beginning to sound concerned. "I haven't seen her today, and I didn't get a chance to wish Spring luck. Why don't you talk to Ayla while I get dressed? She can fill you in on my new schedule."

* * *

In the chauffeured car, her dad glanced over at her. "You look great."

"Thanks." She smoothed her pink pencil skirt.

"Another couple of pounds off, and you'll be in perfect condition."

"Perfect condition for what? A pedigree dog show?" She looked out of the darkened window at the streets of L.A. "You don't need to come with me, you know."

"I *like* coming. It gives me a chance to meet the crew and the producers and get a sense of whether it's going to be a good vehicle for you." He studied her carefully. "Are you okay?"

"I'm fine." Silver looked back out of the window at a young couple with their arms around each other. "If you hadn't ended up managing my career, Dad, what would you have done?"

Silence greeted her question and eventually she turned to look at him.

"I haven't really thought about it." He chuckled. "Everything happened so fast. Your mom took you to your first baby commercial tryout, and that was that."

"But there must have been something," Silver persisted. She wasn't sure why. "No one wakes up and decides they want this crazy life."

"Are you sure you're feeling okay?" He sat back and studied her. "If this is about the indie movie you want to be involved with? I've talked with your mom and Ayla and I'm not going to stand in your way if you want to do it."

"But that's the point, Dad." Silver sat forward, her hands clasped together. "It's not up to you what projects I decide to take on anyway. I'm turning twenty-six next week. I've *earned* the right to make my own decisions."

He went to speak, and she kept on talking.

"I want you to step back. I want you to spend more time with Mom doing the things that you like to do together."

"But you kids are our *life,*" he objected.

"I'm not a kid anymore. I'm a fully grown woman who wants to take control of her own life and career." She met his gaze as the car drew to a halt. "Will you at least *think* about what I've said?"

He pointed at the door. "I told you there would be cameras. No one's seen you for a month."

"Great." Silver put on her sunglasses, straightened her skirt, held her designer purse so it could be seen in the photos, and advanced toward the entrance. She blinked as a volley of cameras clicked and flashed, and kept her smile fixed firmly in place.

"Where've you been?" one of the men yelled. "We missed you!"

Her father came up alongside her, took her arm, and guided her through the narrowing gap into the building. "Gotta go!"

In the lobby, a group of people gawked and whispered as she was ushered past. It was the first time she'd been out in public since being at the ranch, and she felt way too exposed. Everyone knew who she was here. No one thought she worked at the bank or the doctor's office, like Ben's dad had thought, or made an effort to treat her like she was a normal person. Not that she'd been very good at that. Ben Miller had seen right through her.

She'd get through the audition, decide for herself whether she really wanted to be stuck in the routine of filming a TV show, and get back home as soon as possible.

Drew Zarek, the producer of the show, met her at the studio door.

"Hey, beautiful! So glad you could come in to read for us today! How've you been?"

"Great, thanks." Silver had worked with Drew before. He was a decent guy who had never made a pass at her, which made him a rarity in her business. "How about you?"

He made a face. "Just broke up with Madera so if you need an escort for anything, let me know. I'm free."

They'd kept each other company on several occasions when a partner was required, and she was glad he'd made the offer.

"Sorry about that, but I'll definitely keep you in mind." Silver found her script and followed him into a room where three people sat behind a table with one empty chair.

"Hi, everyone."

Drew took his seat and the guy next to him looked Silver up and down. "Don't you think she's looking a bit old for this part, Drew? Maybe we should have her read for the mother instead."

Silver raised an eyebrow. "Who have you cast as your leading man again?"

"Tex Calmundo," Drew told her.

"He's ten years older than I am. If he's supposed to be my love interest that's a big enough age gap."

"But Tex looks twenty." Obnoxious Oscar wasn't giving up. "He needs someone in their teens to play off."

Silver let out a long, slow breath as the four of them started arguing. She didn't need this job, and she was sick and tired of all the bullshit.

She walked up to the table and carefully placed her script in front of Drew.

"I don't have time for this."

Drew's head came up. "I beg your pardon?"

"If you want me to play this part, let me know, okay? I'm not going to stand here like a piece of meat with no feelings while you discuss how old I look."

"Silver . . ." Drew shot to his feet.

"Have a great day!" She smiled, turned around, and walked out, aware of the silence behind her that swiftly developed into a shouting match the moment she closed the door.

Her dad, who was chatting with Drew's personal assistant, looked up as she came toward him.

"That was quick. How did it go?"

"Really well." She gestured at the door. "Can we get going? I have another audition in two hours."

Ben hastily put his phone away as Adam called him for dinner. He'd been staring at a picture of Silver going into one of the television networks. She'd looked beautiful and was smiling like she didn't have a care in the world. But why shouldn't she? She was back in her natural habitat and had probably forgotten all about him and Morgan Valley.

He'd spent way too many restless hours going over what he'd said to make her leave and wishing he could have a do-over. But even in his most selfish moments he still knew he'd done the right thing.

He went into the kitchen where, for a change, everyone was present for dinner. Daisy had just returned from Silicon Valley and Kaiden and Evan, who worked in Morgantown, were also there. As Adam dished up huge bowls of spaghetti and sauce, Ben got the beverages out of the refrigerator and set them on the table with the plastic glasses Auntie Rae had bought when they were kids.

"Thanks." Adam glanced up briefly as Ben also doled

out napkins. “Knowing the way this lot eat, we’ll need those.”

“This looks good.” Jeff came in rubbing his hands together as they all sat at the table. “I think we’re done with calving this year. Danny’s been a great help.”

“Thanks, Dad.” Danny looked over at Ben and rolled his eyes. “I can’t wait to get back to construction in town. My boss doesn’t shout at me half as much, and the pay is twice as good.”

Ben patted his ribs. “Great timing because Dr. Tio says I’m good to go, so I’ll be able to take up where you left off.”

“Cool.” Danny turned to their father. “You hear that, Dad? Ben’s back.”

“Maybe.” Jeff helped himself to a bowlful of spaghetti and sauce.

“Maybe?” Adam who was the last to sit down, glanced questioningly over at his father.

“Pablo Gomez came up to me in the feed store today and asked me if it was true that Ben was looking for a new job. He’s considering hiring a ranch manager.”

Everyone turned to look at Ben who carefully set down his fork. “What did you tell him?”

“I told him he’d have to ask you.” Jeff scowled. “I’m getting sick and tired of hearing what you’re up to from other people. What’s wrong with telling me to my face?”

“Because you’re terrifying?” Kaiden said mildly. “Because most of us would rather face a raging bull than have a conversation with you?”

“I’m not that bad.” Jeff waved the complaint away. “You all know my bark is worse than my bite.” He pointed his fork at Ben. “Is it true?”

“You told me that if I went on that trail ride that you

couldn't guarantee you'd have a job for me when I got back," Ben replied evenly. "I put some feelers out before I left and Pablo must have found out."

"I was angry because you were walking out on us at calving time," Jeff objected. "You must've known I didn't mean it."

"Obviously I didn't." Ben held his father's gaze. "You told me you'd already given me one chance to come back, and that I shouldn't assume I'd get a second."

"I *did* let you back after you fooled around with that girl and got kicked out of college."

"Dad." Adam spoke up. "That was a long time ago. Ben's a different person now."

Ben glanced over at his big brother whom he knew was trying to help, and wondered whether he should apologize to him, too. The Ben they all thought was dead and buried had returned with a vengeance during his time with Silver and done stuff they would never believe he was capable of. What if they found out about that? Would they all look as disappointed and horrified as they had when he'd finally returned home the first time?

"I'll go over and speak to Pablo tomorrow." Ben dug his fork into his pasta and made himself chew, aware of the uncomfortable silence around him.

"You'll do no such thing," Jeff snapped. "You've been lazing around for a month since you came back from that trail ride. If you hadn't disobeyed me and taken it on, you wouldn't have been injured in the first place. You owe me your goddamn labor."

"I'll go after I've finished my work here, okay?" Ben said. "Look, you've already said you don't need me here, and that Danny does a better job than me, so why are you mad? If I'm that useless, surely you'll be glad to be rid of me?"

"Maybe I would." His father stood and glared down at him. "I never thought I'd live to see one of my sons be so damned ungrateful." He picked up his bowl. "I'm going to finish my dinner in my office before I say something I shouldn't."

Ben winced as the door slammed behind his father and kept his attention on his plate. If he didn't look up, no one could catch his eye and start talking at him.

"One has to wonder what Dad thinks he hasn't already said." Kaiden filled up Ben's glass with iced tea. "I suppose it's an indicator that Mom really is a good influence on him because he did actually leave before he lost it completely."

"Maybe he's planning a bonfire of my stuff like he did with Mom's." Ben gratefully took a sip of tea and then sighed. "I'm sorry, guys. I didn't mean to spoil Daisy's homecoming and this great meal Adam cooked for us."

"Spoil it?" Kaiden sat back. "Spaghetti and a show? Life doesn't get much better than this."

"Kaiden, this isn't funny," Daisy said severely. "I think Dad is actually quite hurt."

Everyone looked at her.

"Hurt?" Kaiden took the bait. "He's annoyed because Ben got sick of him disparaging him and took it upon himself to look for another job."

"He doesn't disparage Ben," Daisy objected. "He just . . . struggles to know how to praise people and make them feel valued."

Kaiden snorted. "He treats Ben like an afterthought, and you know it."

"Thanks for spelling it out, bro." Ben winced.

"But it's true, isn't it? Dad idolizes Adam and you,

Daisy, but the rest of us?" Kaiden looked around the table. "We're just work units who need to do his bidding when required, and to hell with what we think about that. Why do you think three of us don't work full-time on the ranch?"

Daisy bit her lip. "I . . . hadn't thought of it like that before."

"Hey, don't look like that." Kaiden reached across the table and grabbed her hand. "I'm sorry, Daisy. That wasn't fair of me, okay?"

"But it's the truth." Adam spoke up, his gaze on Ben. "Dad even left the ranch to me without even thinking it necessary to consult with any of you. I had to make him slow down and tell you all what he planned."

Ben rose to his feet and threw his napkin onto the table. "I'm going to talk to him. If he kicks me out, it's been nice knowing you all."

"Ben—" Adam started to rise, but Ben was too quick for him.

He walked down the hallway to the farm office, knocked on the door, ignored his dad's growl to go away, and went inside. The old-fashioned computer screen was lit up, illuminating the walls of shelving where all the account books and livestock registers were stored, and one of the lamps was on. His dad was sitting behind the desk, his empty pasta bowl beside him.

"What do you want?" Jeff folded his arms across his chest.

"I wanted to ask you something."

His father shrugged. "Can't stop you asking seeing as you're between me and the door."

"Why shouldn't I go and work for Pablo if he needs a ranch manager?"

"Because your place is here, working for me and

supporting your family. I brought you up to be useful, not to take your skills off to another ranch."

"What skills? I do all the shit jobs that no one else wants to do," Ben said.

"Maybe because that's what's needed here right now."

"And what about what I want?" Ben asked.

Jeff sighed. "Here we go again. It's not all about you, Ben. We all have obligations in life, and this ranch—this family—is part of yours. Do you think I wanted to keep going after your mother left me? Did you think dealing with six kids and running a ranch on my own was *fun?*" He pointed his finger at Ben. "I stuck it out because I wanted you boys to have this place when I'm gone."

"Correction. You wanted Adam to have this place."

Jeff stood up. "You know what, son? If you'd hated the idea of Adam being in control of the ranch you should've spoken up earlier instead of sulking like a kid and making everyone else suffer."

"I *wanted*—"

"You don't know what you want!" Jeff raised his voice a fraction. "It's way easier to complain and moan and do nothing than it is to take control of things and forge your own path in this world. You've let yourself stay in Adam's shadow for years, and now suddenly that's everyone else's fault?"

Ben slowly closed his mouth and just glared at his father.

"That girl you took on the trail ride! She was head over heels for you, and what do you do about it, eh? Nothing! Because it's easier, Ben, because that's the way you've lived your life since you screwed up when you were at college."

"That's not true. I—"

"That other girl, Cassie. You let her spin you around

her little finger until you didn't know which way was up anymore! She almost killed you!"

"She—" Ben turned on his heel. "I'm not listening to this."

"Of course you aren't because it's hard, isn't it, Ben? Much easier to avoid it and pretend nothing's wrong and repeat the same mistakes over and over."

Ben made the mistake of looking back. "You're a fine one to talk. Look what you did to our family!"

"And I've learned from it! I'm talking to my ex-wife and I've apologized to her!"

"What a hero." Ben wasn't feeling kindly toward his father right now. "What do you want, a goddam medal?"

"Look." Jeff approached Ben, his hands held out wide. "Go and talk to Pablo. Maybe talk to that Silver woman, too, because I can see that you miss her. Make some real hard choices. I might not like them, but I'll live with your decisions, okay?"

Ben could only manage a nod before he left the office and headed straight to his bedroom. The house was super quiet, probably because everyone was busy eavesdropping on him and their dad. He locked both doors just in case Kaiden decided to come and chat, lay down on his bed, and stared up at the ceiling. He wasn't going to think about any of the stupid accusations his dad had just flung at him in his usual rage.

But how could he not? There had been something there . . . some truth that had exploded in his head like a bomb and illuminated a lot of the darkness he usually preferred to remain hidden. Was that who he was? A man who preferred others to take on responsibility while he passive-aggressively complained and did nothing? After the debacle of his relationship with Cassie, he'd come home and wanted nothing but the security of his work on the ranch and his family. Had he buried himself here? Had he really hidden who he was and what he wanted until circumstances changed to reveal that he wasn't really safe after all?

Ben groaned and pressed his hands over his eyes. He'd been busy telling Silver she couldn't always get what she wanted while he was too much of a coward to even admit he even wanted anything at all. He might not want to think about what his father had said, but he sure as hell couldn't get it out of his head, and he doubted it was going to get any better.

Chapter Fifteen

Silver dropped her keys in the bowl on the kitchen countertop and walked into the family room where her parents, Ayla, and both her siblings were hunched over their phones. They all looked up when they saw her, and she frowned.

"What's up? Did someone die?"

"Maybe just your career?" Her brother, Aaron, who wasn't part of the family acting dynasty and therefore didn't take it quite as seriously as everyone else, spoke up.

"Ha ha. What did I supposedly do?" Silver helped herself to some juice and hopped up on one of the stools. She'd been to the gym and was feeling quite good about herself. Punching and kicking her trainer while imagining it was Ben had somehow inspired her.

Ayla came over and handed Silver her tablet. "There's a lot of . . . gossip about where you've been for the last month and a half."

"So what?"

"Mr. Meadows is worried that it might spiral out of control unless we do something."

Silver looked over at her dad who for once wasn't smiling. "What's up?"

He sighed. "The rumor is that you have . . . relapsed,

and that you spent a month in rehab. There are photos of some blond woman they claim is you in Serenity Heights."

"But we know I wasn't there, and so does this rehab place. Just put out a joint statement." She looked at her mother who wasn't smiling either. "It's not like the first time this has happened, is it?"

"The thing is . . . news has also gotten out that you walked out of that audition the other day," her father said carefully. "Oscar Palmer is telling everyone you were hysterical, and difficult to understand, and that you threatened him when he wasn't sure you were the right fit for the part."

"None of that is true. Ask Drew," Silver suggested.

"No one's going to listen to Drew when what Oscar is saying will drive more clicks," Ayla reminded her.

"I think we should tell the press where you were," her father said.

"And subject Morgan Ranch to all that scrutiny? No way." Silver frowned. "That's hardly fair."

Silver still hadn't exactly told her dad what had gone down the last couple of days of her trip. The last thing she wanted was the media descending on Morgan Valley, finding that out, and making a big deal out of it.

"Let's just ignore it. I'm sure there'll be a bigger scandal in the next day or so." Silver slid off the stool. "I've got to shower, and then I need to speak to you, Ayla."

"Silver . . ."

"What?" She faced her dad.

"Are you one hundred percent certain that these rumors aren't true?"

Her smile faded. "That I was in rehab? You know I wasn't."

"I meant that you've started using again." She went to interrupt him, and he held up his hand. "I know you think

I'm being incredibly invasive, but I need to know. You did walk out of a highly lucrative job opportunity."

"I walked out because Oscar suggested I was too old to play opposite Tex Calmundo who is ten years my senior, and that they should get a teenager instead." She held her dad's gaze. "If that's being 'difficult' then, sure, I was difficult. I don't need the money, Dad. I only auditioned in the first place because you insisted on it. I'd rather not work with someone who thinks I'm too old to play someone my actual age."

"And what about the rest of what I asked you?" Her father wasn't a coward. Somewhere beneath her rising anger she knew that, but it didn't really matter right now because she was so damn hurt.

"If you think I'm back on drugs then I'm not going to argue with you." She shrugged. "I would hope that you'd know me better than that. I made a promise to all of you." Her gaze swept her family. "I know in my heart that I haven't broken it."

She walked away before the tears that threatened behind her eyes actually fell. The lack of *trust* . . . that hurt more than anything.

Even after her shower she still felt sick to her stomach. When she entered her office again she was relieved to find only Ayla there.

"I'm sorry you got to witness all our family drama," Silver said.

"It's okay." Ayla looked uncomfortable. "I hope you don't mind, but your dad and I did talk about several ways we could deal with this issue. He asked me to present them to you."

"Because he's scared I wouldn't listen to him?" Silver sat down next to Ayla and sighed. "Go on, then. Tell me."

"Well, firstly he's going to talk to your publicist and make sure we are all on the same page."

"Sure." Silver nodded.

"But he also thinks we should make some kind of statement—maybe not naming the ranch, but saying what you'd been doing, and why."

"But how would the indie movie people react to that when I haven't even been offered the part?" Silver objected. "It might even push them to publicly declare they would never consider me for such a role."

"I had the same thought," Ayla admitted. "I was wondering whether you'd like me to talk to Inola and get a sense of where they are in all this."

"If you can manage it without making things worse, then please go ahead," Silver said. "I can't believe this is all happening right now when I thought things were going well."

"Life sucks sometimes, doesn't it?" Ayla agreed and hesitated. "Do you want me to put a call through to Morgan Ranch just to give them a heads-up that things might get busy their way soon?"

"Only if you must." Silver groaned. "I feel so bad for them."

"They might welcome the publicity for their dude ranch."

"I suppose so," Silver said dubiously. "But it still feels like a betrayal. Let's hope that some other celebrity does something monumentally stupid tomorrow, and all this gets forgotten."

Unfortunately, no one obliged, and the next morning, Silver faced a "crisis" meeting with her team, including her publicist who was screaming for something she could put out to the media.

Silver looked at the headlines and wanted to crawl away and die. Apparently, she'd been seen at more than one rehab *and* down on the streets of L.A. soliciting drugs. The fact that she'd done nothing wrong seemed irrelevant now. She knew how things went. The story would take on a life of its own and the more she tried to deny it, the worse it would get.

She broke through what her publicist was saying.

"Okay, put out a statement. Say I took two weeks off to go on a trail ride. That's the truth."

"But who's going to believe that?" Aaron piped up. "You're not exactly known for your interest in the Wild West, sis. It's going to sound like a scam."

Silver looked over at Ayla. "Any news from Inola?"

"She said they were very impressed by your answers to their questions, so maybe a hint that you really were at a ranch researching for a movie role with them would work?" Ayla looked over at Nadeem the publicist. "It could give the film good publicity too, right?"

"If we handled it properly." Nadeem nodded and turned to Silver. "We'll need to use the real name of the ranch, to make sure we sound authentic."

"This *is* authentic!" Silver glared at all of them. "That's what I actually did! Please don't forget the truth among all these lies."

Her dad cleared his throat. "Look, how about I put in a call to Morgan Ranch and give them a heads-up? Hopefully, that will be the end of it. The indie movie will get a boost, the ranch will get new guests, and we can go back to worrying about whether it's ever going to rain again in L.A. this century."

Everyone but Silver laughed, but then why shouldn't

they? They weren't having their name smeared and their career trashed for nothing. She abruptly got to her feet.

"I'm going down to the gym to meet my trainer." She raised her chin. "If that's okay with everyone? I promise I won't try and score any drugs on my way down the stairs."

She'd barely made it into the home gym before her father caught up with her.

"Silver . . ."

She fiddled around lacing her shoes so she didn't have to look at him.

He sighed and leaned against the door. "I'm sorry."

"For which particular part?" she asked, focusing hard on achieving the perfect loop ratio.

"All of it. I should've trusted you. I just . . . overreacted because I was scared."

She started on her second shoe. For the first time in her life she wasn't willing to simply roll over and forgive him. She loved him, but she couldn't live the rest of her life with him constantly looking over her shoulder, and accidentally or deliberately, undermining what she had achieved.

"My trainer will be here in five, Dad. Why don't you go and call the Morgans?"

Ben pulled his Jeep up in front of the Gomez ranch house and got out to the sound of barking dogs and honking geese. He stayed where he was for a moment and let the dogs check him out before looking around for Pablo.

"Hey!" Pablo came out of the house and whistled to his dogs who obediently came back to him. The geese stayed where they were, their mean eyes focused on Ben. "Come on in, Ben. It's good to see you."

Carefully edging past the guard geese who would happily kneecap him if they took a sudden dislike to him, Ben went into the ranch house which was of a similar age to his family home, but about a third of the size. Pablo only had one daughter who lived in the Bay Area and worked as a doctor.

"Coffee?" Pablo held out the pot. His family had arrived in California from Mexico in the early twentieth century and had quickly established their ranch in Morgan Valley. Pablo now specialized in organic beef. His place was a lot smaller than the Millers' and the Morgans', but he still managed to survive.

"Thanks." Ben took his mug and sat opposite Pablo at the table. As promised, he'd done all his work, had his dinner, and come over to Pablo's on his own time.

"Jeff didn't seem very happy at the thought of you not working for him," Pablo commented.

"That's my dad for you." Ben shrugged. "He's got five sons. Adam works full-time along with him and Danny's perfectly capable of taking on my job if I decide to branch out."

"I only have my daughter and she has no interest in working here." Pablo sighed. "I tried to get my nephew involved, but he hates living in such a remote place. He wants to move back to the coast as soon as I can find a replacement for him. What I'm looking for is an experienced person to run the everyday operation of the ranch with me. Knowing Jeff"—Pablo grinned—"I guess you've been well trained."

Ben sipped his coffee. "I definitely know the work, and I wouldn't let you down."

Pablo nodded and slid a piece of paper over to Ben. "This is what I'm going to put in the paper if I can't get you on board. It sets out the pay rate, the minimum hours—although you know how ranching goes—and that the job comes with a place to live."

"Yeah?" Ben looked up from the paper. "Because if I do take this job, I don't see my dad letting me live at home."

"Neither do I." Pablo grinned. "It's a separate structure on the other side of the barn. It's nothing fancy, but I did it up for my nephew. You're welcome to take a look if you like."

"I'll come back during daylight if that's okay with you, Pablo?" Ben asked. "I don't want your nephew thinking I'm a burglar and shooting me."

"Ha!" Pablo sat back and studied Ben. "I'm going to be honest, Ben. I can't think of anyone I'd rather have working here with me than the son of my old friend Jeff."

"Even if it pisses him off?"

"After the way he treats his friends?" Pablo winked. "That's a bonus."

Ben took the paper, folded it in quarters, and stuck it in the pocket of his jeans. "It's a big change for me and a decision I don't want to take lightly. I hope you'll give me some time to think things over."

"Absolutely." Pablo stood and shook Ben's hand. "Let me know when you make your decision. With you working alongside me I bet we could make this place stand out."

Ben finished his coffee and Pablo escorted him to his Jeep. Ben took his time driving home, his mind busy trying to consider all the angles of taking the opportunity Pablo was offering him. He'd earn more money, have the chance to directly implement his ideas on how a ranch should be run, and have somewhere to live without his family but close enough to visit them.

He parked his Jeep at home but didn't get out. He stared into the well-lit house, idly counting the parked trucks to work out who was home, and who was still out.

Jackson, Daisy's fiancé, was obviously around, which meant his dad would have to be a little more polite to Ben when he came in.

Just as he was about to get out, his cell buzzed and he checked the caller and picked up.

"Hey, BB. What's up?"

"Nothing much." BB hesitated. "You home?"

"Yeah, why?"

"Because I just had a call from Phil Meadows. I really think you should hear what he has to say."

Ben's stomach dropped. He put his seat belt back on and started the engine. "I'm coming right over."

"Apparently, the fact that Silver Meadows went missing for two weeks got social media in a frenzy." BB handed Ben a mug of coffee and sat opposite him in the deserted kitchen. Jenna was out on call and Maria was probably in her bedroom. "I know it sounds crazy to us, but that's her life."

"What does that have to do with Morgan Ranch?" Ben asked.

"Phil said the media is speculating that Silver was in rehab again, and that she's unstable."

"That's a load of bull," Ben said flatly. "She isn't like that at all."

"Which is what I told her dad." BB nodded. "He says that her publicist needs to put out a statement saying where she was, and that they wanted us to know they'd be mentioning Morgan Ranch."

"Okay, so what's the problem?" Ben asked. "Won't that be good for business?"

"He said it could get a little crazy around here with news media."

"Like they'd come all the way out here for what exactly?" Ben scoffed. "No one knew she was here except you guys and me. There's no gossip to find."

"Which is why I'm telling you what's happening." BB drummed his fingers on the table. "There's a bit more to it than just the media thing. When I was talking to Phil I mentioned how brave Silver had been on the trail ride, and that there was no way she was doing drugs. To say he was surprised is putting it mildly."

Ben stared at his employer in growing horror. "He didn't know?"

"Nope. She hadn't told him about it."

"Shit," Ben said slowly. "Was he angry?"

"I have no idea." BB held Ben's gaze. "But your name might get out there as well as Morgan Ranch, so I just want you to be prepared."

Chapter Sixteen

Just before dawn, after a restless night, Ben went into the farm office, fired up the computer, and spent half an hour scrolling through the gossip sites. The statement from Silver's publicist sat front and center in all the news, and speculation about its authenticity was never-ending. Ben felt sick just reading some of the comments and couldn't even imagine how bad Silver must be feeling.

His life had come crashing down when he was twenty so he knew how it felt to have your character called into question, your intentions misunderstood, and your guilt established before anyone bothered to learn the facts. And he had been in the wrong about some things. Silver hadn't done a thing, and yet thousands of idiots on the Internet felt like they had the right to criticize and belittle her for nothing.

His cell rang and he picked up.

"Yeah?"

"Is this Ben Miller? I'm sorry to bother you, but my name is Ayla. I'm Silver Meadows's personal assistant."

"Come again?" Ben frowned even though she couldn't see him.

"I just wanted to talk to you about the current situation Silver is going through."

"Does she know you're calling me?" Ben asked suspiciously.

"Not yet. I'm calling at the behest of her father, Phil, who I think you met when he picked Silver up from Morgan Ranch?"

"Okay, so what's up?"

"Firstly, after we finish our call, I'm going to recommend that you only answer your cell phone if you know the caller because your name is about to get out there."

"*My* name?" Ben breathed out hard as he remembered what BB had told him. "What the hell?"

She started talking faster. "Phil really wants Silver to get this movie role with the indie film company. Releasing the information about what went down at the end of your trail ride will make her look really good and might make certain that she gets the part."

"What's that got to do with me?" Ben demanded.

"Because you're part of the story, and the media will want to find you and interview you."

"Right . . ." Ben almost laughed. "I doubt that."

"Trust me, they will. I'm going to give you my personal number. If things get too hectic down there, or you get worried about your safety or the safety of your family, call me and we'll help."

"I still think you're overreacting, but give me your number, and I'll stick it in my contacts." He wrote down what she said. "If Silver doesn't know you're calling me, she's going to be pissed when she finds out."

"I know." Ayla sighed. "But I think this is for the best. She really wants that role, and I guess this is the only way she's going to make sure she gets it. Free publicity for the movie, great publicity for her, and increased interest in Morgan Ranch trail rides. What could go wrong?"

Three hours later, Ben had turned his phone off completely and was convinced he was in some kind of alternate universe. One of the last calls he'd taken had been from BB telling him that there had been reporters nosing around the gates of Morgan Ranch and seen in Morgantown. It was so stupid and pointless, he couldn't even get his head around it.

By the time he got home for dinner and turned his phone back on he'd accumulated two hundred messages and a similar amount of texts and dropped calls. He deleted almost all of them before he entered the house and took off his work boots and Stetson in the mudroom. There was no sign of Kaiden in the bathroom, so he took a quick shower and got dressed again, his thought straying to Silver and what she must be going through as they had all day.

Just as he was pulling up his jeans, Kaiden came barging into his bedroom.

"What the hell's going on?"

Ben raised an eyebrow as he zipped up his jeans.

Kaiden held out his phone. "You're on *Reality Bites*, the number-one gossip site on the Internet."

"Yeah? Is that good?" Ben inquired as he sat down to pull on some socks.

"It's fricking crazy! But what's even funnier is that you're the doofus in this story and Silver's the heroine who saved you from imminent death."

"She did save me." Ben stood up. "If she hadn't been there, I wouldn't have gotten out of that tree and climbed back up the slope. If she's claiming credit for what happened and it does her some good, then I'm okay with it."

"I like your attitude," Kaiden said as he punched him on the shoulder. "You coming for dinner? Lizzie's here with Roman and she's helping Adam cook."

"Cool, what are we having?" Ben followed Kaiden out into the hallway and down to the large family kitchen diner where, from the sound of it, there was already a crowd. He tried to pretend that everything was the same and that the whole world wasn't going crazy. "Smells like roast beef to me."

Roman, Lizzie's son, who was about to enter kindergarten in the fall, danced over to tug on Ben's T-shirt. "There were people with cameras at the gate! Adam told them to go away!"

Ben glanced swiftly over at his brother who nodded. "Yeah, that's what happened. Lizzie says your name is all over Facebook or something. What did you do?"

"He didn't do anything." Lizzie wrapped an arm around Adam's waist and smiled at Ben. "For some reason he's got caught up in some celebrity nonsense. Yvonne says it's the same at Morgan Ranch."

"Ben Miller!" His father came through into the kitchen already in full-on yell mode. "What the hell have you been up to *now!*"

Ben winced as Adam frowned at their dad. "Roman's here, so mind your language, okay?"

Jeff patted Roman's head. "Sorry, son." He turned back to Ben. "What's going on? I was in town at Maureen's and there was a man asking her all sorts of questions about the Morgans and us. She told him nothing, but I still don't like it."

Ben cleared his throat. "Okay, so you all should hear this. I took Silver Meadows on a trail ride a month or so ago. The media have gotten hold of that information, found out about the accident, and now they're after me. I'm sorry for all the disruption this stupid mess is causing."

"Silver Meadows?" Jeff asked. "That pretty girl I met at the Morgans?"

"Yup, that one." Ben nodded. It was ironic that he was the one who had promised not to blab about anything that had happened during their trail ride and yet Silver was the one to renege on that assurance.

"Well, no wonder she didn't want to hang around with you." Jeff shook his head. "She's gone back to her Hollywood lifestyle and can go out with anyone."

"Thanks, Dad," Ben said. "I appreciate the support. Hopefully, once they realize that they can't get to me here, they'll go away, or focus on the Morgans." He glanced over at Adam. "Can I help with anything for dinner?"

"What did you do?" Silver marched into the family dining room and fixed her father with an accusing stare. "Why is Ben Miller's name plastered all over the gossip sites?"

Her father sighed. "Can we all sit down and eat our dinner before we get into this?" He glanced over at his wife. "Alva's been cooking all afternoon."

Silver took a seat and sent her mom an apologetic glance. "Sorry."

"It's all right, my love. You know how I love to cook when Dee has her afternoon off."

In an attempt to be civil, Silver looked over at her sister. "How are the auditions going?"

"They aren't." Spring continued to cut up her fish into bite-sized pieces. "No one wants to talk about me at the moment. All they want is info about you, and I'm not playing that game." She ate a tiny amount. "And, to be honest, I think I'm over this whole acting thing anyway. I'm never going to be as good at it as you are, and I'm tired of having to pretend everything is okay."

Silver looked at her dad. "Did you know about this?"

He shrugged. "I've been trying to persuade her it's just a phase because she hasn't been as successful as she'd like recently."

"Maybe she wants out," Aaron said, and turned to Spring. "You should go to college like I did, and get out of this weird bubble."

"I think I'd like that." Spring ate another minuscule portion of fish.

"Then you should do it," Silver urged her. "There's plenty of money to pay for college. What do you want to study?"

"I'd like to be a teacher," Spring said.

"You'd be awesome at it," Silver agreed before she smiled at her parents. "Think about how much free time you'll have to spend together when Spring's at college and I'm managing my own career."

Neither of her parents looked thrilled at the idea, but Silver was not going to let it go. "You could travel the world, buy an RV, and visit all the states in the USA!"

Her father set down his glass. "We have to sort out the current media issue before we think about anything else."

"We're going to talk about that now?" Silver focused in on her father. "Who told you what happened when I was on the trail ride?"

"Surely the question should be, why didn't you tell *me?*" her father replied. "If I'd known . . ."

"If you'd known, you would've gone in there suing everyone in sight. It was nobody's fault, and we all got out alive," Silver said firmly. "I intended to tell you when I got back. It just slipped my mind."

She'd been too upset to even mention Ben's name in case she started crying and revealed far more than she wanted to. . . .

"Who told you?" she repeated.

"It was a combination of people. When I called BB Morgan, he said that you'd been extraordinarily brave. When I asked Ayla about it, she showed me your answers to the indie film producers confirming what BB had said." He paused. "Ayla only told me because she thought it would help your case with the movie, not to get you into trouble."

"Does Ben know?" Silver asked.

"Ayla spoke to him this morning. He was fine about it."

"Of course he was," Silver muttered. "He won't even care that everyone is making me out to be the hero of the story when, if it wasn't for him, we wouldn't even have gotten out of the valley."

Her father chuckled. "He doesn't need fame or fortune, or to look good at this particular moment, Silver. You do."

"So we'll use him to make me look good?"

Her father shrugged. "If we have to."

"I don't like it." Silver held his gaze. "He isn't equipped to deal with all the shit that is likely coming his way right now, and it's all my fault."

"Then call him up and apologize if it makes you feel better. Buy him a new horse or something." Her father waved a negligent hand. "Whatever it takes to ensure he stays on our side and doesn't decide to take the biggest payday of his life and do a tell-all article about his ten days with a megastar or something."

"He signed an NDA." Silver set down her fork and stood up, her whole body shaking. "He's a good and honorable man. I don't appreciate the way you are speaking about him, as if he only exists to serve your purposes and can then be discarded."

"Hey, come on," her father protested. "That's taking what I said completely out of context."

"She's right. You've changed, Dad." Spring stood, too. "You used to be a good, kind man who encouraged us, but never pushed too hard. These days all you care about is keeping me and Silver working to keep the money flowing in."

Aaron also rose. "Count me in as well. I'm glad I got out when I was younger." He turned to his sisters. "Anyone want to come and play Dragonlandia with me? It's a super cool game."

Their father sat as still as stone, a shocked look on his face, as they all marched out. As Silver went to close the door behind them, Alva rushed over to sit next to him and took his hand. Silver almost felt sorry for her dad, but perhaps it was time he learned to listen a bit more to the people in his life he professed to love.

She didn't even have Ben's cell number. She hadn't asked for it because she was afraid that she wouldn't be able to stop herself from checking in with him. She pressed a hand to her heart. Even though he'd let her walk away, she wouldn't wish what might happen to him on anyone. She hoped he was okay and hated the thought that he must be thinking really badly of her right now.

"Silver?" Aaron called out to her. "Are you coming?"

"Yes." She made herself move. "I'll be right there."

"Back off!"

Ben fought to control Calder who was leaping around

like he was at a rodeo and faced the men in the all-terrain vehicle who were still taking pictures of him.

Adam had already confronted them and he was rightfully furious. "This is private land. If you don't leave immediately, I'll call the sheriff."

Ben rode up beside him. "And expect a bill for the damage you've caused to our livestock!"

"Anything to say about Silver Meadows, Ben?" one of the guys called out to both of them.

"Get off our ranch," Adam said and got out his phone. "Right now."

He signaled to Ben to ride off with him. The cows and calves they'd been checking were huddled down in the corner of the field. When the vehicle had roared down the hill, half the calves had panicked and run, causing a stampede that had spooked both horses and set the dogs off.

Adam was still cursing under his breath as he slowed down and spoke into his phone.

"Yeah, Nate. We've got trespassers. They must have come up through the Garcias' place. They are the only ranch with fences down that side onto ours." He listened for a second. "Thanks. Let me know what happens, and what we can do to stop this happening again."

Ben groaned and met his brother's gaze. "I'm sorry, Adam. I had no idea it would get this crazy or that these fools would go to such lengths just to get a look at me."

"It's okay." Adam stowed his phone away and glanced at the cows. "We'd better leave them where they are, today. I don't want to upset them any further."

They left the field and took a circuitous route back to the house just in case there were any other unexpected surprises. Kaiden had reported that there were a couple of people camped out at their gate and more in Morgantown, but no one had asked him for his opinion on anything yet. He'd sounded quite disappointed.

"I can't stay here if this is going to affect the ranch," Ben said abruptly.

Adam gave him a sideways glance. "This is probably the safest place to be right now."

"Not if someone I love gets hurt. Imagine what will happen if Dad comes across any of these guys." Ben blew out a breath. "When we get home, I'll call Silver's PA, and tell her what's going on. Maybe she can suggest something."

"You sure you don't want to hunker down here and wait them out?" Adam looked concerned. "They can't hang around forever."

"Maybe not, but I don't like it," Ben said. "If I can do something to make things better, I'll do it."

They reached the barn and Ben dismounted and checked Calder over. He seemed fine but was still a little overheated. Ben patted his neck.

"You missed your calling, Calder. You should've been at the NPR finals in the bucking chutes."

Calder nuzzled his face and Ben offered him a carrot stick.

Adam came over. "I'll look after him, if you want to go and call Silver's PA."

"Thanks, bro." Ben tried to smile. "I appreciate it."

He went into the house, which was quiet because he and Adam had returned early, took his cell into the farm office, and closed the door.

She answered immediately. "This is Ayla. How may I help you?"

Ben parked himself on the edge of the desk. "We're having problems here with the press invading our ranch and scaring our cattle and horses."

"Gosh, Ben, I'm so sorry." Ayla paused. "Do you think you need to get out for a while until things settle down?"

"Yeah."

"Can you hold on a sec?" Ayla asked.

He waited for what felt like an hour for her to come back to him and then a different voice spoke in his ear.

"Hey, Ben, this is Phil Meadows. I'm really sorry for all the hassle."

Ben didn't have anything to say to that so he kept quiet.

"I was wondering whether you would consider doing this—we'll fly you out to L.A., you do one public news conference confirming Silver's story, and then we send you off on a two-week vacation somewhere warm until everything blows over."

Ben considered the idea. "Why do I need to do the news thing?"

"Because everyone will get what they want in one hit, and then they'll be off to the next thing. Silver's reputation will not only be restored, but enhanced, and you'll be free of any further issues." Phil paused. "It would mean a lot to Silver to get this movie role. She really wants to change direction, and I want her to be happy."

So did Ben, but he wasn't going to share that with her old man.

"Are you sure Silver is okay with this?"

"Of course she is," Phil said firmly. "In fact, she's looking forward to seeing you."

Ben's heart leapt at that comment and he knew he was smiling like a fool. The thought of seeing her again—of her being grateful to him was really motivating.

"Okay, then. I'll do it."

Chapter Seventeen

Nadeem came into Silver's office and looked expectantly at her.

"You ready to go?"

"And do what?" Silver pointed at her phone. "No one wants to talk to me right now so I'm hardly busy."

"For the press conference." Nadeem frowned. "Didn't Mr. Meadows tell you?"

"No." Silver folded her arms over her chest. Her dad hadn't been speaking to her much since the revolt over the dinner table.

"I was thinking you could go casual, like maybe even in jeans and a T-shirt? The kind of stuff you wore on the trail ride? That would give a great visual."

"Nadeem, slow down. What are we having a press conference for?" Silver asked.

"To present both sides of the story." Nadeem blinked at her. "It's a genius idea, and I don't know why I didn't think of it."

Silver was beginning to get a bad feeling. Ayla had called to say she was busy organizing something, and would see her later, and her dad had disappeared completely.

"Is my dad back?" Silver asked slowly.

"No, he's meeting us there." Nadeem checked her cell. "You've got about fifteen minutes, so we really need to be going soon."

"I still don't understand—"

Nadeem headed for the door like the house was on fire. "I'll go and make sure our driver will be ready in ten, okay?"

Silver contemplated the space where Nadeem had been. Her publicist was being deliberately evasive, which didn't bode well for the whole press conference thing. She had a suspicion that her dad was up to something, but what? Was it possible that he'd got BB Morgan to come to L.A. and talk about Morgan Ranch? Or was it even worse than that . . . ?

She ran out of the room and up to her bedroom. If she was about to face the press, she'd better be looking her best.

There was no one at the back door when she and Nadeem were ushered through, which was unusual, until Silver realized that every single gossipmonger was probably seated out front just salivating for the latest news. She spotted her dad looking relaxed and chatting with some guy about the lighting and went right up to him.

"What's going on?"

He smiled, patted her arm, and drew her into a quiet corner. "Calm down, honey. Remember, we want them to think you are sane, lucid, and drug-free, not flaming mad."

Silver just glared at him until his smile faded.

"Look, it's no big deal, Silver. I thought the best way to get all this out in the open was to get the man himself to come here and answer questions about how you saved his life on that trail ride."

"No. Big. Deal?" Silver struggled to draw breath as she looked frantically around her. "You forced Ben Miller to come all the way out here just to make me look good? Don't you remember a *word* about what we talked about?"

"Hold on. It wasn't my idea. *He* called Ayla because there were some problems on his ranch. See, here?" Her dad fumbled for his cell phone and showed her the short sequence of the two men on horseback being confronted by an ATV full of idiots.

"Oh my God, don't they know how dangerous that was?" Silver said. "Those horses could have bolted, the cattle could have stampeded. What a stupid, *irresponsible* thing to do."

"Which is why Ben called Ayla. He wanted to get away. I offered to bring him out here to set the record straight before he went on a well-earned vacation."

"Ranchers don't take vacations," Silver said. "His dad will be furious."

"Not our problem, sweetness. He agreed to do this to help clear your name and help you get the role in the indie film, which was really nice of him, right?"

"Where is he?"

Her dad frowned. "In one of the dressing rooms. Why?"

"I need to speak to him. I need to make sure that he's doing this of his own free will, and that you haven't forced him into it," Silver said grimly.

"He's in the second room on the left, but you don't have a lot of time, Silver. You need to visit makeup, and we're set to go in less than five minutes."

She was already walking away and she didn't bother to turn around. "As they are all here to see me, they can damn well wait."

* * *

Ben adjusted the collar of his new, green checked shirt in the mirror and wondered whether he'd already sweated through the powder they'd insisted on puffing all over his face. The speed and efficiency with which he'd been picked up at the ranch, flown in on a private plane, cleared airport security, and driven in a limo to this studio had struck him dumb.

When the door opened, he turned, expecting to see either Ayla, who had picked him up at the airport, or Mr. Meadows, and instead found himself staring right at Silver.

"Hey." He smiled at her like a fool. "Long time no see."

She leaned up against the door and regarded him steadily while he just drank her in. She was wearing a simple pink top and white jeans, and her blond hair was loose around her shoulders. Her expression wasn't altogether friendly.

"Were you coerced into doing this?"

"As in made to come here?" He shrugged. "I was offered the opportunity, and I thought that if it cleared the air for you, *and* stopped my family having to deal with trespassers, then it was worth a shot."

She sighed. "I'm so sorry about what happened on your ranch. Is Calder all right? Was Adam okay?"

He'd forgotten how sweet she could be, and had to restrain himself from marching over and taking her in his arms.

"Spooked a few calves and their mommas, but they got over it."

She bit her lip. "That's terrible."

"It's all good." He shrugged. "Hopefully, we can put it all to rest when we do this press thing." He sat on the edge of the table. “I was surprised that you were okay with seeing me here.”

“I wasn’t.”

“Okay.” Jeez, that hurt more than he had anticipated. “I just thought you might need my help, but if I was wrong—”

“No.” She took a step toward him and then stopped. “That’s not what I meant. No one told me you were going to be here. They probably knew I would freak out and tell them to stop bothering you.”

“We don’t have to go through with this if you don’t want to,” he pointed out. “I can walk out, hop on the bus, and be home in a couple of days, no questions asked.”

“But the press might still come after you.”

“Then let’s do this thing.” He held out his hand. “We’ve got nothing to hide.”

She raised an eyebrow, reminding him that they did, in fact, have a lot to hide, and he didn’t regret a single moment of it.

He couldn’t help but smile at her. “You know what I mean.”

She came toward him and took his outstretched hand, her fingers curling around his.

“You haven’t changed a bit.”

“As I said, it’s only been six weeks.” He drew her even closer until she stood between his thighs. “Everyone sends their love, by the way.”

“Even your dad? I bet he wants to kill me right about now.” She reached out and placed her palm on the front of his shirt. “How are your ribs?”

“All healed up, thanks.”

“How about your head?”

“Concussion’s all gone.”

“You sure about that?” She met his gaze. “Because the

last time I saw you, you appeared to be under the delusion that you were some kind of sex god I would never be able to forget."

"I . . ." He sighed. "I meant it for the best."

"As in, how can I get this annoying woman out of my life as quickly as possible?"

"Yeah, that—without the annoying part."

She considered him for a long moment, her fingers tracing a circle over his heart. "Thank you for coming to help me out here."

"You're welcome." He couldn't look away from her mouth, and leaned very slowly toward her, giving her plenty of time to back away. What was that his dad had said about him hiding from everything because he was too much of a coward to live his own life? "I missed you."

She licked her lips like he was a treat she was looking forward to. "I missed you, too."

A loud knock on the door had her leaping away from him like a gazelle. Mr. Meadows came in, his anxious gaze fixed on Silver.

"You guys ready? The crowd is getting restless out there."

Silver looked back at Ben. "Are you sure you are okay about this? It's going to be wild."

"I'm good if you are." He slid down off the table. "Let's do it."

Two hours later, Silver poured Ben a glass of lemonade and sat down beside him on the couch in her suite. He still had the dazed look of a man caught in the headlights and she couldn't blame him.

"That was . . . unbelievable." He shook his head. "How the hell do you deal with that every day?"

She shrugged. "I've never really known anything else. It doesn't mean I like it, though." She patted his knee. "You did great." He really had. He'd been calm and charming and radiated the kind of honesty that couldn't be rattled by any of the deliberately provocative questions he'd been peppered with.

After the press conference and despite her father's protestations, she'd grabbed hold of Ben's hand, commandeered a car, and brought him back to her house where she knew he'd be safe and she could lock the doors.

"I doubt it. I felt like a fool."

"Only because you made me out to be some kind of hero when I didn't do much at all," Silver scolded him.

His smile was so warm it took her breath away. "I don't care how stupid I look if I get to go back home, and these guys stop bothering me."

"Dad said he'd offered you a two-week vacation in Hawaii," Silver said casually. "Are you going to take it?"

"I wish." He grimaced. "My dad would kill me. I'm hoping to leave as soon as Adam lets me know the coast is clear back home." He cleared his throat. "I think Ayla booked me a hotel somewhere quiet?"

Silver bit her lip. "I was kind of hoping you'd stay here with me—I mean us. We have *way* better security than any hotel, and no one will bother you."

He turned to look at her, his brown eyes wary. "You sure you want me here?"

"It's okay. I'm not going to proposition you or anything." She moved her hand off his knee and scooted back on the couch. "I have two bedrooms in this suite. Ayla sometimes stays over if we're traveling together the next day."

He met her gaze unflinchingly. "The reasons why I

backed off at home haven't changed now that I'm here. I can't live here, and you work here."

Silver just managed to stop her jaw from dropping. "Hold on. Are you trying to say you *considered* having a long-term relationship with me?"

He looked insulted. "Of course I did."

"But you *said* . . ."

"I said what needed to be said at the time to make sure you left mad at me, and nothing has changed, has it?"

She glowered at him, her arms crossed over her chest. "You flat-out lied to me, and let me walk away thinking maybe you'd done this before, and that I was just one of many trail-riding guests you'd slept with?"

"Where the hell did all that come from?" He scowled right back at her. "I've *never* behaved like that with any guests except you! It was totally out of character, and you know it! And, by the way, you walked away looking like you didn't give a damn, either."

She rose up on her knees and pointed at her chest. "Meet the greatest actor in the world!"

He lunged for her at the same time she went for him, and they only narrowly avoided cracking heads before he started kissing her and that was that. She straddled his lap and let him have it, her hands roaming over him, relearning every taut muscle in his body and luxuriating in the feel of him. His hand cupped her ass, pressing her against the hard bulge behind the fly of his jeans as she rocked against him.

"Silver." He finally came up for air. "We shouldn't—"

"Shut up."

She bit his lip and kissed him, her fingernails scratching his scalp as he groaned and let her have her way with him. She inched one hand under his shirt and he shuddered.

"Silver." This time he held on to her hands. "We really do need to talk about this."

She undulated against him. "Then talk."

Ben struggled to draw a breath that didn't smell like Silver, and the heat of her, and the *need* . . .

"I can't give you anything, but sex."

She studied him carefully. "Okay."

"I can't stay in L.A. and be with you."

"So you said." She kissed his nose.

He angled his head against the back of the couch to give him more distance from her, but when she was sitting in his lap with his favorite parts right over his really excited dick it was difficult to think straight.

"You don't care if it's just sex?" he asked cautiously.

"It sounds like that's all you're offering. . . ."

He cupped her chin. "I can't live here, Silver, so how can we have a relationship?"

Her smile faltered and she climbed off his lap, making him want to howl like a wounded animal.

"You're right." She got completely off the couch and started walking away from him. "The spare bedroom is the one on the left, okay? I'll leave you to get settled in while I go and tell my parents you're staying here for a few days."

She walked out, and he closed his eyes, kind of annoyed with himself for being honest, and yet proud that he hadn't just gone ahead and jumped into bed with her. She deserved better. She deserved a man who was always by her side, who supported her one hundred percent, and loved her more than anything in the world.

He could be that man. . . .

He *wanted* to be that man.

Ben got off the couch and headed to the spare room. He'd take his stupid dreams and fantasies, have a cold shower, and remind himself exactly why he preferred to stay out of the limelight. Getting involved with someone again, hurting them, and not being able to do a damn thing about it was too much for him to bear. His father would be annoyed with him for not reaching for what he desperately wanted, but what was new? He'd done what he'd set out to do, which was help Silver out, and that was the end of it.

Silver's mom glanced up as she came into the kitchen. "Would you like something to eat, dear? Dee left us a late lunch, and dinner is already prepped and in the refrigerator."

"I'm not hungry right now." Silver tried to smile. "Ben's going to be staying with us for a few days until he gets the all-clear to go home, okay?"

"I think Ayla booked him a hotel."

"She did, but Ben is staying here. You know as well as I do that the moment he walks out of his hotel room, the press will be all over him. He's much safer with us. I'll go and fetch him in a minute so that you can say hello properly, and he can have some lunch."

"That sounds lovely." She hesitated. "What's wrong, sweetie? I thought it went well today."

Silver sat at the table. "Mom, have you ever really wanted something and you just can't think of a way to have it?"

Her mom joined her. "It depends what you mean by wanting. Sometimes there's a good reason why you can't always get what you want."

"I knew you'd say that." Silver heaved a sigh. "You sound just like Ben."

There was quite a long silence before her mom replied. "He's a very nice young man, Silver. You can see that he has been properly brought up."

"He is nice," Silver agreed. "And way too responsible and honest for his own good."

"Do you like him, sweetie?"

"Yes, but please don't tell Dad. You know what he's like and, as I can't have Ben anyway, you'd just get him all riled up for no reason."

"I'm not sure you can truly *have* anyone," her mom said thoughtfully. "Relationships are built on many things, and one person seeing the other person as a thing to have like a possession isn't going to make for an equal partnership."

"That's not what I meant."

"Well, it sure sounded like it."

Silver sometimes forgot that her sweet-voiced mother had some strong opinions of her own.

"I can't change who I am."

"And neither can Ben," her mom reminded her. "If he's sensible enough to realize that he can't give you what you want, you should respect that."

Silver shoved a hand through her hair and blew out a breath. "I know you're right. I know *he's* right, but it hurts, Mom." Tears gathered in her eyes. "It's been so hard to meet someone I actually like and admire, and when I finally do—somehow I'm not allowed to be happy."

Her mom took hold of her hand. "If you really think he's the right man for you, then you're going to have to think of a way for one of you to compromise, right?"

"I can't think of any way to do that right now," Silver confessed.

"Then maybe this isn't the right time for you both." The

soft regret in her mother's voice made her tears start to fall. "Maybe you should just stay friends."

Later that day, Ben took his place at the table for dinner and was introduced to Aaron and Spring, Silver's siblings. He'd met her mother at lunch and had liked her immediately. She looked like her two blond daughters and seemed happy to stay in the background and not draw attention to herself. Mr. Meadows, who had told Ben to call him Phil, was way more outgoing and was currently dominating the conversation around the table.

Coming from a big family himself, Ben quickly became aware that there were some definite undercurrents buzzing through the interactions, and that maybe there was a reason why Phil was talking so much.

"Well, I have to tell you all that the press conference was a smash hit." Phil smiled broadly at Silver. "Everyone thought Ben was adorable."

"Great. Then hopefully I can go home and not have to deal with those idiots anymore," Ben said.

"So what do you do on your ranch, Ben?" Phil turned to him.

"We're a cattle ranch. We breed cattle and sell beef. That's about it."

"And do you like your job?"

"Ranching is more of a lifestyle choice than a job, Mr. Meadows. You don't get to clock in and out for regular hours, the workload can sometimes be overwhelming and the rewards sparse."

"Sounds a lot like the acting profession," Aaron muttered. "Including all the bullshit."

Ben had to smile at that. Aaron reminded him a lot of

Kaiden. "I've never felt the urge to act so I'll take your word for it."

"So, why do you do it if it's so hard?" Spring spoke up. She was quieter like her mother.

"Because it's in my blood, I suppose," Ben replied. "I can't think of anything I'd rather do."

"Did you ever even try anything else?"

Silver poked her sister. "This isn't an interrogation, Spring."

"It's okay. It's a reasonable question and I don't mind answering it," Ben said. "I went to college on a football scholarship. Realized I wasn't ever going to be good enough to compete professionally and kind of lost interest in the whole idea." He winced. "I dropped out after a couple of years. I missed my home."

"Well, at least you tried something *different*." Spring looked pointedly at her father as she spoke. "Which is what I'm going to do."

"Good for you." Ben nodded, aware again that there was something going on that he was missing. "Ranching might be hard work, but staying in this business must be crazy hard."

"It is," Silver said, and also looked toward her father. "I'm thinking about starting a production company where I can acquire projects that I love rather than having to deal with another person's vision."

Phil set down his fork. "Where did that idea come from?" He glanced at his wife and then at Silver. "You've never mentioned being interested in that before."

"Maybe because I'm twenty-six and I'm now being cast as someone's mother while my male costars get to play parts when they are forty years older than the woman? I'm sick of it, Dad."

"It's only happened once, Silver, and Drew has apologized for Oscar's behavior, and he still wants you for that part." Phil paused. "He called me today to ask why he hadn't heard back from you."

Silver gave an exasperated sigh. "Why is he calling you? Why isn't he calling me directly? I'm not a child and I don't need you controlling my career."

"You *know* why I took control." Phil glanced over at Ben. "And I don't think it's fair for us to be having these discussions in front of our guest, do you?"

Ben met Silver's frustrated gaze and held up his hands. "Hey, don't mind me. I'm from a big family. Sometimes stuff needs to be said."

"You also know that I was telling the truth about not going back on drugs, so you owe me, Dad." Silver pointed her fork at him. "You need to take a step back."

"Yeah," Aaron and Spring chimed in at the same time. "Silver's got this."

"I'm not sure why all this hostility is suddenly being turned on me, but I sure don't appreciate it." Phil stood up. "If you want to talk to Drew, Silver, I suggest you go ahead, and I'll keep out of it."

He nodded stiffly at Ben. "It's been a pleasure getting to know you, son. I hope to see you tomorrow before you go."

As soon as the door shut behind him, Aaron whistled. "Wow, he's in a snit. Maybe we're finally getting through to him."

"You're not being fair." Mrs. Meadows spoke up. "He's very upset that all his hard work for you over the years is suddenly being called into question."

"No one's saying that, Mom," Spring said patiently. "We just all want to do different things, and Dad seems stuck in the past. Silver and I aren't little girls anymore who can be pushed into any project he wants. We've paid our dues and made our money. Silver doesn't need to work for the rest of her life!"

Ben hadn't thought about how wealthy Silver might be, but he sure was thinking about it now. It was just another huge chasm between them when he barely had five thousand bucks in his savings account. She could probably buy the whole of Morgan Valley and not even notice.

"I think you are all being very mean to him," Mrs. Meadows continued. "He's always wanted the best for you."

Silver reached out and took her mom's hand. "Then help him understand that he needs to move on. Don't you want to spend more time with him? Wouldn't you like not to have to be going to auditions and premieres and all that stupid stuff?"

"I suppose that would be nice," Mrs. Meadows admitted. "He's been working so hard for the last twenty years to advance your careers, and he never takes a break or thinks of himself."

"Maybe it's time he did," Silver said softly. "You've raised three, strong-willed successful children, and that's *awesome!* Now it's time to think about what you two want to do with the rest of your lives."

Aaron and Spring were nodding along sympathetically. Ben was struck anew by how kind Silver could be. It was an underrated value, but one that he for one appreciated.

Mrs. Meadows sighed, her expression thoughtful. "I'll think about what you've said, Silver." She glanced over at her other children. "And I'll do my best to help your father understand where you are all coming from. He loves you all very much."

"And we love him," Silver said instantly. "Make sure he knows that, too." She rose to her feet and glanced over at

Ben. "Would you like to come out to the rooftop and watch the sun go down? It's pretty awesome."

"I'd love to."

He went to pick up his plate and Mrs. Meadows reached out to stop him. "Don't worry about any of that. My housekeeper, Dee, will be coming in to clean up."

"Okay, thanks."

Ben cast a dubious eye on the cluttered table and joined Silver who was waiting for him by the door. He hadn't seen much of her since she'd introduced him to her mom and left him there to have lunch. She looked tired and she was definitely back to being careful around him. He couldn't blame her. He hadn't exactly been the perfect guest.

"Follow me."

She led him up three flights of stairs, which left him puffing, and her still breathing easily. They emerged onto the flat roof that had a lap pool on one side, a fake lawn and a putting green on the other.

"This is nice." Ben took his time and turned a slow circle to appreciate the entire view before he focused on the sea and the setting sun.

"I like it. It's why I chose this house." Silver pointed downward. "There are three smaller properties around the main residence. One houses the garage block, and our chauffeur, Mario, and his family live there. Dee lives in the second, and the third was supposed to be my mom and dad's, but they, along with Aaron and Spring moved back into this house after I got addicted and haven't left."

"Would you like them to move back out again?" Ben asked, keeping his gaze on the horizon where the sun was rapidly descending over the Pacific Ocean.

"I think so." She sighed. "Do you think I'm being too harsh with my parents?"

"It's really not my place to comment," he said carefully. "But if you want my opinion? I think you're totally in the right."

She looked up at him and smiled. "Thanks. It's hard to make changes, isn't it? Hard and frightening."

"Yeah." He couldn't help himself and reached out to rub her hunched shoulders. "You're doing okay, Silver, you really are."

She leaned back against him and they watched the sun slide lower and lower until it hit the ocean, and the sky exploded into a kaleidoscope of oranges, pinks, reds, and yellows that rivaled the most amazing art treasures in the world.

She turned in his arms and looked up at him.

"Will you kiss me?"

"Silver—" His regret dripped off his voice.

She put her finger on his lips. "I know it looks like we can't be together. I know that you are going back home soon. I don't like it, and I don't see a way to solve it right now, but I still want to be with you. Does that make sense?"

"But don't you think it will just make things harder?" He cupped her chin. "Like if we do this again, we'll want even more?"

Her slow smile took him by surprise.

"Well, that's kind of my plan, that at some point we'll *have* to work out a solution because we can't bear not being together." Her gaze was both shy and uncertain now. "Do you think I'm nuts?"

He thought through her logic and looked consideringly back at her. Maybe she was on to something. "Nope."

"No, you don't agree?"

"No, you're not nuts."

"That's great." She leaned in and kissed him gently on the lips. "Will you come to bed with me?"

He nodded like a fool. "I'd like that very much."

Chapter Eighteen

Silver made sure that every door and window to her suite was locked, and that the blinds and drapes were firmly closed. She loved her family, but this thing between her and Ben was way too precious and private to share. She knew her mom would keep her secrets, and that was enough family involvement for now.

He'd stopped by the fireplace and stood looking down at her, his brown eyes heating as she slowly stripped off her T-shirt. She pointed at the couch.

"Sit."

He did what she asked and leaned his head back so that he could still look at her. He made a gesture with his hand. "Keep going."

She was proud of her body—she'd worked hard for it—and the thought of stripping for him was totally turning her on. She shimmied out of her white jeans and strolled over toward him. He licked his lips as if he was already anticipating tasting her. His breath hitched as she straddled him, her lace-covered breasts just grazing his chest.

"May I touch?" he asked hoarsely.

"Not yet." She eased one button of his shirt free. "Is this new?"

"Yeah, Ayla gave me a couple of shirts to wear at the

press thing when I arrived. She said this one made my eyes look good, but I liked the green one better." He paused as she started on the second button. "Do you think she wants it back?"

Silver concealed a smile as she nuzzled his throat. He smelled like sunshine and leather. "No, I don't think it would fit her. It's all yours."

She slowly pulled the shirt aside to reveal his chest and abs and sighed. "I'd forgotten how great you look." She leaned in and kissed his ribs. "Did your ribs heal okay?"

"Apparently." He breathed out hard as she bit his nipple. "Are you sure I can't touch you?"

She undid his cuffs and pulled the back of his shirt free from his jeans before taking it completely off. His jeans sat low on his hips and she could see the beginning of his Adonis lines disappearing below his belt. She hummed low in her throat and pressed her breasts against his chest, capturing his mouth in a searing, needy kiss.

He groaned her name, one of his hands coming down to touch her hair before he pulled it back. "You're killing me, here."

"You deserve everything you get, Mr. Sex God," she reminded him severely as she figured out how to undo the silver buckle on his belt and slip the leather free. Her fingers brushed against the hard bulge in his jeans and he instinctively rocked his hips. She took her time unzipping his jeans to reveal black, cotton boxers that were straining to contain his growing shaft.

She pushed him down onto his back and licked a slow trail from his now-hard nipples, over his hips, and down to her ultimate goal. If this was going to be the last time she made love with him, she was going to savor every second. He was watching her through half-closed eyes, his hands clenched into fists with his effort not to touch her or take over. She licked the wet patch on his boxers and used her teeth to pull down the fabric.

Suddenly anxious, she looked up at him. "Am I doing this right?"

His smile was desperate. "If you do it any more right, I'll come right now."

"Oh, don't do that. I've got a lot planned for you."

His laugh broke off as she sucked the crown into her mouth, remembering the taste of him, the scent of the outdoors that hadn't left him even in the heart of the city. She took more, gripping his hip as he tried not to surge forward and allowed her to take him at her own pace and in her own time.

She hummed her appreciation, and he buried his hand in her hair, his fingers flexing with each pull of her lips as she brought him closer and closer to completion. His hand tightened on her scalp.

"You don't have to—"

She wasn't listening. She'd already decided to have it all and no one was going to stop her. He surged forward and that was it; he came hard, and she took everything he gave her, only easing away when he finally went still.

"Are you okay?" Silver asked, studying his bemused face. "Did I do it right?"

"You—" He sat up so suddenly that she almost shrieked and rolled her onto her back. "You are going to pay for that."

She smiled sweetly at him as he took off his jeans and boxers and crouched naked over her. Her smile faltered as he cupped her between the legs.

"You're wet for me."

"Well, duh."

He bent down to kiss her, sharing his taste, giving her so much more. "I'm going to go so slow that you are going to be begging me, *begging* me, Silver, to let you come."

"I think I'm ready to come right now, actually," she murmured between his kisses, pushing shamelessly against the palm of his hand. "Just stay right where you are. . . ."

He removed his hand and slowly shook his head. "Not happening yet, babe." His appreciative gaze swept her body. "I've got a lot of territory to cover before I get to there, so settle down, and buckle up."

Ben woke up in Silver's bed and smiled into the darkness. They'd made love three times. Once on the couch and twice in the vast California king-sized bed. He was tired, but also deeply happy. He wasn't sure what to make of their current relationship, but as Silver said, if it worked for them then it was no one else's business.

He glanced down at her tousled blond hair and kissed the top of her head. She was special and he didn't want to lose her. He hadn't heard back from Adam yet. He wondered whether he'd get the all-clear to return when he checked his phone in the morning. There was no reason for anyone to hang out at their ranch now that the media had met him and heard the true story of where Silver had been. Hopefully she'd get the movie role she'd been after, her reputation restored, and he'd get to go home and get shouted at by his father.

Unless he took the job at Pablo's place. . . .

He'd told Silver about it earlier, and she'd thought he should take it, too. If he had his own place, and if she could get away, maybe she could come and see him occasionally.

The realization that they still hadn't really solved

anything except the sex hit him hard. Could he live with it? Did he have a choice? If they stayed together could they somehow find a way to make it work? He was a world champ at not stirring the waters and of letting things slide so he should be good at this. No one at home would understand what he was doing, and his father would pick at him endlessly.

"Are you awake?" Silver whispered.

"Yeah."

"I thought so." She stroked his chest. "I could hear you thinking too much. Your body got all tense."

"You know me, always looking for ways to make myself miserable," he said lightly, which didn't even fool himself.

"So, tell me." She rolled onto her side and looked at him, pushing her hair out of her eyes.

"There's no point in making you miserable, too."

"Ben . . . if we're going to make this work, we're going to have to be honest with each other, okay?" She reached out and stroked his nose. "If you're worried about something, just say it."

He took a deep breath. "Okay, what do I tell my family? Are we keeping this a secret?"

"I wasn't planning on mentioning it to mine, but I think that's up to you."

"Why won't you tell your family?" Ben asked. "Don't you think they might notice that we've been holed up in here together for two days?"

"I've sort of told my mom," Silver admitted. "I'll probably tell Aaron and Spring later, but not my dad."

"And how come Aaron didn't get a stupid name like you and Spring did?" Ben demanded.

"Oh, he did." She grinned. "He just refuses to answer

to it, and this has nothing to do with him, so please stop changing the subject. What else?"

"The logistics."

"Of getting together?" She nodded. "Yes, I can see where that might get a little complicated, but you'd be amazed what money can do for your privacy and security. The Morgans have a fully functional landing strip on their ranch, don't they?"

"Yeah, Chase Morgan has a private jet and he flies back and forth from the Bay Area all the time. Daisy sometimes hitches a ride. What about it?"

"I can arrive there with no one the wiser. You can meet me and we can go back to your place." She shrugged. "Or I can send the plane, you can get on it, and we can meet anywhere you like."

"You make it sound so easy, but how am I going to explain that to my dad?" Ben asked.

"That's up to you." Her smile dimmed. "As I said, if you want this to work, you're going to have to make some choices as well."

"What if it all gets too much?" Now that he'd started yakking Ben didn't seem able to shut up.

"Then we'll say good-bye and know that we did everything we could to try and make it work, and that it just wasn't meant to be."

He stared at her, aware of the lightening sky behind the shades and the promise of dawn.

"You're pretty amazing, you know that?" Ben said quietly. "I'm supposed to be older than you, and yet you outthink and outshine me at every turn."

"I had to grow up fast." She shrugged. "In an industry that doesn't like failure and where you're completely expendable."

"And I grew up on a ranch where my dad ran my mom

off the property when I was eleven, and nothing was the same after that." He sighed. "Maybe that's why I'm always looking for the problems." Every time he stepped out of his comfort zone and tried to be more spontaneous, he messed up.

"Can I ask you something?" Silver looked at him expectantly.

Ben nodded.

"You said your mom left, but when I was at the ranch you were talking to her on the phone."

"She came back into our lives a year or so ago. She lives in New York and has another daughter."

"Seven kids?" Silver shuddered. "What a hero. So, is she nice?"

"Yeah, and she's a lot happier, and she doesn't take any shit from my dad anymore."

"Was it weird for you—her coming back like that?"

Ben considered what to say. "I thought I'd be okay about it, but when she actually turned up? It kind of churned things up for me a bit."

"Like old memories and resentments and fear?"

"How did you know?" Ben asked.

She shrugged. "Because childhood trauma is a big deal according to every therapist I've ever visited, and your mom walking out? That's a doozy."

"She didn't really want to leave. She wanted to teach my dad a lesson—except he didn't get it, and made no effort to apologize, or ask her to come back, so she really left him and went to live in New York with her brother." Ben grimaced. "Dad basically refused to speak her name, so for years we all thought she was dead, except—" He abruptly stopped talking.

"Except what?"

Ben just stared at her until she jabbed him in the chest with her fingernail.

"Ouch." He glared at her. "What was that for?"

"Honesty, remember? You can tell me anything, and I promise I will never tell another soul."

He rubbed a hand over the back of his neck. "I've never told anyone this before, but when I walked out of college, I decided I'd take a trip to the East Coast to see my mom. I accidentally saw a letter she'd written to Dad once, and I . . . copied the address, and kept it. I was angry with her and I had this stupid idea in my head that I was going to confront her and tell her how I felt."

"And?"

"Things kind of went wrong on the road trip. I ended up having to give my mom's address to the cops in Pennsylvania, and thank God, she came to get me." He grimaced. "She also called my dad. You can imagine how that went down."

"But she did come and get you," Silver said softly.

"Yeah." He met her gaze as he thought about that for the first time. "She did."

His phone buzzed and he rolled over to turn it off. "Forgot to cancel my alarm." He noticed a text from Adam and paused to read it. "Excuse me."

He set the phone down and turned to Silver who was watching him intently.

"Adam says I should give it another day just to be sure, and then I can head back."

Silver's smile was glorious. "Then if you are willing to get rid of your cowboy hat and blend in with the crowd, you and I can spend the day together."

* * *

Silver had learned long ago how to dress down and not draw attention to herself. Despite some celebrities saying they could never get out without being spotted, Silver tended to think those people just couldn't bear not to be noticed. Ben had only been in Southern California once on a school trip, and, as Silver had lived there her whole life, she was eager to show him her city. She'd also found that a lot of the places she liked to go were perfectly happy to let her be, and not get in her face.

It was even more fun showing Ben the small restaurants, the ice cream place she loved, the stretch of beach not overwhelmed by tourists and flashy locals. They picked up lunch and went and sat on the flat rocks overlooking the sea just like any other young couple.

"It's beautiful out here," Ben reluctantly admitted, and she did a little dance of triumph and stuck her finger in his face.

"You see? I told you it wasn't all bad."

He grinned at her. "You're still the best part of it, though."

She leaned in and kissed him, and that took a while before she sat back and finished her lunch.

"What are we going to do this afternoon?" Ben asked as he finished his bottle of water.

"Are you up for some culture?"

"As in what?" He looked wary.

"Have you ever been to the Getty?" Silver asked.

His brow creased. "Nope. Do I want to?"

"Haven't I done you right so far?" she demanded. "It's the most fabulous place, and the views over the city are spectacular."

"Okay, I trust you." He allowed her to pull him to his feet. "But we'd better get back soon, because we definitely need a nap before dinner."

Chapter Nineteen

Ben woke up at his usual time of five A.M. and realized he was starving. Seeing as Silver had told him to help himself to breakfast whenever he wanted, he decided to leave her to sleep and go and eat. He'd bring her a tray up with a flower and everything; she'd probably like that.

He took a quick shower and got dressed before padding out in his socks down the hallways and stairs to the lower level where the huge kitchen and family room occupied half the floor.

"Oh!" A diminutive woman pressed her hand to her chest and stared at him from behind the countertop. "Who are you?"

"I'm Ben Miller. I've been staying here for a couple of days." He smiled reassuringly at her. "Silver said it would be okay for me to come down and get some breakfast. I'm used to getting up early."

"You're Silver's young man! The cowboy who was on the news with her!" She finally smiled at him. "I'm Dee, the housekeeper. Now, what can I get you to eat? I've already started the coffee. Mr. Meadows sometimes gets up early so I'm always ready for him."

"I can get something myself; I don't need to bother

you." Ben was speaking to air as she opened the huge refrigerator and started getting stuff out.

"I have fresh fruit and granola, or I can cook you eggs, or maybe a breakfast burrito?" She eyed him speculatively. "If you work outside you can probably eat a lot. My brother works on a ranch out in the Gold Country up north."

"Yeah?" Ben gave up his attempts to be independent and settled down on one of the stools drawn up against the countertop. "I live in Morgan Valley. It's near Bridgeport."

"I know where that is." She nodded and passed him a bowl. "Help yourself to the fruit and yogurt while I get to work on your eggs."

Ben was just finishing up his second plateful of food when Silver's dad came in. He halted when he saw Ben, a strange expression on his face.

"Just the person I was looking for! Is Silver up?"

"I think she was still asleep. Her door was closed when I went past." Ben wasn't really lying. He'd shut the door himself.

"Good." Phil turned to Dee. "Good morning, my dear. Can I have my coffee to go?" He nodded at Ben. "I need to have a chat with this guy before I can eat properly."

Ben slid off the stool, thanked Dee profusely, picked up his own coffee, and followed Phil through the silent house to his office. Ben paused on the threshold, taking in the photos of Silver and her siblings, the awards they'd won, and the film posters.

"Wow, this is some collection," Ben said as he closed the door.

Phil was now sitting behind his desk, his hands folded in front of him. He gestured at the chair.

"Please sit."

"Thanks." Ben took the chair. "If you're worried about

me overstaying my welcome, I'm expecting to leave today. Adam said everything's cool at home."

Phil made a face. "I'm sorry to have to tell you this, Ben, but that might not be the case for much longer."

"What's happened?" Ben set his coffee down.

"After you appeared at the press conference, a lot of the sites wanted to know all about you because they decided there was something going on between you and Silver." He sighed. "Unfortunately, they found out quite a lot more than they bargained for."

There was a hollow sensation in Ben's gut, which made him wish he hadn't eaten so much breakfast.

"I'm not following."

Phil picked up a sheet of paper. "'Ben Miller, not the hometown sweetheart Silver might think he is.' That's the headline on *Reality Bites* this morning. Would you like me to go on?" He started reading again. "'Ben Miller, the oh-so-charming cowboy rescued by Silver Meadows, isn't exactly a stranger to captivating wealthy women. The last time he got entangled with a rich beauty, she ended up dead, and dear sweet Ben was sued by his honey's parents. Maybe someone should warn Silver before it's too late.'"

Ben met Phil's gaze. "That's not what happened."

"Ben." Phil set down the pen he'd been fiddling with. "I got Ayla to do some checking, and this might be a sensationalized version of what did occur, but you *were* sued, and Cassie Walker, one of the Walker stores' heiresses, was in your company when she died."

"I wasn't convicted of anything. Cassie's parents were mad with grief and looking for someone to blame. I just happened to be there at the end, and they went after me." Ben kept his voice low and calm. "I was nineteen, Mr. Meadows, and so was she. We went to Stanford together. Her life was a mess long before she met me. I got dragged into a situation that was way too heavy for me to deal with."

"Look, son." Mr. Meadows sat forward. "I'm not here to argue the ins and outs of something that happened all those years ago. All I know is that this mustn't hurt Silver. She's barely managed to get through the latest scandal, and I don't want her being hit by another."

"I get that." Ben nodded. "You're her father, you want the best for her and so do I."

"Which is why I'd like you to leave right away." Phil watched him intently. "And I want your promise that you won't attempt to contact her again."

"I don't think that's up to you, Mr. Meadows," Ben said slowly. "Silver's a grown woman. She deserves to be treated like one. If I'm going to leave, she deserves to know why."

The door opened and Silver came in carrying a mug of coffee. "What's going on, Dad?" She glanced over at Ben. "Dee said you hadn't eaten because you needed to talk to Ben."

Phil smiled at his daughter. "There's nothing for you to worry about, honey. I was just making sure Ben had all the necessary details for his ride home. I've got to go out early this morning, and I didn't want anything to get messed up."

Silver turned to Ben, her smile bright. "It's a shame you've got to leave. I really enjoyed seeing you again."

"Likewise." Ben shifted in his seat. Despite Phil's insinuations, he wasn't ready to give up on her that easily. "Maybe we can keep in touch?"

"Oh, I don't know about that, Ben," Phil said quickly. "Silver's a very busy woman."

"That's not your decision to make, Dad." Silver met her father's gaze. "If I want to see Ben again, I will."

Phil sighed. "I wish I'd never suggested you do that trail ride."

"You didn't." Silver said. "It was my idea. You just organized the details and you did a great job." She paused. "What's your problem?"

Phil ignored his daughter and continued looking at Ben. "When I told you Silver had a drug problem and asked for your help, I didn't realize I was asking completely the wrong guy to keep her safe."

Silver stiffened. "You knew about that, Ben?"

"Yeah." Ben met her gaze. "But—"

"And you didn't mention it when I was pouring my heart out to you about how I thought my dad was deliberately trying to sabotage my interest in a more versatile career?"

Phil stood up. "Hey! I—"

Silver ignored her father and focused on Ben. "Answer the damn question."

"I promised him I wouldn't tell you I knew." Ben wasn't going to lie about something that now seemed so unimportant compared to the rest of the deep shit he was currently in.

"Did you send back reports on me to him?"

Shit. From the stricken expression on her face, Silver obviously didn't think it was minor at all.

He shrugged. "I did go through your stuff right at the beginning of the trip just to make sure you hadn't brought anything illegal with you, but after that? I just kept my eye on you."

She looked so damn hurt that he wanted to go over, take her in his arms, and just apologize again and again until she forgave him, but if he did that, Phil would know that they were more than friends and bring out the big guns.

"I *trusted* you," Silver said.

"And I told your dad when we got back that you didn't do anything on the whole trip to make me think you were still doing drugs," Ben countered.

"That's not the point and you know it." She glared at him. "We promised to be honest with each other."

Phil cleared his throat and looked from Silver to Ben. "Are you trying to tell me that you two are involved?"

"No!" Silver flung out her hand and spoke over Ben. "We're supposed to be friends!"

Ben almost wished she'd said yes because the thought that she didn't want to admit to her father that they were seeing each other stung. It was his turn to look at her.

"Honesty?"

She had the grace to blush. "You *know* why I'm doing this. What I don't understand is why you lied to me. I feel like I was spied on the whole time. I thought Dad was finally starting to believe I could take care of myself, but instead he'd just set me up with an alternative nanny."

"It wasn't like that." Ben desperately tried to regroup. "Maybe you should have more faith in me."

"Like you do in me?" She shook her head.

"I'm trying." He held her gaze, ignoring her father as best he could. "This isn't a big deal, *okay?* There are way worse things—"

She turned to her father, tied the sash of her robe more tightly around her waist, and headed for the door.

"I'm really disappointed in you, Dad, but I suppose I should've expected this."

"Silver . . ." Phil reached out his hand but she ignored him and looked at Ben.

"I'm going to work out with my trainer. Let me know when you're leaving, so that I can come and say good-bye."

She stormed out and Ben took one step toward the door. "Silver . . ."

"Hold on there, son." Phil came around the desk and blocked his path. "Let's just think this through before you go rushing off upsetting her again."

"You upset her. You refuse to allow her to be a fully functioning adult." Ben was beyond being polite now. "I need to explain before she reads all this stuff about me—"

"Why?" Phil spread his hands wide. "Why not leave it as it is? Go home, have a good life, let Silver have hers, and I won't say a single thing about what you did when you were a teen."

Ben felt like someone had sucked all the air out of his lungs.

"Excuse me?"

"You know what I'm saying, Ben. Ayla and I will make sure Silver doesn't see any of the gossip about you that's out there, and in return, you will go back home and leave her be." Phil smiled at him. "If you really are her friend, wouldn't that be for the best?"

"How can she not see stuff?" Ben protested. "If it really is out there, someone will eventually tell her."

"But by that time, you'll be home and, Ben, I hate to say this, but when she reads about what you did, I doubt she's going to want to call you." Phil sounded almost sympathetic, but Ben wasn't buying it. "If you leave now, she might be in a snit with you, but if she gets over it you might hear from her again." Phil returned to sit behind his desk. "Although, if you're the kind of man I think you are, you won't respond to her."

Ben swallowed hard. "You've got this all planned out, then?"

"I love my daughter very much, and I just want the best for her." Phil held his gaze; the sincerity in his voice was undeniable.

"And you think you know what she needs better than she does?"

"In this case, yes." He sighed. "Ben, I've got to be honest here, I don't want her hanging around with anyone who enables drug use."

"I never did that," Ben repeated. He'd been put through hell once by the Walkers' lawyers and survived with his reputation intact. He wasn't going to let Phil Meadows undermine him. "Despite all the Walker family's power and money, I was not prosecuted because no judge found any evidence that I aided or abetted Cassie's drug use."

Phil nodded. "As I said, I'm not here to argue about that. All I care about is Silver, and I'll do what I have to do to keep her safe, happy, and well." His gaze hardened. "Please, take my advice, and leave, and Silver will never need to know anything."

Ben didn't answer directly, but walked out, his mind circling in an endless spiral of conflicting arguments. He should tell Silver himself; she'd believe him—wouldn't she? She'd asked for honesty, but right now she thought he'd gone behind her back and sided with her father and might not be amenable to him trying to justify what had happened with Cassie. He wasn't very good at keeping people around or keeping them safe, so why the hell would Silver want to stick with him anyway?

He went up to the suite, packed his bag, and paced the carpet in an agony of indecision. Eventually, he picked up his phone, and called the last person in the world he really wanted to talk to, but the only person who knew the whole story of what had gone down in his teens.

"Dad?"

"Who else? What's wrong, son?"

Ben sank down onto the couch where he'd recently made love to Silver.

"I need your advice."

Jeff snorted. "First time in a long while you've needed that, but go ahead. What mess have you gotten yourself into now?"

"Silver's dad found out about what happened with Cassie. He's threatening to tell Silver unless I come home and never talk to her again."

"Well, crap."

Ben waited for what seemed like an age before his father started speaking again.

"Why can't you just tell her yourself?"

"Because she's already pissed with me because she found out I was keeping an eye out for drug use on our trail ride." Ben hesitated. "She's going to hate me when she finds out about Cassie. You know what the Walkers did to me in the press. Now it's all been turned up again and I look like a complete shit."

"Then come home."

"Without trying to sort it out with her?"

"Yeah."

Ben waited hopefully, but there was nothing but air. "That's *it?* That's your advice?"

"No point beating a dead horse. Come home, take that job with Pablo, and get yourself together."

"But what about Silver?"

"You care for her, right?"

"*Yes.*"

"Then if she's as smart as you think she is, she'll work it out and come and find you. If she doesn't, then you've lost nothing."

Ben opened and closed his mouth a few times, and then shook his head even though his father couldn't see him.

"Thanks for nothing."

"You're welcome. I'll see you later today and you can

get started on the eastern fence line. You'll get a lot done before the light fades."

Silver finished her workout and went back up to her suite to take a shower and change. She'd asked her trainer to make things tough for her, which had stopped her from thinking too hard about both her dad and Ben's behavior. But she couldn't avoid the subject forever, and she still didn't know what to do.

Ben hadn't been honest with her about his role on their trip, but she had flat-out denied they were in a relationship to her father right in front of him. She was fairly certain he'd been about to say yes, and she'd almost shouted over him to get her father's attention.

It hurt that despite their closeness, he hadn't told her that he'd been both guide and watchdog. She'd thought he was different—that he valued her over Team Meadows. But, now that she'd calmed down, she was still willing to listen to his side of the story—if he wanted to give it to her. She might have overreacted a bit to get her dad from thinking there was something going on between them.

"Ben?" She walked into her suite and immediately knew he wasn't there. She forced herself to check out the bedrooms and bathroom before she returned to the couch beside the fireplace and noticed the note with her name on it. She picked it up, her hands trembling, and unfolded it.

Dear Silver, thanks for everything. <u>I mean it.</u> You are an amazing woman, and I'm proud that you allowed me to get to know you. I'm sorry for letting you down and I wish you nothing but the best. All my love, Ben. X.

She refolded the note and dropped it onto the couch, her mind slowing as she struggled to deal with the fact that he'd gone without saying good-bye to her.

"How *could* you?" she whispered. "Why aren't you here giving me some lame-ass excuses that I'll believe because I care about you?"

She turned around and went back down the stairs to her office where Ayla was typing away on her tablet.

"Silver!" Ayla jumped like the guilty person she was. "Is everything okay?"

"You know it isn't." Silver kept her voice low and calm. "What time did Ben leave?"

"About forty-five minutes ago." Ayla swallowed hard. "He's already in the air."

Silver nodded as her throat closed. Ayla set down her tablet. "Mr. Meadows arranged everything. He just told me to follow through."

She wanted to ask how Ben had been, how he'd looked, whether he'd given any damn indication that he cared about leaving her, but she wasn't sure she was in the right mindset to expose herself to Ayla by asking the questions.

"I'm sorry, Silver," Ayla whispered. "I didn't know what to do, and you don't usually like being interrupted when you're in the gym."

"That's a really lame excuse." Silver said. "Maybe you'd better work out where your allegiances lie because I don't need someone around me who carries out my father's orders without consulting me."

Ayla's lip wobbled. "I thought—*we* thought it was for the best, because . . ."

"Because all you care about is my career, right?" Silver went to find her phone, which she'd left recharging on the desk. "Where's my cell?"

"Mr. Meadows knocked it off the desk this morning

and broke the screen. He took it with him when he left." Ayla looked like she was about to burst into tears. "He said to say sorry and that he'd ordered you a new one, and he'd pick it up on his way home tonight."

Silver fought the urge to scream at yet another example of her father's high-handedness.

"I'm going to take a shower. Text my dad and make sure he knows I'm waiting on that phone."

She turned away and Ayla cleared her throat.

"There is one more thing."

"What's that? Did you arrange to have Ben's plane blow up in the air or something? So that he wouldn't bother me again?"

A tear slid down Ayla's cheek. "I'm so sorry, Silver."

Silver held up her hand. She really wasn't interested in making her assistant feel better about her choices when it felt like someone was jumping all over her heart.

"What thing?"

"Inola called. She wants you to meet her, the production team, and the rest of the potential cast in Utah."

Even the thought that she'd possibly gotten the role of her life didn't make her feel better. "Sure. When do I need to go?"

"This afternoon, actually." Ayla rushed to show her two sets of travel documents. "It's top secret so they've only told people today."

"Fine. Call me when it's time to leave."

"Oh, and Silver?" Ayla said. "The Internet and electricity will be down for the next few hours. Dee reported a problem in the kitchen and health and safety said we have to turn everything off."

"Great." She turned to the door. "I'm going to take a nap. Wake me up when we're leaving."

She made her way back up the stairs, aware that her

body was hurting, and that all she really wanted to do was go to bed and cry herself to sleep. She hadn't slept much the night before because she and Ben . . . She pushed the thought of him smiling down at her away. If he could walk out without a care in the world over such a minor disagreement, then he didn't deserve her thoughts.

She turned on the shower and stripped off her workout clothes, her gaze settling on her reflection where the rough abrasions of Ben's beard still showed on her skin. She was not going to cry over him. If he didn't have the balls to stand up and have it out with her, then he wasn't the man she'd thought he was, and he didn't deserve her.

She'd told him that their relationship would only survive if they both tried their best to make it work. It seemed that he'd given up at the first roadblock. She knew he doubted he was worthy of being loved, and that he feared being abandoned, but at some point he had to believe in *something*. . . .

Obviously, it wasn't her.

She'd pushed him too hard. She'd demanded he respond to her because she still thought she was a star who could get anything she wanted. Maybe he hadn't agreed with anything she'd said, and he'd just gone along with her stupid fantasies to avoid an argument. She stepped into the shower and turned her face into the water where she could pretend she wasn't crying at all.

Ben had been right all along. She couldn't have everything she wanted. And, in his own particular way, he'd made damn sure to drive that message home.

Chapter Twenty

Whenever he entered the house, Ben obsessively checked his cell just in case there was a text or a call from Silver. As the days went by, and she didn't contact him, he only felt more anxious about her. Had she seen the news stories? To his relief, they'd only lasted a day or so before some other fool had captured the media's obsessive attention. He wondered whether Phil Meadows had anything to do with that, and wouldn't have been surprised. Despite everything, Ben truly did believe that Phil would do anything for his children.

His dad had welcomed him back with his usual lack of enthusiasm and a to-do list as long as his arm. Ben sometimes wondered whether his father was using his old trick of making him so exhausted that he fell into bed every night and slept like the dead. He had no time to check up on social media, and he guessed his father had told his siblings not to ask him anything because they'd all remained unusually quiet.

Ben put his cell away and went into the kitchen. He was ravenous because he'd been out at five and hadn't had much time to eat with his father shouting at him to get a move on. It was now noon, and Jeff had reluctantly allowed him to go back to the ranch for an hour to pick up fresh fencing supplies and check that his mother had arrived for her visit.

"Ben! Darling!" Leanne came over and gave him a hug. She was the only one in the family who had as much red in her hair as he did. She was petite like Daisy, but her father had been very tall, which was where all her sons got their height from, much to his dad's annoyance. "I hear you've been to L.A.!"

"Yeah." He hugged her awkwardly back. She didn't seem at all surprised to see him and he wondered if his dad had set him up. "How was your trip?"

"It was great!" She went over to the refrigerator and looked at him expectantly. "What can I get you to eat?"

He followed her over. "It's okay, I can feed myself. Why don't you sit down and relax?"

"Because I've been sitting down for eight hours?" She smiled up at him. "And I missed out on taking care of you for twenty years so let me coddle you just a little bit?"

He sat down at the table and scrubbed a hand over his hat-flattened hair. Everyone else was still out, which meant it was just him and his mom, which was kind of weird.

"There are some hamburgers, or I can make you a sandwich?" Leanne looked back at him inquiringly.

"A sandwich sounds good. I don't care what you put in it."

"As long as it's not pickles, right? You always hated those."

She poured him a glass of milk like he was five, set out a bowl of chips, and eventually handed him three rounds of sandwiches.

"Thanks."

"I know how hard you work, and how hungry you get." Leanne sat opposite him, a cup of coffee in her hand and her own small sandwich on a plate in front of her. "Jeff said he was keeping you real busy."

"He's trying to get his money's worth out of me before I go off and work for Pablo." Ben bit into his first sandwich and devoured it in three bites. "This is great. Thanks."

"He thinks it will be good for you." Leanne sipped her coffee. "He says it's time for you to step out from Adam's shadow and make your own life."

Ben stopped chewing. "Dad said that?"

"He might be difficult sometimes, Ben, but he is very aware with what's going on with all you kids." She sighed. "After I left, he had no choice but to be involved, whether he wanted to or not. He told me about what's been happening with Silver Meadows."

Ben just stared at her. She was the first member of his family to mention Silver's name since he'd got back a week ago.

"I saw the press conference you did with her." Leanne continued as if unaware that she was treading on dangerous ground. "She really likes you."

"She did." Ben drank some milk.

"Did she read all that crap about you and Cassie Walker and believe it?" Leanne shook her head. "Well, if she did, she wasn't the right woman for you anyway."

"I'd forgotten you knew about that," Ben confessed as he wiped away his milk moustache.

"How could I forget?" She shuddered. "You and that . . . girl in that awful, squalid hotel. You were so afraid. I'm so glad I brought Declan with me, and we were able to get everything straightened out with the police."

"Yeah, because if you hadn't insisted that the police and medics do everything by the book, I would be in jail right now." His appetite faded and he met her gaze properly for the first time. "I don't think I've ever said thank you for that."

She shrugged. "You didn't need to. I'm just glad you had my address and reached out to me."

"I was coming to see you," Ben said. "Did I tell you that? I found out you weren't dead, and that Dad was communicating with you, and I kept it to myself. When I got kicked out of Stanford, I was so screwed up that I decided I'd drive across the country to find you and tell you to your face what an awful person you were." He grimaced. "What a stupid ass."

"You almost made it," she said. "I would've been delighted to see you even if you had been mad at me. You had cause."

"I thought I did, but Dad wasn't exactly honest about why you left, and why you stayed away, was he?" Ben reminded her. "If you hadn't come back, we would never have known that he ran you off and refused to let you see your own kids."

"We both made mistakes, Ben, and we've both owned up to them and forgiven each other." She sighed. "The worst thing is the damage that it did to all you kids. I *hate* that."

"We're okay." Ben took another sip of milk. "We survived."

He didn't need to tell her how hard it had been for them, the knowledge of that was already etched on her face, and he'd never been the kind of guy who deliberately set out to hurt people. If his parents could finally work out how to get along, he wasn't going to spoil it.

"After Dad came and took me home, I just wanted to hide away and die," Ben confessed. "But I wasn't even allowed to do that because the Walker family came after me." He paused. "Did you pay for my lawyers?"

"Declan did," Leanne confirmed. "He knew how much you all meant to me, and he also knew the Walkers personally." She hesitated. "Having been through losing his own son to drugs, he knew they would focus their anger on someone, and he guessed it would be you."

She found a smile. "In the end, when they were flatly refusing to accept defeat even though not a court in the state would touch the case, Declan went to see them and laid it all out there. He told them that destroying another life would not bring their daughter back, that they'd be better off joining him in fighting the drug dealers and cartels who had provided the drugs to her. Mrs. Walker finally listened to him, and that was the end of it."

"Thanks, Mom." Ben reached across the table and took her hand. "I wish I'd had a chance to thank Declan, too."

Tears filled her eyes. "Don't worry. I thanked him enough for both of us."

"I'm glad you found him, Mom. I really am. He was a good man."

"Thank you." She patted his hand and smiled brightly. "Now, tell me all about Silver Meadows, and why everything went wrong."

Silver took a swig of water and went over to where Inola was standing staring down at her script. She'd been in Utah for a week, and the experience had been both terrifying and enlightening. Maybe because her personal life was in disarray, she hadn't had time to be nervous and had just jumped right in with the rehearsals and enjoyed everything immensely.

"Is everything okay?" Silver asked.

"Not really." Inola grimaced. "We're on a really tight

budget for this movie and one of our co-producers from one of the cable networks just pulled out."

"Crap." Silver meant it. "Does that mean we can't go ahead?"

"I'm hoping we can find someone else to invest in us." Inola looked up at Silver. "By the way, you're doing great. Everyone likes you, you don't put on any airs, and you're nailing the part."

Silver clasped her water bottle like someone had handed her an Oscar. "Really? That means a lot. I get what Minnie is going through so well right now." The movie was set during the desperate struggle for survival of the women who had followed their men out west into a dust bowl.

"Silver? Can you run through this with Kaya?" Mike, the director called out to her.

She handed off her water to Inola and went to join her fellow actor, Kaya. Her name came from the Hopi language and meant Big Sister, and she certainly liked to mother the crew even though she was the same age as Silver. Kaya grinned at her. "In this scene we're fighting over who gets to eat this skinny rabbit."

"This should be fun." Silver grinned back and looked over at Mike. "Can we really go for it?"

"Sure. We can always dial it back when we shoot the scene."

An hour later, after the toy they'd been practicing with was nothing more than a pile of stuffing, Silver went to her tent. It was the same brand she'd shared with Ben. Every time she crawled in she kind of hoped he'd be in there, too. Inola and Mike had chosen to set up camp in the middle of a desert as far away from civilization as they could manage. Her ability to not only put up her own tent, but start a fire and cook over it had definitely impressed them, so she should thank Ben for something. . . .

She still didn't have her phone, and she couldn't say she was missing it much. If it was in her hand right now she'd probably be checking up on Ben or re-watching the press conference when he'd sat alongside her in his new green shirt, his hard thigh touching hers, and answered questions with his usual calm humor.

She lay on her back and looked up at the roof. Ayla had wanted to stay with her, but Silver had sent her back to L.A. to get on with their new business venture. She needed to be away from everyone because her focus was on the movie, and not thinking about Ben. It was easier not to think about him and the fact that she'd run away rather than deal with it.

"Which you are doing right now, by the way." Silver spoke to herself out loud.

She still couldn't believe he'd left in a huff about something she'd been prepared to forgive him for. She sighed. But maybe he'd weighed their chances of making it again and gone back to believing it was impossible. For the hundredth time, she ran the conversation back in her head, trying to picture his face, to work out exactly when he'd decided he'd had enough.

Why had her dad looked so guilty when she'd walked in on his conversation with Ben? Neither of the men had looked as though they were just chatting amiably about what time Ben had to leave. Had her father been applying extra pressure on him to go, and not contact her again? He'd certainly been the one to drop Ben in it about the whole you were supposed to look after my drug-addicted daughter thing.

And what about the Internet going down and her phone magically disappearing? She'd been in such a rush to leave, she'd just seen those things as further catastrophes to avoid in her distress.

Silver groaned and spoke aloud to herself. "You've been a fool, haven't you? You let your emotions rule your choices and forgot to use your brain. No wonder your dad thinks you're easy to manipulate and Ben walked away from you."

But what could her dad have said to make Ben go without at least talking to her first? Silver sat up and went back out of her tent toward Kaya's. She fake knocked on the door and called out.

"Hey, can I borrow your phone for a minute?"

Kaya unzipped her tent and beckoned her inside. "Sure. What's up?"

"I just wanted to check in with my assistant," Silver said, which wasn't a complete lie because Ayla was working on something important for her. "My phone died just before I left for here, and I didn't get a chance to replace it."

Kaya shuddered. "I don't think I'd survive without my phone." She tapped in her password and handed it over. "Here you go."

Silver took care of the business side of things and then took a deep breath, typed her and Ben's names together, and started reading. No wonder her father hadn't wanted her to have her cell phone after Ben had left, and the house Internet had mysteriously died. She'd made it so easy for him to manipulate her by running away to the desert without thinking things through.

She looked up at Kaya. "Have you ever felt like really stupid?"

"All the time." Kaya's brow creased. "Is everything okay?"

"Not really."

By the time Silver finished reading, she was so angry she wanted to walk right out of the camp, flag down a ride, and get back to L.A. to sort out a few things.

But she didn't have that luxury. She'd stay here, pour all her emotions into her character, secure the role, and then go and kick some ass.

Inola clapped her hands and grinned at the faces around the campfire.

"I have some great news! We've been approached by a new production company called Ladybug who want to invest in our movie. We'll be meeting with them when we get back to L.A., so keep your fingers crossed." She looked up at Mike who had come to join her. "Over to you, boss."

"I just wanted to thank you all for coming out here in the middle of nowhere just to humor me and Inola, and the rest of the creative team."

Everyone laughed and hollered and Mike smiled.

"We'd like to confirm that all of you are our current first choices for your roles, so if you're willing to sign on with us, let us know, and we'll talk schedules and the joys of guild wages."

"Cool!" Silver and Kaya hugged each other and jumped up and down.

Kaya met Silver's gaze. "We're going to be fantastic in this, I just know it."

"Yes, we are." Silver grinned back at her. "I can't wait to get started, can you?"

After the beer started circulating and an impromptu singing circle emerged around the campfire, Silver went to find Inola and Mike who were sitting away from the noise. She joined the line of happy actors waiting to talk to them, and eventually sat opposite them.

"I'd love to be in your movie. Where do I sign up?" Silver asked.

"That's great! We'll talk to your agent as soon as we get back," Inola promised. "You do know that we're not going to be able to pay you much?"

"You can pay me the same as you're paying Kaya," Silver said firmly. "I'll tell my agent the same thing."

"Wow." Mike and Inola glanced at each other. "That's really good of you."

"You might change your mind when you hear the rest of it." Silver sat up straight. "I have something to confess, and I want to bring it out in the open before it becomes an issue."

"What is it?" Now Inola looked nervous again. Getting a movie made if you were a small, independent filmmaker was never easy.

"Ladybug is my production company." Silver sat back and watched their faces. "I want to invest in the film. Even if you don't want me in it now, I'd like to do that."

"What exactly are you looking for in return for your investment?" Mike asked carefully.

"Just the opportunity to speak up if I think I can help with anything." Silver shrugged. "I don't want creative control, or to have you make my part bigger, or anything like that. I just want to learn this side of the business with people I already feel comfortable with." She searched their faces. "I really believe in this project, and if you'll let me act in it, I'll be incredibly grateful."

"Maybe when we get back to L.A. we can all sit down together and go through everything," Inola suggested with a glance at Mike who was looking worried. "If we can't accept the money from your production company, would you still be willing to take the job?"

"Absolutely." Silver nodded. "Look, I'd be okay if you really needed the money, and you didn't want me in the movie. I'd hate it, but I'd do whatever it takes to make sure this thing gets made."

She stood up, aware that there were other people who needed to talk to them. "Call me when you get back to L.A., okay?"

At Inola's nod, Silver turned back to the campfire. Tomorrow, the whole place would cease to exist and everyone she'd formed a bond with would be scattered to all four corners of the country. Knowing she had a lot to accomplish when she went back to L.A., Silver went to spend her last evening with her new friends. She'd see them all again once they started filming, but that could be a while.

She stared at the flickering flames and drew an unsteady breath. Everything was changing again, and very soon she would have to make some hard choices about what she wanted and stick with them.

"You should call her."

Ben turned to see his mom walking down the length of the barn toward him. He'd gone to check the horses before he turned in for the night, and to make sure his gear was in good order because he was heading out to see Pablo early the next morning to start his new job. Adam wasn't particularly happy about him leaving, but everyone else had been supportive, even Danny, who would have to step up his hours on the ranch.

"I tried." Ben came out of Calder's stall and latched the door. "Her dad answered and I hung up."

"Ouch." Leanne winced. "Why does he have her phone?"

"Maybe she gave it to him to stop me calling her," Ben said gloomily. "I wish I'd stayed and fought it out with her, but I was too much of a coward."

His mom patted his arm. "You were put in the middle of a very unexpected situation and you handled yourself well. If Silver was already mad at you for something, making her madder wouldn't have solved anything, would it?"

"No, but—"

"Jeff's right. If she's the woman you think she is, then she'll work out what's happened and come and see you for herself."

"Number one, I can't believe Dad is right about my love life, and two, if she comes here, he's going to open his mouth and ruin it for me somehow, isn't he?" Ben asked.

"Don't be so negative, Ben." Leanne said bracingly. "Under his rough exterior your father has a very good heart, and you know it. Why, he was the first one to notice that you really liked Silver!" She paused. "Apart from Ruth Morgan of course, with whom I had a *very* interesting chat after church yesterday."

"Mrs. Morgan knows?" Ben groaned. "If she tells BB he'll kill me—and I mean that literally."

"She won't tell a soul. She's been keeping the secrets of Morgan Valley for at least fifty years, and she wishes you and Silver all the best." She looked up at him. "Are you coming in?"

"I've got a couple of things to finish up first." Ben gestured vaguely at the tack room. "What time are you going tomorrow?"

"Around noon. Adam's driving me to the airport. You know how bad a driver your father is."

"Cool." He bent down to kiss her cheek and draw her into a hug. "It's been good to see you."

She cupped his chin so that he had to look at her. "Now, promise me that if Silver *does* turn up here, you'll talk to her?"

"Mom, if she turns up here, I'll get down on my knees and kiss her feet," Ben promised. "I might even cry."

"Because you love her, that's why," his mom said with way more confidence than he had in himself. "I can't wait to meet her. Jeff said he kept thinking he knew her and thought she worked in the bank." She chuckled.

"She says that happens a lot," Ben agreed. "But she handles it really well." He hesitated. "The thing is, we're still living in completely different worlds, and I don't know if it's possible to bridge that gap."

Her face softened. "Ben, when I met Declan, I was a forty-two-year-old divorcée with six kids, living in my brother's apartment, waitressing to make some money, and helping out in a soup kitchen. I had no idea who he was, just that everyone treated him with respect, and that he never had to raise his voice to get something accomplished." Leanne smiled. "You can imagine why I appreciated that."

"Absolutely." Ben nodded.

"The first time he asked me out, I said no, and I kept saying it for months before he finally persuaded me to go to a book signing event with him. I went because it was an author I'd long admired, and Declan and I had bonded over reading the latest book." She smiled. "I had no idea that Declan had moved heaven and earth to get this particular author to appear at that particular shop mainly for my benefit."

"Wow."

"I had no idea how wealthy he was until I was well and

truly in love with him for who he was." She looked up at his face. "Can you imagine me chairing galas and chatting away to billionaires, socialites, and Broadway stars? Me neither. But I did it because that was part of Declan's life, and in return he gave me his love, my totally unexpected new daughter, and a quiet house out in the countryside where I could ride my horse and tend to my garden. If we could make it work, then so can you. Don't give up before you even start, love."

She patted his cheek and half-turned away. "That's enough of me lecturing you for one night. I'm going to make myself a hot drink and go to bed."

"Night, Mom," Ben called out softly as she walked away from him. "Love you."

She raised her hand to signify that she had heard him and kept on going. Ben checked the other horses were all good for the night, and then went into the tack room to make sure everything had been put back in the right place. Adam hated it when things were all muddled up.

As he hung up a bridle and shook out a blanket that had ended up on the floor, Ben thought about what his mom had told him, turning it around in his head to examine it from every angle. He'd known who Silver was from the word *go,* but he'd also spent a lot of time with her when she was just being herself, and he *liked* her. When he'd needed her help, she'd stayed calm, and stopped a stupid accident from turning into a full-scale disaster.

Ben paused, his unseeing gaze on the pile of blankets. But did he *love* her? He missed her so badly his heart hurt, and he couldn't stop thinking about her. All he wanted was the chance to set things right even if she never wanted to see him again. He wanted her to be happy, but most of all he wanted her to be happy with him.

"Jeez . . . of course you love her." Ben shook his head. "You're an idiot."

"Can't argue with that." Adam's dry voice drifted in from the doorway. "Standing out here in the middle of the night talking to yourself. What will people think?"

"That I'm just one of those crazy Miller brothers?" Ben did another quick survey of the tack room, but everything looked okay. "It's all done. I'm just about ready to turn in."

"Thanks." Adam didn't move out of the way. "Are you looking forward to working with Pablo tomorrow?"

"No, I'm scared shitless." Ben met his big brother's gaze. "I've always had you to hide behind if things went wrong, and now it will all be on me."

"You'll do great." Adam grimaced. "I'm sorry I've been acting like an ass about this."

"What's new?" Ben raised an eyebrow.

"I've just gotten used to always having you at my back. It'll be weird not having you here to depend on." Adam let out a breath. "Lizzie says I should make sure you know that I'm really proud of you for stepping up, and that whatever happens, I'll always support you."

"*Lizzie* says?" Ben teased. "How that woman puts up with you I'll never know. But I'm glad she does because she's the only one who can talk some sense into you."

Adam stepped out into the barn and Ben joined him. "Yeah, I know. She's way better than me at all this emotional stuff."

"That's because Dad told us emotions were for sissies, so we're all petrified of showing any," Ben reminded his brother, who chuckled.

"There is that." Adam paused. "Are you really keen on that Silver Meadows woman?"

"Yeah, I am."

"So what are you going to do about it?"

Ben groaned. "I wish you'd all stop asking me that. Like I even know where she is right now or whether she wants to hear from me, or if she's got a new man, or—"

"Call her."

"She's not answering her phone."

"Write her a letter, hitch a ride on Chase's jet next time he goes to L.A., and look her up. . . ."

Ben halted and looked up at his big brother. "You know when you screwed up really badly with Lizzie, and I ended up taking her home because she was so upset with you?"

A crease appeared on Adam's brow. "What the hell does that have to do with anything?"

"Remember how you felt right then when you knew you'd messed up, and you weren't sure she'd ever let you see her again?"

Adam slowly nodded. "It was one of the worst days of my life."

"Then you know how I'm feeling right now, so stop with the helpful suggestions. If Silver wants me, she'll reach out to me. I'm not going to turn into some kind of stalker. She has enough of those to deal with already."

Adam studied him for a long time. "Okay, got it." He gestured at the house. "Are you coming in? It looks like it's going to rain."

Chapter Twenty-One

Silver put on her sunglasses, hid her hair under a baseball cap, and descended the steps of the private jet she'd hired to bring her to Morgan Valley. She'd turned off her phone because after their last discussion, her dad hadn't stopped texting her, trying to explain and justify the decisions he'd made about Ben. She already knew he'd done it with the best of intentions, and she loved him dearly, but she wasn't ready to talk to him quite yet.

She needed to speak to the man himself.

An ancient truck pulled up at the end of the runway and an equally ancient cowboy slowly got out and waved at her.

"Welcome back to Morgan Ranch!" he shouted. "Ruth's expecting you."

She thanked the pilot and told him she'd be in touch about the return journey, shouldered her backpack, and walked toward the old man.

"I'm Roy." He held out his hand and smiled to display two missing teeth. "Good to meet you, ma'am."

She climbed into the truck and they were soon heading down the dusty path toward the ranch house. The sky was a clear blue without any of L.A.'s haze and the sun was bright enough to blind her. She inhaled the now-familiar scents of the great outdoors, and realized she'd missed it almost as much as she'd missed Ben.

They pulled up in front of the house, and Roy came around to open her door, before stomping up the steps to the porch and holding the screen door wide.

"I've got her, Ruth!" he shouted into the coolness of the interior. "Can't stop to chat! Got to get back to my pigs!"

He tipped his hat to Silver as she reached the door. "Let me know if you need a ride back, okay?"

"Thank you." Silver smiled at him and he winked.

"Come on in. Silver"—Mrs. Morgan appeared in the hallway, wiping her hands on her apron—"it's so good to see you again."

Half an hour later, she was drinking a tall glass of lemonade and helping Mrs. Morgan prepare lunch.

"I thought, if it was okay, that I could stay here tonight just in case everything goes horribly wrong, and Ben doesn't want to see me again?" Silver asked her companion.

"I doubt it will go wrong, but you are more than welcome to stay." Mrs. Morgan put something in the oven. "Have some lunch, and then you can borrow my truck, and I'll give you directions to the Millers' place. It's not far."

"You think I should just turn up?" Silver asked nervously.

Mrs. Morgan gave her a funny look. "Isn't that why you came here?"

"Well, yes, it is," Silver babbled. "But I was thinking maybe I should work up to it, or—"

"I saw Leanne, Ben's mother, at church last week, and we had a good chat about you two. She said Ben is missing you dreadfully, and that he did try and call you, but your father answered so he didn't leave a message."

Mrs. Morgan handed Silver a lettuce to wash and started cutting up tomatoes and cucumber. "All that nonsense in the papers about Ben and that Cassie Walker wasn't fair to him at all. The Walkers had a lot of money and they were determined to blacken Ben's name."

"I just wish he'd told me about her," Silver admitted as she set the washed leaves in the salad spinner.

"He's not a great talker, that Ben Miller, but he feels things very deeply. I think he would've told you in his own good time. He's spent his whole life trying to live with what happened and I think he took it hard. Certainly changed him from the wildest of the Millers to the one you sometimes don't even notice was there."

Mrs. Morgan checked the timer and took out the freshly toasted garlic croutons from the oven. Silver's mouth watered. "Mustn't burn them. Ten seconds too long, and they're black and crispy."

She turned to Silver. "Do you know how to make a dressing for a Caesar salad?"

"No, I don't."

"Then it's a good time to learn." Mrs. Morgan placed a handwritten recipe down on the kitchen table between them. "We'll start with a good-sized bowl."

Three hours later, after a lively lunch with Ruth's great-grandson Chase William and his mom, January, Silver was sitting on the drive leading up to the Miller Ranch trying to get the nerve to get out, open the gate, and go through onto their property.

She could turn around right now, go back to the Morgans, send Ben a text like a civilized person, and wait politely for his response. But what if he didn't get back to her? Would she keep making excuses for both herself and him? And then what?

"Dammit!"

She got out of the truck, checked the code Mrs. Morgan had written on her hand, and tapped it in the padlock, releasing the chain that kept the gate shut. She pushed the gate open and hurried to get back in and drive through before she had to get out and repeat the whole process again.

There was only a single, rutted track, which went upward so she wasn't likely to get lost. When she pulled up outside the low-lying ranch house, she cut the engine and took a cautious look around. The house wasn't as pretty as the Morgans', but apart from that, the layout of the ranch was very similar. House, cow barn, horse barn, and fenced paddocks radiating away from the house. There was also a chicken run where several interested spectators had gathered to watch her arrival.

She checked the time. There were two parked trucks and space for at least a dozen more. Would Ben be back by now? Mrs. Morgan had seemed pretty confident that someone would be there to talk to her. She got out of the truck. She had nothing to lose and a lot to gain.

As she approached the house, wondering where on earth the front door was, someone called out to her.

"Come through this way, and wipe your feet!"

She jumped and turned, one hand plastered to her heart, and saw Mr. Miller beckoning to her impatiently.

"Hi!" she squeaked. "I hope you don't mind me barging in like this, but—"

Her voice died as she realized he'd disappeared into the house leaving the door wide open for her.

She went inside and took off her boots in the mudroom, walked out into the hallway, and then stopped, confused by the number of doors and passageways leading away from her. Whoever had built this house hadn't thought things through very logically.

"I'm in the kitchen!" Mr. Miller shouted out.

She followed the smell of coffee and emerged into a huge kitchen that wouldn't have looked out of place in a magazine spread. It had the most beautiful handmade cabinets she had ever seen.

"This is lovely." She stroked the wood. "And so unexpected."

"Kaiden did the work." Mr. Miller was standing beside a pot of coffee he held up to her. "Want some?"

"Yes, please." She headed for the long pine table and took a seat.

"Cream and sugar?"

"No, thanks, just as it is."

She accepted the mug he handed her and waited for him to sit on the other side of the table. Even close up, he didn't look much like Ben, but there was something in his direct gaze that reminded her of her reluctant lover.

"What brings you to Morgan Valley?" Mr. Miller asked.

"I came to see Ben," Silver replied. "We parted on bad terms and I wanted to sort things out with him."

"Why's that?"

She frowned at him. "I don't understand."

"Why do you want to sort things out with him when you're going to hightail it back to L.A.?"

She sat up straight. "That's between me and Ben."

"It's a legitimate question." He sipped his coffee. "I don't want him getting all lovey-dovey about you again, and then getting hurt."

"He's a big boy." Silver met Mr. Miller's direct gaze head-on and reminded herself that just like her own father,

Ben's dad really did care for his son. "I think he'll work out what he wants to do."

"I damn well hope so. That boy's been scared to make any decisions since he was nineteen and he got tangled up with that other rich girl." He snorted. "She came here once and complained the whole time about how *rural* it was, and how *basic* and *quaint.* Darn well made Ben ashamed of his roots."

"I'm not like that." Silver wasn't backing down. "I like it here."

"Enough to stay?" Mr. Miller wasn't backing down either. "He won't thrive if you take him away from here for good."

For a moment, they stared each other down like two gunslingers, before Silver risked a smile.

"Then we'd better think of a way to keep him here, hadn't we?"

Mr. Miller grinned back and held out his hand. "I *knew* I liked you. Call me Jeff, and I've thought of just the thing."

Ben settled Calder into his new stall at the Gomez ranch, made sure the barn was clean and tidy, and walked up to the house to report to his boss. His cell buzzed as he was approaching the side door and he stopped to check it.

> Unexpected meeting in town so I won't be back.
> Will check in with you tomorrow morning.
> Take the night off ☺ Pablo.

Ben retraced his steps to the small cabin on the other side of the barn, which was now all his. It was only the second time in his life that he'd lived away from home, but this time he was going to make it stick. The work he was doing was familiar, the only difference being that he was now the one who decided who would do what, and which tasks to prioritize. As the ranch was smaller, as was the herd, it wasn't as hard to take inventory, something he was very grateful for.

He'd spent his first week following Pablo around, just listening and watching, getting to know the hands, the beef cattle, and the lay of the land. Next week, he planned to ask Daisy to help him set up the ranch files and records on the Internet and update the very basic website. Despite worrying that having the power to make decisions would be too much for him, the opposite was true. He was enjoying himself.

He halted at the side door of his place, wiped his boots off on the mat, and went inside. The faint smell of toast and coffee greeted him and he found himself smiling at the silence. He liked being part of a big family, but sometimes being able to come in and not have to speak to anyone was kind of nice. And, if he wanted noise, all he had to do was get in his truck and drive a couple of miles around to his old home.

He hung up his hat and sheepskin jacket in the mudroom and heel and toed his boots off. The house was basically three rooms, a kitchen/family room, a bedroom, and a bathroom, which suited him just fine. Pablo's cleaning lady had offered to come in once a week just to keep things neat like she had with the previous occupant, but Ben had decided not to bother. After years of being shouted at by his father and Kaiden, he was pretty tidy.

He took the mail he'd picked up earlier from the ranch box and walked into the kitchen, his head down as he sorted through the junk. A flash of movement caught his eye, and he looked up with a start.

"Hey."

Ben blinked and stared hard at the apparition sitting at his kitchen countertop.

Silver's already-anxious smile dimmed. "It's me, Silver."

Ben nodded like a dimwit and slowly put the letters down on the table.

"Your dad told me you'd moved over here."

"You saw my dad?"

"I went to your home, thinking you'd be there, and Jeff was there instead. We had coffee together and he gave me a ride over here."

Ben tried to imagine how that had gone and failed miserably.

"He said you'd been here just over a week. How's it going?"

"It's going good." Wow, he'd managed to get another whole sentence out. "Silver, forgive me if this sounds rude, but what the hell are you doing here?"

She folded her arms over her chest. "I thought you might like to talk to me."

"About what?"

"Take your pick." She shrugged. "My dad, maybe? Your past? Your decision that we weren't even worth fighting for?"

He rubbed his hand over the back of his neck, still not really believing she was sitting in his place looking so darn hot he wanted to jump her bones, but he couldn't because of the mountain of stuff between them.

"Your dad did what he thought was best for you." When the silence started to stretch again, Ben made a valiant effort to end it. "I get that."

"What was best for me . . ." She raised an eyebrow. "So you two made a joint decision to protect the little woman?"

"I would never do that," Ben said quickly. "Your dad kind of blindsided me about Cassie and that seemed way more important than what I had or hadn't done on the trail ride. You were already mad about me knowing about the drug thing. I thought the Cassie thing would make everything worse."

She regarded him solemnly but didn't speak so he stumbled on.

"You've got every reason in the world not to trust anyone who enables drug use." He blew out a frustrated breath. "I read the news reports the Walkers put out there, Silver. I *know* how I looked. Why would you think any different?"

She slid off her stool. "Maybe because I thought we'd decided to be honest with each other? That we liked and trusted each other?"

"I *knew* I shouldn't have run away. I thought about contacting you all the time. I was even thinking about coming out to L.A. again," Ben said. "And then this happened. Stay there." He went into his bedroom, found the envelope he'd tucked under his socks, and brought it out with him.

"If you trusted me, how come I got this in the mail the other day, forwarded on from my dad's?" He handed over the envelope and waited until she opened it. "That's your signature on that check, right? Did you think I'd cash a fifty-thousand-dollar check and walk away smiling, and forget you?"

She raised her head and her appalled expression slightly eased the hurt he'd been hiding inside him.

"I didn't—I had *no* idea . . . God, Ben, my dad must've used one of my presigned checks. He probably thought he was doing something nice." Her voice broke. "I am *so* sorry." She turned toward the door. "I shouldn't have come, you must really hate me, but I swear I didn't know he'd tried to buy you off. I'm going to kill him when I see him—if I ever see him again."

"Hold up." Ben blocked her way. If he let her walk out, all the changes he'd tried to make in his life would be meaningless. "I don't hate you. Can we just sit down and talk this through? *Please?"* He gestured at the two chairs on either side of the wood-burning fire.

She sat, her shoulders hunched and her face hidden behind her hair. Ben took the chair opposite and tried to think of where to begin. If he was ever going to step up, then this was the moment to do it.

"When I got the check, I tried to be angry about it, and convince myself that I'd done the right thing by walking away—that you obviously didn't need me if you thought you could buy me off."

She went to speak and he held up his hand.

"Just let me finish, okay? But I couldn't do it, Silver, because some part of me couldn't believe you would do that to me." He looked up at her. "Some crazy part of me was still convinced you'd come back. And here you are, sitting in my kitchen, and I'm messing it all up again."

"But I felt the same," Silver blurted out. "Even after what happened in L.A. I couldn't believe that was the end of it. I knew that somewhere, *something* had gone wrong and that maybe it wasn't us who'd caused it." She gripped her fingers together and stared at them. "The day you left, my dad said the Internet was down in the house, that he'd needed to take my phone to replace it, and that I had to immediately fly out to Utah for a run-through with the indie film people. I was an idiot and totally fell for it."

She looked up. "I was stuck in the middle of the desert

for over a week with no way to check in with you or with the outside world. I had no idea about the stuff that was written about you after the press conference until I borrowed a phone, found out what was going on and what my father had tried to keep from me."

"Which is exactly why I agreed to leave quietly," Ben said gently. "Your dad promised me you would never know what was being said about me. I thought it was better if you didn't know because"—he struggled to continue—"once you heard about what I'd done, you wouldn't want me around anyway."

Silver didn't look away. "I know how the media works, Ben. I *know* how they twist things. I wish you'd trusted me to believe the truth."

"I just wasn't expecting it all to blow up like that again," Ben explained. "I felt like I'd been hit by a wrecking ball, and I panicked because back when it happened, the only people who stood by me were my family, and the folks from Morgan Valley. Everyone else believed the Walkers. I couldn't even get into another school because everyone was convinced I was some kind of sleazy murderer."

She continued to study him and he let her, hoping that somewhere in his open gaze she'd see the truth.

"Can I tell you about her?" Ben asked softly. "About Cassie?"

Part of Silver wanted to say no because so far they'd cleared the air beautifully, and she was afraid that hearing him talk about another woman might break that spell. But if he didn't tell her, she'd always wonder. . . . Better to know everything and make a clear-eyed decision than leave things to fester. She couldn't believe her dad had tried to bribe Ben . . . she wasn't sure if she would ever be able to forgive him for that.

"Okay." She gestured for him to start talking and tucked her feet up on the chair. His place lacked furniture and, well everything, so she was glad the chairs were at least comfortable. "Tell me."

"I met Cassie on my first day at Stanford. She was full of excitement and so confident that when she grabbed my hand and towed me around with her, I felt less alone, you know? She was everything I wasn't, rich, super smart, sophisticated, and she had parents who adored her. I was there on a full scholarship, barely keeping my GPA above the minimum required to stay in the program, well aware that my dad was just waiting for me to fail so that he could haul me back home to keep working for him."

Silver nodded and tried hard not to imagine him and Cassie hanging out together.

"Things were great during the first year, and then she started to complain that me and our friends were boring, and she drifted away toward a group of the really rich and entitled kids." He grimaced. "She got into drugs, but every time I tried to warn her, she'd tell me I was worrying over nothing, that she had it completely under control. But she didn't, of course. And because I cared about her, I started lying and covering for her—even doing some of her schoolwork, which meant I wasn't doing my own, and that's when things got really difficult."

"Because you got kicked out," Silver said.

"Yeah, I already kind of knew that I didn't have it in me to be a professional football player, but I didn't expect to get cut for not turning up enough to practice or failing my classes because I was too busy trying to save Cassie's ass. I was terrified of telling my dad, and I was so angry with all of it—with Cassie thinking it was all a big joke, with her friends agreeing with her and sabotaging everything good I tried to do for her."

Silver swallowed hard at the pain in his eyes.

"When I got kicked out, I decided I'd drive across America and confront my mom instead of going home." He shook his head and risked a glance at her. "Stupid, I know. Cassie decided she'd come with me. I agreed because her parents lived in New York, and I thought that if I had my eye on her for the whole journey, she might be drug-free by the time we got there. But things just got worse. I'd been so busy trying to salvage my college career that I hadn't realized just how bad an addict she'd become. I didn't have a lot of money so we stayed in cheap hotels in places where she'd just disappear on me for hours and come back with a new friend, or barely make it through the door before she passed out." Ben looked down at the floor.

"She knew I hated what she was doing, and that made her even more devious about concealing exactly what she was up to." He shoved his hands through his hair. "I tried everything, Silver. Bribing, threatening, cajoling, locking her in . . . Nothing worked, and I was getting so scared."

"You were nineteen. You shouldn't have been put in that position," Silver reminded him gently. "And for the record, when I was addicted there was nothing anyone could do to stop me getting that hit or that high either. My parents were *right there* and I still managed to get around them."

"When we got to Pennsylvania, I'd just about had it," Ben continued. "We had a bad argument, and I told her I was going to call her parents to come get her. I went out to get us something to eat, and when I came back, she'd locked the door on me and I couldn't get back in because

I'd stupidly left my key in the room. I banged on the door for about half an hour and eventually I went to reception and asked them for help.

"By the time we got in there Cassie was already dead." His voice shook and Silver wanted to go to him so badly. "I don't remember much more until the cops turned up, and guess who they wanted to talk to first? I remembered I had my mom's address and they called her. Things got marginally better after that because her husband, Declan, made damned sure that the cops and the medics followed procedure. I was blood tested and came up clean. He also got me a hot-shit lawyer. They got statements from the hotel owner, various guests who'd seen me banging on the door for ages, and the takeout place where I'd waited for almost an hour for food. I still had the receipt in my pocket. The medics believed she'd died not long after I'd left the room."

"Thank goodness for your mom and Declan," Silver murmured.

"Yeah, because the Walkers wanted blood, and they did their very best to get me convicted of murder. When they couldn't get the authorities to agree to prosecute the case, they tried to sue me personally." He set his jaw. "We could've lost the ranch just in lawyer's fees, but Declan stepped up and took care of everything. My dad never let me forget it."

"Declan sounds like a good man."

"He was. His only son died of a drug overdose so he knew all about addicts and he never ever made me feel like it was my fault." He abruptly stopped talking and his throat worked. "But I still felt like it was—that I could've done something more."

Silver scrambled out of her chair, almost falling in her haste, and rushed over to put her hands on his shoulders.

"Declan was right. Take it from someone who knows. You did everything you could for her. The only person who could've stopped her using was *her*."

He gazed at her solemnly. "Everyone kept telling me that, but I kept thinking, what if I'd stayed with her? What if I'd called her parents and not walked out because I was so angry and scared for her? What if—"

He gulped and lurched forward, burying his face in her shoulder. She held him tight as his whole body convulsed and his tears flowed. She rocked him gently and told him over and over, "It's not your fault, Ben. It's not." She smoothed his hair, her fingers curving into his curls. "She wouldn't want you to feel like this. She loved you, right? She made some terrible choices but they were her *own,* and nothing to do with you."

He finally raised his head. "But—"

"No buts." She held his gaze. "She hid what she was doing because she knew at some level that what she was doing was wrong—that she was hurting those she loved, and she still couldn't stop." Now she was the one with tears pouring down her face. "I know how that goes. I hurt the people I loved so badly, Ben. I made them so *afraid* for me, and I'll *never* make that right."

It was his turn to comfort her and within seconds she was safely settled on his lap while he held her and kissed the top of her head.

Eventually she stopped crying and pushed the hair out of her eyes.

"Oh God. Way to make everything about me."

"I think you needed to say that." Ben stroked her cheek. "I'm glad you felt safe enough to say it in front of me and help me understand both sides a little better."

"We're a real pair, aren't we?" She leaned against his chest and just appreciated the solid beat of his heart.

"Life and soul of the party," Ben murmured, and she gave a watery chuckle.

"Maybe that's why we like each other so much."

"Because we make each other cry?" Ben asked.

"No, because we can cry in front of each other, and it's okay." She stroked his beard.

"My dad wasn't a big believer in tears."

"Surprise, surprise," Silver said. "Neither was mine. From the first time I acted in a commercial when I was a baby I was *always* supposed to look happy."

"I like you when you get mad." Ben kissed her reddened nose. "You keep me honest."

"Right back at you." Her breath shuddered out and she allowed herself to relax against him. She didn't ever want to move again. She felt more at home with him in his almost-empty cabin than she did in her L.A. house.

Eventually, he stirred. "Do you want to come to bed, or do you need to be somewhere else?"

"You'd like me to stay?" Silver asked carefully.

He shrugged. "You've seen me cry. I can't ever let you out of here, so you'd better get comfortable." He gestured at the bathroom. "I'm going to take a quick shower while you decide what you want to do, okay? No pressure."

Silver scrambled to find her cell and sent a text to Mrs. Morgan and to Ben's father so they'd know where she was, and not worry. By the time Ben came back, she'd gone into his bedroom, which had only a twin-sized bed and a chest of drawers, stripped down to her bra and panties, and got under the sheets.

He sat on the edge of the bed and stared down at her, his hair damp from the shower.

"I still can't believe you're actually here."

"I'm most definitely here." She patted the sheets. "And so should you be."

He cupped her chin, his expression so full of awe that she almost wanted to cry again. “I can’t think of anywhere else I’d rather be right now.”

“Then get in and hold me while I fall asleep.” Silver tried to speak lightly even though her heart was stuffed full of emotions she was afraid to unpack right now.

“That I can do.” He climbed in beside her and frowned as he gathered her close. “I’m going to have to get a bigger bed.”

“Damn straight,” Silver murmured and promptly fell asleep.

Chapter Twenty-Two

"Ben?"

Ben groaned and forced his eyes to open as he held his phone to his ear.

"What's up, Dad?"

"You'd better get back here right now, and bring Silver with you, or I won't be responsible for what happens next."

Before Ben could even attempt a reply, his father had ended the call, leaving him blinking like a fool.

Beside him, Silver stirred. "What's wrong?"

"My dad's got a mad on, and is demanding we meet him at the ranch." Ben checked the time. He'd forgotten to set his alarm, and it was already past seven in the morning. He'd slept better than he had in weeks with Silver wrapped in his arms. "Do you want to shower first?"

She ran the tip of her finger over his bare chest. "Maybe we could do that together?"

"Honey, you haven't seen the size of my shower. I have no intention of getting stuck in there and having to get the volunteer firefighters of Morgantown out to cut us free. I'd never live it down."

"Okay." She sighed. "Then, sure, I'll go first."

He wasn't normally this slow in the mornings, but as

she went to climb over him, he put his hands on her hips so that she was straddling him.

"Or we could just stay here a while longer?"

"Won't Jeff be mad?"

He smiled up at her as he hooked a finger in the side of her panties. "He's already mad. Maybe we need to give him some time to cool off."

After checking in with Pablo, Ben took Silver and drove his truck back home. There were several other vehicles in the yard, including a fancy rental he wasn't familiar with.

"Come on." He held out his hand to Silver as she climbed out. "Brace yourself."

They went through the mudroom and took off their boots and hats. It was eerily quiet inside the house and Ben wondered what on earth was going on. He went on through to the kitchen and then stopped so fast that Silver, who was following behind, bumped into his back.

She peered around him and gasped.

"Dad? What are you doing here?"

Before Mr. Meadows could answer her, Ben's dad spoke up.

"Good question! This guy barges in here like he owns the place and starts accusing me of abducting his daughter!" He glared ferociously at his companion. "Then, when I tell him to simmer down, he starts threatening to call the cops on me! In my own home!"

Silver marched over to her father. "Why on earth are you here disrupting Mr. Miller's morning?"

Ben's startled gaze met his father's as Silver squared up to her father.

"Can't you just leave me alone for *five* minutes without interfering?"

"Silver, if you would just calm down . . ."

Ben winced as somewhat predictably Mr. Meadows's words had the absolutely opposite effect on his already-furious daughter.

"Go away, Dad. Go home, and when I've calmed down—if I ever calm down—I will contact you and we can talk!"

"You turned your phone off! I was worried about you. I—"

"I asked you to give me some space to try and sort out the mess you'd made between me and Ben, so why are you here?" Silver had her hands on her hips. "And why did you send Ben a check for fifty thousand dollars like you were paying off a prostitute?"

Mr. Meadows gulped. "I was trying to help."

"Fifty thousand dollars?" Ben's dad murmured and looked at him. "You never mentioned that to me."

"Because it was none of your business," Ben replied equally quietly. "And I'm not going to cash it."

"Why not?" Jeff rounded on him, totally forgetting Mr. Meadows. "Silver won't mind, and I could put that to good use on the ranch."

"But it's not for you, Dad, and I'm not going to allow Mr. Meadows to pay me off when I have every intention of having a relationship with his daughter."

Ben made sure his gaze included Silver's father when he was speaking, and addressed his next remarks directly to him.

"I appreciate that you meant well, sir, but I don't want Silver's money."

A dull, red flush rose on Phil Meadows's cheeks. "Silver, I need to talk to you alone, okay?"

"You can say anything you like right here out in the open, Dad, or I don't want to hear it," Silver snapped. Ben's dad obviously wasn't the only one with a mad on.

"Okay, then. I don't want you hanging around with a man who enables drug use."

There was a sudden silence and then Ben's dad spoke up, his voice quiet, which was alarming enough to raise the hairs on the back of Ben's neck.

"Are you saying my son is some kind of drug dealer?"

"Maybe." Phil shrugged. "I read all the evidence brought against him, and the Walkers said that when he went out to get 'food' maybe he procured the drugs that killed their daughter."

Jeff's lunge at the other man was so out of left field that Ben almost didn't get in the way quick enough to stop him.

"Dad, this won't solve anything, okay?" He hung on to his father's raised fist. "Mr. Meadows is one hundred percent wrong, and we know that because not a single prosecutor believed that lie. If you hit him, he'll call the cops and sue the pants off you."

Silver went over to her father, who was staring in shock at Jeff Miller. "Come outside right now, and I will talk to you."

He nodded and walked out, leaving Ben still holding on to his father. Silver met his gaze.

"I'll deal with my annoying parent, if you can take care of yours?"

"Sure." Ben nodded.

"I'm really sorry, Mr. Miller," Silver said. "My dad had no right to turn up here and behave the way he has. I'll make sure he doesn't bother you again."

She walked out into the yard and found her father pacing by his rental.

"That man is insane! He should be locked up!"

"You walked into his house, uninvited, and accused him of kidnapping a grown woman. How would you expect him to behave?" Silver shook her head. "I'm so ashamed of you."

"Of *me*?" Her father echoed her words in disbelief. "He was the one who wanted to beat me up!"

"Because you suggested his son was a drug dealer. The Walkers used their guilt over their daughter's death to try and destroy a nineteen-year-old boy who had been doing his best to bring his friend home because he was so afraid for her. *That's* what happened, Dad. You of all people should know that if an addict wants to get high, they'll find a way despite everyone around them."

"I do know that, which is why I don't want you hanging around with someone who has enabled a drug user!"

"Ben didn't do that." Silver made her dad look her right in the eye. "I know you care about me, and that I scared you very badly, and that it's hard to let go of that fear. But, even if I did start using again, it still wouldn't be your fault. It would be on *me*. It would be *my* failure, not yours."

A muscle moved in his jaw. "I'll always blame myself for being so caught up in your success that I didn't notice the toll it was taking on you—that you felt you couldn't tell me what was going on—that I let you down." He swallowed hard. "I *never* want that to happen again."

God, he sounded just like Ben the night before. . . . Addicts like her really did have a lot to answer for.

"And you won't let me down if you back off and let me make my own mistakes," Silver said earnestly. "You're smothering me and interfering in my personal life. If you keep this up, we won't be able to have a relationship at all."

She took a deep breath and stepped away from him. "I want you to go home, talk to Mom, and either make the decision to move back into your own house, or move away entirely."

His eyes widened. "You're shutting me out?"

"No, I'm asking for some space. If you can't give me that, then, yes, we might have to consult our lawyers, and separate our business interests. But I don't want to do that, Dad. Do you? I just want to be allowed to live my own life and make my own mistakes just like everyone else."

He stared down at her for a long time, his face a mask of indecision, and slowly nodded.

"Okay. I'll leave you in peace. Apologize to the Millers for me and call me when you get back."

She went on tiptoe and kissed his averted cheek. "Take care, now. I love you, and love to everyone."

He opened the car door and then swung around to look at her again. "I never wanted to hurt you, Silver. I've always tried to do what I thought was best for you."

"I know that, Dad." She risked a smile. "You haven't even run off with all my money, which puts you right up there among stage parents."

She surprised an answering smile out of him and he shook his head. "That's my girl. Are you sure Ben Miller is the right guy for you?"

"Yes, Dad. I am. I love him very much."

"Then that's good." He blew her a kiss, his voice shaking. "Speak to you soon."

She stayed where she was, watching his car drive away, images of him laughing down at her in movie studios, arguing on her behalf, protecting her from the wrath of directors and fellow actors. . . . He'd done his best and she would always be grateful for that. But he needed to understand that things were changing, and he needed to find a new direction for his own life. Her mom would help him with that; Silver knew it in her soul.

"So, you love that Ben Miller guy, yeah?"

She swung around to see that Ben had emerged from the house and was leaning against the wall in the shadows. She walked toward him and stopped where she could still look up at him.

"Yes, I do love you. Is that okay?"

He reached out a hand and cupped her chin, his brown gaze serious. "You have to ask? I love you like crazy."

She melted into his arms. "Then that's definitely okay."

He kissed her quickly and fiercely. "I don't know how we're going to make this work, but—"

She stopped his words with her mouth and he didn't attempt to argue her out of it.

"Jeez!" She buried her face in Ben's shoulder as Jeff Miller came through the door. "You're worse than Adam and Lizzie!" He raised his eyebrows. "Are you coming, then?"

"Coming where?" Silver asked.

"Back to Pablo's." He winked at her. "He's got a big plot of land that he's more than willing to sell you so that you can build yourselves a decent house."

"What?" Ben looked between the two of them. "What have you been up to?"

"You can't expect a movie star to live in a hovel, Ben, so I had a chat with Pablo last night, and he's got some land to show you." Jeff started for his truck. "He also says that he might be willing to sell the whole place to you when he decides to retire."

"What?" This time it was Silver who answered him. "Really? That's fantastic!"

She turned back to Ben who had gone quiet and was staring at her in shock.

"That's okay, isn't it?" Silver asked. "Me being here with you—you managing the Gomez ranch—me running my production company and taking the occasional movie role?"

His smile came so slowly that she almost forgot to breathe.

"Did I ever tell you that you are amazing?"

"I don't think you did," Silver replied demurely. "But if you'd rather live in L.A.—"

She squeaked as he came in low, picked her up over his shoulder, one hand firmly placed on her butt, and headed after his father. Her life might be about to get way more complicated, but she wasn't going to regret a single thing. She'd found a man who loved her as much as she loved him, a place where they could be together and a future.

What more could any world-famous movie star ask for?

Epilogue

"I think I look okay," Silver said as she did a final twirl in front of the mirror. Her custom gown was pale blue with silver embroidery and made her look like an old-time movie star. She gazed regretfully at the sandwich on the table. "I can't eat anything now or I'll have a bump and the media will start all that stupid stuff up again about me being pregnant."

Ayla held up a cup with a straw. "You can have water."

"Then I'll have to pee, and there is no way that's going to happen without a team of people helping me."

The door into her bedroom opened and Ben emerged, his expression dubious.

"You sure I look okay in this tux?"

He wore the classic black and white version with a blue bow tie that matched her dress. His beard had been trimmed and shaped and the curls in his hair tamed.

"I feel like I'm at prom." He grimaced and rubbed a finger over his neck. "And I hate not having my hat."

Silver placed her palm over her heart and stared at him. "You look . . . beautiful. Who would've guessed you'd clean up so well?"

She knew how much he hated accompanying her to movie star things, but he'd agreed to be pampered and dressed for this occasion, and looked so fine, she wanted to jump his bones. Which she couldn't do because the corset of the dress was holding her upright like steel armor.

She walked over to him, her high heels making her feel tall, and he took her in with a comprehensive gaze from head to toe.

"You're the one who looks beautiful." He smiled as she readjusted his tie. "I suppose I can't touch?"

"Correct." She ran her finger along his lower lip. "But whatever happens tonight I promise you can undress me later, and I'll even keep my shoes on just for you."

"Just the shoes?"

"If you like." She smiled into his eyes. "God, I'm so nervous I want to puke."

He held her gaze. "It's going to be fine. Everyone is rooting for you back home."

She shrugged. "Well, if the whole of Morgan Valley wants me to win an Oscar then how can I lose?"

"Your mom and dad called to say they'll be sitting up and watching the ceremony in England and to send you their love."

It had taken a while for Silver to establish a new relationship with her dad, but with her mom and Ben's help, he'd eventually come around and stepped back. He and Alva were currently on a tour of Europe and weren't expected back for at least another two months.

There was a knock on the door of the suite and Ayla went to answer it. She returned with two security guards, and a woman bearing a jewelry book.

"Miss Meadows? I have your jewelry."

Ayla signed the paperwork and took possession of the box. "Thank you so much. We will make sure to return it tomorrow."

"Jeez . . ." Ben breathed as Silver opened the lid and revealed a sapphire and diamond set comprising earrings, a necklace, a bracelet, and twenty gem-studded hairpins. "How much is that worth?"

"It's probably best not to know," Silver said. "Just pray that I don't lose anything, or we'll literally be selling the ranch." She looked over at Ayla. "Can you see if Shareem is still there? I need her to put the hairpins in place."

"Sure." Ayla disappeared deeper into the enormous suite and Silver turned to Ben.

"Can you help me with the rest of it?"

She moved to stand in front of the floor-length mirror and he stood behind her. His hands looked huge as he fumbled with the clasp of the necklace before placing it carefully around her throat.

"You look like an ice princess." He daringly kissed her neck. "You did say you could keep these until tomorrow, right?"

"Yes, why?"

"Just thinking about later. . . ." He winked and she smiled back at him in the mirror.

"Of course, I might be a sobbing mess sitting in my bathrobe eating dairy-free ice cream straight out of the tub."

"Which is also fine, as long as you share." He bent over her wrist as he fastened the bracelet. "I don't care if you win or lose, you know that."

"I do, and I love you for that, but I really want to win this one," Silver confided.

"You've already got all the critical acclaim for your performance as Minnie, and no one doubts you can act your socks off." Ben held her gaze. "The movie has won every other award out there, both in the U.S. and the rest of the world. You've done okay, kid. You really have."

She risked a kiss on his nose and then backed away as Shareem came to deal with the placement of the hairpins. She hadn't looked at the clock for ages, and Ben had confiscated her phone so she had no idea how close they were to leaving. At this point she just wanted to go and get it over with. . . .

"Car will be here in ten, Mr. Miller!" One of Silver's bodyguards who'd taken quite a shine to Ben called out to him.

"Not sure why we have to get there so early," Ben muttered to no one in particular as he paced the carpet and tried to get used to his fancy new shoes.

"Because you need to be seen and admired," Ayla reminded him. "Well, Silver does, and it's your job to show her off."

"I can do that," Ben replied. He'd attended a few of these red carpet events in the last year and had just about got used to the noise, and the unbelievable amount of flashing lights. He was still working on not looking like "a scared coyote caught in the crosshairs."

He smiled as he remembered his father's latest text about his last outing. Jeff had taken to Silver, and even if they occasionally got into it, his father always enjoyed a good fight. She also got on with his mother, which pleased him more than he'd imagined, but Silver was good at that—she was nice to the core.

He stared at the back of her head as her stylist and hairdresser decided where each pin should go for maximum effect. He could no longer imagine her in his bed or riding tandem with him on Calder, her arms wrapped around his waist as they checked the beef cattle at home. Yet, when she was there, she pulled her weight, nurturing the baby calves, mucking out the horse barn, and tending the chickens.

When the new house was finished, and they'd moved in, he'd caved and gotten a housekeeper because neither of them enjoyed cooking and cleaning. Sometimes, like all couples, they still argued about money, but Silver never made him feel like the leech the tabloids tried to portray him as in their relationship. The ranch was thriving under his ownership and turning enough profit that he could afford to pay all his bills.

He was damn lucky. But he still couldn't wait to get out of his tux. . . .

"Five minutes, Silver." Ayla had her headphone on and looked all business. "Shareem and Bree will follow your limo and meet you at the front to make sure everything has survived the journey."

Silver made one last check that everything was secure and then turned to Ben. Her hair had been swept up on her head, and her long dangling earrings caught the light. She looked like the movie star she was, and for a moment, he just stared at her like any other long-term fan.

"Are you ready, Ben?"

He heard the anxiety in her voice and held out his hand. He'd seen the movie she'd helped to produce and co-starred in. It had been an eye-opener about how good an actress she really was. He had nothing but total respect for her skills.

"I'm good. Let's do this thing."

A torturous hour later they were on the red carpet and between the massive gold statues. His head was ringing from the screams and all the flashing lights had half blinded him. He concentrated on looking attentive as Silver spoke to what felt like a million idiots with a mike as they slowly progressed into the theater.

As he was taller than a lot of people—who knew that male movie stars tended to be on the short side in real life?—he spotted Mike, Inola, Kaya, and the rest of the film crew ahead of them. They weren't moving much faster than he and Silver were, which meant it was still going to be a while before they were out of public view.

He resisted the urge to stick his finger down his collar. Who thought it was a good idea to dress up like this in the heat of the Californian sun? At least if he'd had his Stetson on, he would have some shade.

"And how are you doing tonight, Ben?"

He jerked his attention back to the smiling woman who was now shoving the mike in his face.

"I'm good, thanks."

She giggled loudly and turned back to Silver. "He doesn't say much, does he?"

"No, but he's really good at lifting heavy things," Silver cooed, and stroked his arm. It was all he could do not to burst out laughing.

"I bet you'd rather be home on the ranch, eh?" the woman persisted.

"Yeah." Ben nodded.

"Riding the range."

Ben just looked at her and then raised an eyebrow at Silver who grinned at him.

"It's okay, sweetie. You can talk to the nice lady. I won't be jealous."

"And who are you wearing tonight, Ben?"

He looked down at his tux. "I have no idea. Does it matter?"

Silver rushed in and supplied the answer, but the conversation turned back to Ben.

"Do you really wish you weren't here tonight, Ben? I bet this isn't your thing at all."

Ben recognized provocation when he heard it and cleared his throat. "I'm here for Silver. She was excellent in *Dust Bowl* and I wish her and all the crew the best of luck."

"How sweet!" The woman turned back to Silver. "I think you've finally got a keeper!"

Silver pressed down hard on Ben's arm and he obediently moved on.

"Jeez . . ." he murmured. "What was her problem?"

"I've no idea," Silver muttered back through her smile. "We're almost done, thank goodness. I see the doors."

"Inola and the gang are just ahead of us," Ben informed her as they rushed past the last few hopefuls, and into the screened-off area where there was at least some shade.

It was crazy inside the theater. Ben tried to keep from gawping like a fool as hundreds of movie stars chattered and bickered and laughed as they settled into their seats. As nominees, Silver and the rest of the crew were seated near the front, and Ben found himself sharing an armrest with Meryl Streep, who was super nice.

As the ceremony progressed, he held on to Silver's hand, and tried to look interested as she'd warned him that the cameras would scan for the audience's reactions at all times.

When Kaya won for best supporting actress, Ben was thrilled to finally stand up and join in the celebrations as she made her way up to the stage. Silver was trying not to cry as Kaya said all kinds of nice things about her and the rest of the cast and crew.

By the time her category came up, Silver was trembling so hard, Ben was worried she was going to pass out. Even though she was smiling serenely, her nails were digging into his wrist. Ben had to admit that she was up against some stiff competition, including his revered seatmate on his left. It seemed to take an age for the idiot up on the stage to get the envelope open. When she read out Silver's name, time speeded up with a roar.

He grabbed Silver, kissed her hard, and then released her so she could celebrate with her castmates and walk up the steps to the stage. His throat closed up as she turned to the audience, and he heard the tears she was holding back in her voice. She thanked everyone, named all the names, mentioned her family, and then looked right at him.

"And last but definitely not least. This is for Ben, who took me out on a trail ride that not only helped me understand how to survive for my role, but also gave me so much more. I love you, Ben Miller. Thank you for everything."

He blew her a kiss and sat down heavily in his chair, swallowing hard. Luckily, Meryl had a spare tissue, and she passed it over to him with a sympathetic press on his hand. There was no sign of Silver, and he wondered where she'd gotten to and how he was supposed to find her again in this crush.

Mike won for best director and called everyone up on the stage with him. Silver and Kaya emerged from the wings, clutching their awards to join him, but she still didn't come back. As things wound down, Ben had way too much time to think about how Silver's life was going to change and wonder whether everything would remain the same.

She'd be in high demand now. Would she want that? Would she allow this place and these people to consume her again? Ben knew he had a tendency to look for the problems, and he'd hate it if he ended up holding her back. She deserved her success, and he was so fricking proud of her right now, that his own stupid needs were going to have to take a rain check.

Someone tapped him on the shoulder and he turned to find Ayla grinning at him.

"Isn't this awesome?"

He gave her a hug. "Yeah, now how do we get out of here and find Silver?"

"She's going to be tied up for quite a while, Ben, so she asked me to come find you." Ayla hesitated. "Do you want to attend any of the after-parties with her? She's been invited to them all."

"Not really my thing," Ben said.

"That's what Silver thought. She's going to have to go to at least one. Shareem and Bree are standing by with a new outfit for her to change into, so she doesn't have to come back to the suite."

"So she'll be okay without me?" Ben clarified, not yet sure how he felt about how things were moving along.

"She'll have the whole cast with her, and her agent. She says she'd love you to come, but if you want to go back to the suite and hang out, she'll see you there."

Ben considered his options as his fears raised their heads to shout down his common sense.

"Tell her I'll meet her back at the hotel, and that I'll be fine, and not to rush back on my account."

When Silver let herself into the suite, it was eerily quiet. Most of her team and the film crew had stayed out partying, but she'd had enough, and had gotten her two bodyguards to take her back.

She took off her second new pair of shoes for the night and winced. Adrenaline had carried her through the rest of the evening, and now all she wanted was to see Ben and go to sleep. The low murmur of a TV caught her attention and, picking up her shoes, she made her way into the bedroom.

Ben was sitting on the bed watching some baseball spring training thing. He'd taken off his jacket and tie, rolled up the sleeves of his white shirt, and removed his shoes. On the side table there was an empty bottle of beer, three full ones and the remains of a hamburger and fries. Silver swallowed hard. She couldn't remember when she'd last eaten.

"Hey," she said softly.

He turned to look at her, his expression slightly more wary than she'd expected.

"Hi." He set his beer down and muted the volume. "Congratulations."

"Thank you." She limped toward the bed. "My feet hurt, and I'm starving."

"I got you some food." He swung his legs over the side of the bed. "Do you want it in here, or shall I set it out on the table?"

"Here's fine."

She hobbled into the bathroom, fought her way out of her Spanx and spent a few minutes in the shower getting the makeup off her face. One of Ben's T-shirts was draped over a chair so she put it on and took the bathrobe off the back of the door.

"Ayla told me what to get for you," Ben said. "It's a protein-rich salad with kale and quinoa."

"Great." She eyed his plate. "Can I have your fries?"

He stopped and looked at her properly for the first time. "Sure. I'll heat them up for you."

"Can I also have one of your beers?"

"Seeing as you're the big winner tonight, help yourself." He picked up his plate. "I'll be right back."

She climbed onto the bed, took the lid off the nutritionally correct salad, and just stared at it. The appetizing smell of hot fries preceded Ben's reentrance into the room.

"Something wrong with your food?" Ben asked.

"I want a hamburger with double fries and ice cream with brownies and fudge sauce."

He nodded, picked up the phone, and was connected directly to the hotel's premium chef.

"It'll be here in fifteen minutes." Ben handed her the fries and a beer. "Start with this."

"Thanks." She drank the whole bottle and he immediately gave her another. She also ate the fries and almost purred as the fatty, salty carbs hit her empty stomach.

He put his arm around her shoulders and continued watching baseball even though the volume was off. She was so tired of talking that the lack of noise was wonderful, and the weight of his arm so comforting that she wanted to stay there forever.

The food was delivered, and Ben went to deal with the waitstaff. He returned with the tray and a grin on his face.

"The guy says this is on the hotel to celebrate your win."

"Nice."

He brought the food around, and she set the tray on the bed between them. "Help yourself."

"I'm pretty stuffed," he admitted. "But I'll have some of the brownie when you get to it."

Silver bit into the burger, aware that the mayo might be running down her chin, and not caring at all.

"Not as good as our beef," she commented thickly, and finished the first half in three more bites.

"What is?" He handed her a napkin. "I suppose what

with you winning and everything, you'll have to put off coming home for a while."

Despite his deliberately casual tone, she wasn't fooled. She should've known that if she left him alone, he'd get worried and work out all the worst-case scenarios.

"Why would you think that?" She wiped her chin and drank more beer. "There's this thing called a phone, you know. I *can* talk to people. And, let's be honest here. There might be a lot of people wanting to talk to me right now, so being elusive and hard to get hold of can only enhance my value."

She'd had a pointed discussion about this very thing earlier with her agent, and managed to convince him that her way was the best way. By the end of the night, he'd reluctantly concluded she might be right.

"Unless you want to stay here, Ben." She hid a smile. "I mean I'm totally okay about going back by myself and leaving you here."

He went quiet long enough for her to finish her burger, fries, and her second beer. She handed him a spoon.

"Help yourself to the brownie."

"I don't want to stay here without you." He met her gaze. "You know that."

"I'm just making sure. I mean, you are getting pretty popular in your own right. You should have seen the fashion bloggers oohing and aahing about how you looked in a tux." She paused just to check if she had one hundred percent of his attention. "With your face and hot bod, you could get into acting."

He removed the tray that was between them and gently took away her spoon.

"What?" Silver fluttered her eyelashes at him. "What did I say?"

"You're"—he framed her face with his hands—"a

complete pain in the ass." He hesitated. "Look, if you need to stay here, I *understand*, okay? I'll—"

"I don't want to stay. I want to go home, decompress, and consider my options."

He eased back a little and picked up her left hand. "Would one of those options you're considering be marrying me?"

Silver gulped in some air. "Really?"

"Yeah, really. My dad doesn't like us living in sin."

"Your dad can take a hike," she said severely. "I've seen what he gets up to with your mother! A woman who divorced him twenty years ago."

"But you will think about it?" Ben asked, his gaze never leaving her face.

"I don't need to think about it," Silver said loftily. "I'm saying yes right now." She pointed a finger at him. "So don't think you can get out of it."

He lunged for her, wrapped her in his arms, and kissed her until she forgot her tiredness and even her own name.

"I love you so much, Silver, and I'm so damned proud of you," he murmured against her lips.

"And I love you, too," she replied, and struggled to sit up.

"What?' he asked, his shirt now deliciously rumpled, and the worried look banished from his face, hopefully forever.

She reclaimed her spoon. "I've got a brownie to eat, a wedding to plan, and then I'm going to go home and sleep for a week."

His slow smile made her heart turn over in the best way. He picked up his own spoon and dug into the melting ice cream.

"I'm not going to argue with any of that."

Ruth's Frosted Animal Cookies for Ben

4 oz. softened butter (1 stick)
8 oz. self-rising flour
1 tsp. vanilla extract
4 oz. sugar
1 large egg, beaten
1 Tbsp. milk

Frosting
4 oz. sifted powdered sugar
1 Tbsp. lemon juice
food coloring (various)

Preheat oven to 375° F/190° C.

In a medium-size bowl, rub butter into flour until it resembles fine breadcrumbs. Add vanilla, sugar, beaten egg, and milk and mix to form a fairly stiff dough. Roll out thinly and cut into animal shapes using cutters. Place shapes on cookie tray, then bake in oven for 10–15 minutes until golden brown. Remove tray, and let cool completely.

To make the icing, put powdered sugar in a bowl and add enough lemon juice to create a spreading consistency. Split between bowls and color accordingly. Use the back of a teaspoon to spread the frosting, or pipe it on if preferred.

Connect with Us

Visit us online at
KensingtonBooks.com
to read more from your favorite authors, see books by series, view reading group guides, and more.

Join us on social media
for sneak peeks, chances to win books and prize packs, and to share your thoughts with other readers.

facebook.com/kensingtonpublishing
twitter.com/kensingtonbooks

Tell us what you think!

To share your thoughts, submit a review, or sign up for our eNewsletters, please visit:
KensingtonBooks.com/TellUs.